GILDING
THE
WATERS

by Catherine Richmond

Also by Catherine Richmond

Spring For Susannah

Through Rushing Waters

ISBN 978-0-9965887-0-6

In loving memory of my mom, Sara Collins, who was always willing to share her wisdom, chocolate, and love of Virginia.

CHAPTER ONE

"Pretty as a peach," drawled a deep voice above the burble of the creek.

Mabel glanced over her shoulder. Sunlight through the elm trees outlined a lanky man wearing a limp-brimmed hat, plaid shirt, and tattered pants. A long-eared hound panted beside him. The man couldn't possibly be speaking to her, but no one else occupied the mountain laurel grove encircling the spring.

The current pulled the Erlenmeyer flask from her hand and floated it out of reach. "Quick! Before it breaks. Do you have anything—"

The mountain man carried a firearm.

Mabel held out her hand while watching the container bob in a circle. "I can reach it with your gun."

He stepped backwards, which, given the length of his legs, put him out of range. "Warrenton House sells bottled water."

Stubborn hillbilly. She worked her way downstream, estimating the trajectory of the container. If it didn't crash against the rocks— "I must collect my own sample." Here it comes. "It's the only way to ensure—" Just a bit closer. "For scientific integrity, one must-"

"Those rocks slippery as deer guts."

"Your warning is duly noted." Mabel stepped over a cluster of yellow flowers, found a flat spot of moss beside the creek, and knelt. The rotten-egg smell of sulphur tweaked her nose.

"So who you fetchin' samples for?"

"President Theodore Roosevelt."

He chuckled. "Suppose the asylum's missing you 'bout now?"

The flask floated into Mabel's hand and she emptied it. Each sample must be taken at the mouth of the spring, to prevent contamination by organisms and minerals from the creek. "You've not heard of the National Conservation Commission?" In these backwoods? Of course not.

"Course." He, or possibly the dog, made a snorting noise. "You can't tell me the president sent you to steal this here water."

"God made the springs. The water belongs to His people."

"Hotel burned down seven years ago." He nodded toward the bare ridge behind them. "Case you didn't notice."

"In case *you* didn't notice, plenty of people still drink this water." Mabel waved her arms. This bumpkin must have noticed the white brick cottages strung like decorative edging on the bowl of the valley. "If Mr. Wade Hampton Alexander truly cared about improving his customers' health, he wouldn't mind having his water tested."

"What makes you so sure it hasn't been tested?"

"By a scientific laboratory? I think not." She marched upstream to the waist-high opening in the hillside.

"You think not? I'm a-guessing you think too much."

"Can anyone think too much?" One hand clutching the capstone, Mabel stretched toward the bubbling which marked the spring's outlet. "We must all, to be worthy of this new century, think as much as—" The flagstone beneath her feet tilted. The pool rose up to meet her face.

"Whoa!" The hillbilly yelled and his dog added an urgent "Woof!"

The water was shallow, no surprise given the low flow of the springs, but the bottom was soft. Her hand sank into malodorous mire up to her elbow. Muck oozed through her riding skirt and shirtwaist, beneath her corset, vest, and drawers. Mabel's thermometer had measured this spring at 54.7 degrees Fahrenheit, but it felt much colder.

As cold as the mud puddle in the schoolyard, where she landed after breaking the swing. The children laughed and called her a cow in a china shop. Clumsy colossal cow—

Large hands grabbed her by the waist and pulled her to the paving stones. "You all right?"

Mud covered her from shirtwaist to shoes. It would brush off when it dried - she hoped. "No! I've lost the flask again."

The hillbilly stepped into the creek, retrieved the flask and her hat, then slapped them into her hand. "You about drownded!"

"Drown in two inches of water? Hardly. I am a competent swimmer." And competent speaker of English. Drownded, indeed.

"But not real handy at filling bottles."

Weighted clothing fought Mabel's effort to stand. The air had been balmy earlier, but now a brisk wind blew down the mountain. She shivered.

He made a noise halfway between a sigh and a groan. "Best get you inside."

Let this strange man escort her to some hillbilly cave? Highly improper. Besides, she had research to conduct. Mabel stepped back. A sharp pain shot up from her foot and her ankle gave way. She tipped backward toward the grotto.

"Don't suppose hitting your head on stone would knock a lick of sense into you." The man steadied her with a hand to her elbow. "'Sides, only one rescue a day."

In the city, Mabel would have to give him the cut and demand he unhand her immediately. But cutting the one who had come to her aid seemed ungrateful and hopping back to civilization was impractical. "Thank you very kindly."

"Seems you twisted your ankle falling in."

Was he looking at her ankle? If it didn't hurt so badly, she'd muster a bit of outrage. "I should empty my shoes and see what's wrong."

"Don't be taking your shoe off until your foot's propped up, lest it swell." He pulled her arm, the drier of the two, across his broad shoulders and supported her weight, an achievement considering her size.

"I don't have time to sit around." Every step made a squishing sound. Her leg throbbed. "If you'll help me to my horse…"

"Old Applejack? He dragged his cart up to the stable, snacking on pansies along the way. That's how we knew to look for you." The man smelled clean, like almond soap.

Water burbled from a jumble of boulders beside the creek. "Oh, another spring. I should test that one, too."

"Purt near same as the first." This hillbilly might be content with imprecision, but Mabel believed in exact measurements.

"Wait - my satchel?" Losing her testing equipment would bring her research to an abrupt end.

"On my other shoulder."

They stepped out of the glade. A gazebo, terraces, and plantings gave a glimpse of the resort Fauquier White Sulphur Springs used to be. The mountain man headed up the hill toward the buildings.

"I'm not dressed for any resort." Even when she wasn't muddy and smelling like a rotten egg. She stole a glimpse of him. And neither was he. Although he was clean-shaven. With an elegant jaw line.

"No putting on airs around here." Cobalt blue eyes twinkled.

A elderly fellow on a second floor porch waved his telescope and called out, "I see you caught the invader, general. Well done."

Mabel couldn't think of anyone less likely to make the rank of general, but the mountain man returned his salute.

A pair of elderly ladies stared from rocking chairs. Young couples paused their tennis and croquet games to gawk. Readers in hammocks and Adirondack chairs peered over their books. So much for being unobtrusive.

The hillbilly led her to Warrenton House and opened the door.

"No. I'm dripping and—"

The dog's toenails clicked on the lobby floor. The desk clerk's eyes widened, but he didn't evict them.

The mountain man handed over his gun. "Clayton, what's open on a first floor?

"Forty-seven."

"Good. That's close to the baths. Send the doctor and Selina." He glanced down at her. "How are you holding up?"

In agony. "If you'll direct me to the horse, I'll be on my way."

"Surefooted as a three-legged pig on greased glass. Can't hitch a horse to a tree. Wet and shivering." He had noticed. How annoying. "In no shape to traipse these hills on your lonesome."

"I've been working alone all week without incident."

"All week? Then you're due for a day off." One arm under her knees, the other around her waist, he scooped her up, and carried her out the door and down the flagstone path.

"Put me down," she said because it was good form, but she rather hoped he didn't. Mabel hadn't been scooped up since... Well, Mother had picked her up when she injured her knee at age four, but no one dared try since. How encouraging to discover she wasn't such a giantess after all. And what a glorious view of this man's profile. No, none of that. She must keep her wits about her. What were they discussing? "There are eighty-two springs in Virginia and I intend to sample them all."

"Is that what Roosevelt asked, *Lewis*?"

5

"Lewis is my father. Wait—" President Roosevelt's letter to her father wasn't in her satchel. It was in her— "You went through my suitcase?" Which contained her underwear. Embarrassment boiled over into outrage. "The nerve!"

They approached a low building. A row of doors opened onto a veranda.

"Does your papa know you're wandering the mountains by yourself?"

"I'm not wandering. I have a well-organized itinerary."

"Which your papa agreed to?"

"Well, he's up in the Hudson Bay, researching icebergs."

"Leaving you to run amok over the hills of Virginia."

"I'm twenty-four years old and a college graduate. Hardly in need of supervision."

His eyebrows raised and he gave her a long look. If he'd intended to reprimand, the effect was spoiled when he grinned. "Hardly," he repeated.

A heavyset man carrying a black Gladstone bag hurried past them and opened door forty-seven. Evening sun through the muslin curtains showed the monastic simplicity of the room: a pine dresser, chair, headboard, and white walls.

Her rescuer set her on the chair, as gently as if she was glass, then left her satchel on the dresser. "Doc Daly, this here is the daughter of one Lewis Easterly. Thought she was on a mission for President Roosevelt even before she hit her head falling into the spring."

"Ignore him." Mabel put the flask on the nightstand and extended her hand to the physician. "Mabel Easterly. My head is fine. My ankle, however, is a bit painful." Incredibly painful, to tell the truth.

An older woman bustled in with a stack of linens. A fringe of steel grey curls escaped from her blue and white checked kerchief. She swatted the hillbilly. "Get along, now. Doc can't do his business, nor can I get this here lady into dry clothes with you hanging about." She nodded at Mabel. "I'm Selina."

"Yes'm." The hillbilly touched his hat and closed the door behind him.

"Oh. I should have thanked him for helping me, but I didn't catch his name."

The doctor's thick mustache twitched.

Selina cocked her head and smiled. "That there's Wade Hampton Alexander, boss man of this here Springs."

Wade yanked off his hunting clothes, damp from holding onto the delectable yet devious Miss Mabel Easterly, and dropped them on the floor of his cottage. "What's she about?" he asked his dog.

Raleigh plopped down on Wade's dirty laundry with a satisfied harumph.

"The Conservation Commission has to do with rivers, not little old springs." He pulled on fresh slacks and a white shirt. "TR knows better than to send a city girl out to these woods." Even if the woman was tall enough to look him in the eye. "The bears and mountain lions will think they've been served dessert, sweet as strawberry pie. Or—" Wade considered the sight of her bending over the spring, the way her skirt hugged her curves. "Or peach. No, the way she fusses, more like lemon meringue." Her hair even waved like meringue, although it was redder than his, the color of cinnamon—

Raleigh licked his chops.

"If'n I keep talking pie, we'll both be a-drooling." Wade scratched the spot that made the dog's back leg kick. "You hanker for pie, but you're happy with kibble. Isn't that the key to life, enjoy what God brings your way?" And Miss Mabel Easterly had come his. Wade grinned.

Wade loped across the grounds. The westering sun polished

the cottages with a golden glow. Father had built most of them, managed all of them until he passed onto to his heavenly reward and Wade inherited the job. Wade had spent winter painting the library, patching slate roofs, and tinkering with plumbing. He'd repaired wiring in the Presidents' cottage, hired and trained thirteen new staff, and scared an opossum out of the Monroe cottage. Guests were pleased, reservations were strong, and investors were talking about building a fashionable new hotel. He surely didn't need some Yankee girl, even a glowing specimen of womanhood, casting aspersions on his spring water.

Especially with Mother's foolish notion of letting Robert E have a turn at running the resort. As Selina said, Lord, give me strength.

Heavenly Father, help me hold onto Fauquier.

The bell rang. Raleigh followed him down to the cottage they were using as a dining hall. Wade took his place at the entrance. "Good evening, Tyler family. Welcome, Mr. and Mrs. Clarke. Nice to see you again, Miss Carter."

The elderly belle fluttered her lashes. "Wade Hampton, I'm having a bit of trouble with the window in my room. It just doesn't want to open. Could you stop by this evening?"

"I'd be glad to. You go on and enjoy your supper and I'll take care of it."

She looked him up and down with a predatory smile, then squeezed his arm. "Oh I do so appreciate having a big strong man come to my aide." Finally she sashayed off to her table.

Mrs. Fitzhugh stuck her head out of the kitchen and whispered, "I'll go, lest she try to corner you again."

"Much appreciated." Wade stepped forward to greet the next gentleman. "Welcome back, mayor. We have fresh cream on your table."

The mayor rubbed his ample belly. "Not this year, Wade. I've got to lay off the heavy stuff." He strolled to his place.

Government folk didn't know if they're coming or going, they were so busy making it difficult for business and talking out of both sides of their mouths. He hoped Miss Easterly wasn't one of those sorts.

Doc Daly dropped his medical bag by the umbrella stand. "Your patient seems all right in the head, for a woman. But her ankle's sprained. She won't be going anywhere for a few days."

Wade grinned. A few days was all he needed.

CHAPTER TWO

Dawn's light gave room 47 a pearly glow. Mabel couldn't remember the last time she'd slept so well. Was it the fresh mountain air? The creek gurgling just beyond the window? Or the famous Fauquier White Sulphur Springs water? Hah. Spring water didn't have medicinal properties. In fact, this water might be toxic — which the world would never discover if she couldn't finish her research.

She pushed herself upright. Her ankle responded with an ache, but much better than yesterday's stabbing pain. The doctor had said it wasn't broken. Selina had wrapped it and propped her leg on a pile of pillows. Surely it would be fully recovered today. She unrolled the bindings. The color had ripened to purple, but the swelling had diminished. It tolerated being put on the floor, being stood upon, but - ouch! - not taking her substantial weight.

Dear Lord, what shall I do?

It seemed she was stuck at Fauquier White Sulphur Springs. Which was better than being stuck in Washington, DC during a hot, sticky summer, scrubbing test-tubes and flasks for the Geophysical Laboratories.

"Miss Mabel?" Selina knocked and opened the door. Today she wore a red and yellow kerchief. She hung Mabel's freshly laundered and pressed clothing on a hook. "How you doing this fine morning? Doc wants you in the bath, first thing. Here's your robe. Let me pin your hair up." She raised the carafe in the window's light, then filled a tumbler and passed it to her. "You haven't had your water yet. Doc says a glass with every meal and another between times. Your chair's out on the veranda. Come along now."

Without rushing, but with a certain unstoppable momentum, Selina whisked Mabel into a wheelchair, down the hall, and into a private bathing room.

Mabel hopped to the edge of the pool to show she could. While she probably weighed twice as much as Selina, those muscular arms gave the impression the woman could scrub a person's skin off. "I can manage from here."

"You do that. I'll be back to wheel you to breakfast."

"I hate to trouble you."

"It's uphill." With a shake of her head, Selina closed the door.

Mabel eased into the water, relieved to find it warmer than the creek she'd fallen into. Was it from a thermal spring or was it heated? And how delightful to fit into the pool without squeezing. Her tub at home allowed only a fourth of her body to soak. Mabel floated out on her back and closed her eyes. How lovely…

"Miss?" Selina burst in, catching her dozing. "Oh, my."

Mabel clambered out and subjected herself to a thorough toweling off. "Yes, I know. Built like a dairy cow."

Nut-brown fingers caught her chin. "God made you to have babies."

"Then he should make a man the right size for me."

Her chuckle sounded too low-pitched for her small frame. "Oh, Miss Mabel. He surely did, surely did. Just got to pray his eyes open."

The older woman spiffed her up and wheeled her across the lawn in no time.

In front of the largest building, the guests sang the "Star

11

Spangled Banner" as a trio of children raised the flag. The men wore golf knickers. The women were elegant in pale colors and light fabrics. Thankfully Mabel's travel clothes, what her father called her safari suit, didn't look entirely out of place - especially now that they were clean. And the wheelchair made her height less noticeable.

One of the children rang the bell, then the guests filed inside. Sunshine streamed through windows on three sides of the dining room.

Selina deposited her at a table set for seven. "Now Mr. Wade say you sit with his kin, seeing as how you don't know no one else here."

Three elderly men in Confederate grey joined her and introductions were made.

"Are you related to the Easterdays in Fredricksburg?" shouted the captain.

The major petted his mustache. "I knew a Maybelle in Roanoke. Prettiest little lady you ever did see. Could she ever make strawberry pie."

"Lemon meringue." Mr. Wade Hampton Alexander slid into the chair next to her. "I mean, good morning." He'd exchanged his hillbilly drawl and getup for a gentleman's refined speech, white linen shirt and light brown slacks. His hair, the red-brown of oxidized copper, was combed behind his ears.

"So, caught you a Yankee." The captain nodded at Mabel.

"Thanks to your sharp eyes." The hotelier explained to Mabel, "The officers guard the resort."

Guard? None of these characters was under seventy. The colonel's eyes were clouded. With every shuffling step, the major winced. The captain was deaf. Hadn't Mr. Alexander said yesterday, the horse had alerted them to her presence?

A woman in a white apron brought platters of fried eggs, ham, and soda biscuits.

"Have you had your water this morning?" Mr. Alexander asked Mabel, holding up the coffee pot.

"Yes. What's in it?" She'd read so many outrageous advertisements, she couldn't remember what Fauquier claimed as their magic ingredient.

"Hydrogen and oxygen, mostly." He puffed out his chest, apparently proud to know the names of two elements.

The colonel passed her the salt and pepper. "Wade attended the University of Virginia."

"Does your school intend to enter the twentieth century and admit women?" Mabel asked the hotelier.

"Wade likes women."

"Especially the pretty ones."

The men stood. "And here's the fairest of them all." Two people entered, both bearing Mr. Alexander's Scottish blade of a nose. The woman stood barely five feet tall. Even in old-fashioned widow's weeds, she couldn't weigh a hundred pounds. She clung to the man's elbow and shuffled so slowly, Mabel considered offering the wheelchair. With a tip of her head, the woman took her place at the head of the table. The man sat on Mabel's left. The arrival of toast and tea merited another regal nod, then she raised an eyebrow in Mabel's direction.

Colonel Drake introduced her. "Mrs. Alexander, may I present Miss Maybelle Easterday, no relation to the Fredrickburg Easterdays."

Wade's mother scrutinized her, taking her apart down to her chemical elements. "Many come from miles around to take our water, Miss Easterly. Few take it head first." She smiled, showing where her son had acquired his sense of humor. "I trust you're recovering?"

"Yes, ma'am. I'll finish my samples and be on my way." She turned to Mr. Alexander. "If you'll direct me to the horse."

"I had one of our caddies return Applejack to the livery last night, to keep charges from accruing. No sign of the rest of your luggage, though."

"The satchel and suitcase contain all I need."

"Well, I'll be." The man studied her a long moment, then grinned. "You, Miss Maybelle, are staying right here today."

Mabel narrowed her gaze at the hotelier. She'd make allowances for the soldiers' loss of hearing. But Mr. Alexander knew perfectly well what her name was. "It's Miss Easterly."

"This is Virginia, Miss Maybelle," he said, his voice lowered to a purr. Then he unfolded a paper. "Doc set up an arduous schedule to restore you to full health."

Mabel held out her hand. "May I see that?"

He returned the paper to his pocket. "Mustn't tax yourself, doctor's orders."

"I am far from being overstrained."

"And even further from relaxed." He gave her a cheeky grin.

Mrs. Alexander's escort said to his plate, "I'm Robert E, Wade's brother." His face was rounder than his brother's and his hair had thinned to a widow's peak. "What are you testing the water for?"

"No alarming the guests," Wade muttered as he whisked Mabel outside.

"I would think questionable water safety would alarm them."

"People come here to escape their worries."

His dog met them on the porch.

Mabel extended her hand for a thorough sniffing. "Well, hello, there. What's your name?"

"Miss Maybelle, this here's Raleigh."

"Pleased to meet you, Rollo."

The hotelier sighed. "Raleigh. As in Sir Walter. Early promoter of Virginia."

"Who brought the scourge of tobacco to England."

"Not everyone's as wholesome as you." He pushed the

wheelchair toward a large chestnut tree.

Wholesome? Was that the latest euphemism for big-boned? "At least I don't pretend to be a hillbilly."

He chuckled without any sign of offense. "Fauquier White Sulphur Springs hosts presidents and Supreme Court justices. But some of our workers never had the benefit of schooling. I have to get along with all."

"You were dressed like a mountain man yesterday."

"And a good thing, too. Those clothes don't mind getting wet rescuing a fair maiden from a dunking in the crick." Grinning seemed to be his customary expression. "City boys like to mosey around the woods with an old hunting rifle, give the squirrels something to laugh about. It's easier to go along than form a search party when they don't show up for supper." He parked the wheelchair beside a hammock.

"Is this what passes for arduous in Virginia?"

He helped her stand. His warm hands, large enough to encompass her waist, held her a moment longer than necessary. And his blue eyes held her gaze. "Miss Maybelle, have you never taken a vacation?"

"My father and I travel for fieldwork, but we do not vacation." Much as she enjoyed this close view of the laugh lines around his eyes, she decided to sit. "I can't just lie around. Perhaps some reading material…"

"We'll have none of that, now." He scooped under her legs and swung her feet up, sending her into the hammock with an undignified flop. "You be on your best behavior. I'll be back directly." Mr. Alexander sauntered off to the hotel, pausing several times along the way to chat with the guests.

How long was "directly?" Mabel glanced at her waist, but her watch was drying out in room forty-seven. "He doesn't expect me to stay here all day, does he?"

Raleigh panted, grinning like his master.

A screen door squeaked. The brother peeked from the nearest cottage. He hurried across the lawn to a spot beside the tree trunk, walking with an odd rolling gait. Sunlight showed a sallow cast to his skin. Without meeting her gaze, he handed her a cane. "It's hickory."

"It doesn't matter what it is as long as it works." Mabel reached for it. "I'm sorry. When I get out of sorts, I forget myself. It's perfect. Thank you, Mr. Alexander." She stood and took a step. Still sore.

"Works better in your other hand."

She switched to the side opposite her swollen ankle. "Of course."

"Now you can finish."

"You don't mind if I analyze the water?" She managed a step-hop. At this pace, it would take her an hour to reach her room and all afternoon to limp to the springs.

"How 'bout if I fetch your kit?"

"That would be so kind. Room forty-seven. The testing equipment is in the satchel on the dresser." Mabel returned to the hammock.

In moments, Robert E returned. "Might could be..." He motioned toward the wheelchair.

"Quite right." She hopped in. The hard tires rattled over the rocky path, scaring the birds from the trees. Raleigh trailed along, investigating scents beside the path.

Robert E pushed her with a vigor that told her he was every bit as strong as his brother despite his appearance.

She asked, "So, did you also attend the University of Virginia?"

"No."

"Your resort is quite beautiful. Have you lived here all your life?"

"No."

16

On to the never-fail topic recommended by etiquette advisors. "I do hope this lovely weather will continue."

"It won't."

Well, then. The Alexander brothers were a mystery for a different sort of scientist, so Mabel settled in to enjoy the ride along formal plantings, around clusters of mountain laurel, past scattered wildflowers in pinks and purples. Robert E brought her to the edge of the spring. Mabel hobbled out, gathered her sample, then he delivered her to her room. She set up her mobile laboratory and ran through her tests. The results showed chalybeated sulphur, as advertised. Nothing toxic, but nothing particularly curative, either. She couldn't suppress a smile as she entered the numbers - such a relief to be back to her work.

Robert E returned in time to help her into the wheelchair. He didn't ask about her analysis. In fact, he didn't say a word. Full speed again, they bounced up the creek to the north. Raleigh raced off after a cottontail.

"How convenient to have a guide who knows these mountains. It would take me twice as long using a map to find this spring."

"Follow the water."

Three words that time. What would it take to set off a conversation? "Virginia has a variety of springs: saline, sulphur, chalybeate, alkaline, calcic, and thermal. What type of spring is this?"

"The same."

Back in her room with another sample, she completed her tests and recorded her findings. Robert E was correct. The tests revealed the same innocuous mix of calcium, magnesium, and various sulphates. Certainly no cure for any disease.

Now what? A breath of perfectly clean air fluttered the curtains. A day as glorious as this should be spent outside. She grabbed the cane and hobbled out to the wheelchair. The dog emerged from beneath the porch. "Well, Raleigh, what resort amusement do you recommend?"

Oh, that Miss Easterly. *Maybelle* suited her better than *Mabel*. Wade liked her look of exasperation, fine eyebrows lowered and the corners of her lips tucked in, when he—

"Wade? Wade. Where's your head?" The head cook planted her hands on her hips. "I've been hollering for you going on ten minutes."

"Yes, Mrs. Fitzhugh." He paused in the doorway by the coal shed, trying to remember what crisis had been brewing. Oh, yes, Margaret near about sliced her finger off while butchering chickens this morning. Doc Daly had sent her home. "What did you figure out with the kitchen staff?"

"Margaret's sister will work for her starting with today's dinner."

"What about her babies?"

"Their cousin's daughter will watch the twins."

"Zaidee's just a baby herself, isn't she?"

"She's twelve. Plenty of experience with her younger brothers. But that's not what I was calling you for." Mrs. Fitzhugh towed him inside. "The electric fans went out in the kitchen and we're like to melt." She swabbed her forehead with her apron.

"Can't have Virginia's best cooks turning into puddles. I'll take care of it." He stomped down to the basement and scowled at the mess of wires and fuses. The guests were outside, so they wouldn't mind if he ran the electricity from their rooms to the kitchen for a few hours. A chorus of voices upstairs broke out in a round of "For He's a Jolly Good Fellow." If he could work out a permanent fix, like paying for a trained electrician, he'd be a jolly *great* fellow.

If he didn't... Wade shuddered. Faulty wiring had burned down the hotel at Cold Sulphur Springs a few months ago, so rumor said. The building was only thirteen years old - much newer than any of the cottages here. Seemed like newspapers could barely print an issue without reporting another fire somewhere. A hundred seventy dead in an opera house in Pennsylvania, 174 in a school in Ohio. Tenements in New York, a house in Pittsburgh, a church in Germany - all burned to the ground with casualties.

For the thousandth time, Wade thanked God no lives had been lost when Fauquier's hotel burned down seven years ago. And for the thousandth time, he wondered about the cause. Had it been a short circuit? A gas leak? A magnifying glass misplaced by a child?

Or… was it Robert E? His brother hated the resort. He resented the guests to the point Doc Daly diagnosed him with a condition called "misanthropy." And on the morning the fire started, he'd been working in the hotel, converting gas fixtures to electricity. Was his brother a firebug?

And as Wade had done every moment since, he prayed, "Dear Jesus, spare us from another fire."

Back upstairs, Wade poured another mug of Fauquier's finest and went to the big chestnut tree. The hammock was missing Maybelle. And what had she done with his dog? He surveyed the grounds. Major Holston signaled from the roof walk. Ah, yes, he spotted his prey, er, his guest. Her straw hat, stiff before her dunking, now curved over her meringue hair. If only she'd loosen up as easily. He crossed the lawn to the tennis courts.

Maybelle sat in her wheelchair at the net, calling out instructions to Hiram Byrd and Stewart Spencer, two of the most uncoordinated children to ever visit the Springs.

"Keep your eye on the ball. Follow through." She propelled herself across the court, adjusted the boy's grip on his racket and showed him a forehand stroke. The woman knew her tennis. When she got back on her feet, he'd challenge her to a game. No, when she got back on her feet, she'd be out of here.

Raleigh, stationed at the entrance to the court, wagged his tail.

"You were supposed to keep her in the hammock."

The dog's head drooped and he lay back down.

"Don't blame him." She pivoted toward him with a confident tilt of her head. "I am incapable of laziness."

"It's not lazy, it's relaxing." He handed her the mug.

"Look Mr. Wade! Miss Maple taught us to hit it over the net!" The last time Wade watched Hiram try to serve, the ball went backwards over his head and landed behind him. This time it floated over the net and hit Stewart's left leg.

"My turn! Let me show him!" Stewart's serve bounced off the post and made a beeline for Hiram, who missed it anyway.

"I'm impressed, Miss Maybelle." Wade pushed the wheelchair out of the court. "I should hire you as a tennis coach."

"If the Geophysical Laboratory gets any more tedious, perhaps I'll take your offer."

The Geophysical Laboratory? The Carnegie Institute studying the earth, its geology and magnetism and mysteries. What a brilliant mind her pretty head must contain. And what trouble her report could cause, with that prestigious organization behind it. He had to stop her.

"Doc told you to keep your foot up." He wheeled her to a chaise lounge beside Barrows Run. And now the fun part. In his experience, the best way to fluster a woman was to take his time with them. Yankees especially weren't used to unhurried, lingering attention. Wade reached beneath the hem of her skirts to lift her ankles off the footrests. Her dark-brown eyes widened. Then he stood, bent, and brought his face close to hers, holding her fathomless dark-brown gaze with his. His hands slipped under her arms to her trim waist. She jumped to her feet, then had to clasp his forearms to keep her balance.

20

"A lot of bother," she muttered.

"Your small parts are worth a good bit of bother." His gaze traveled her face, admiring the dance of freckles across her smooth cheeks, coming to a rest on the peach-kissed bow of her lips until she turned pink. *Got her.* He lowered her - slowly, slowly - to the lounge. "Until lunch," he murmured.

But of course by then Maybelle had upped and run off again. With Major Holston's signals, Wade eventually found her in the children's play area, holding a tea party with the Wythe girls, her leg propped on an apple crate.

"Are you impervious to the effect of Fauquier White Sulphur Springs?" He steered her wheelchair back to the dining hall. "Everyone else, even the most nose-to-the-grindstone worker, relaxes here."

"I suppose you credit your water." The wind loosened a curl of Maybelle's hair and blew it across Wade's hand, causing him to lose his train of thought for a moment.

"It's more than the water. It's the chance to take it easy and enjoy yourself." Unlike the rest of his guests, happy wasn't the goal. Disconcerted and returning to Washington was. "Doctor's orders, remember?"

After lunch, Wade deposited Miss Maybelle in the library, hoping a hefty pile of the latest magazines would keep her in place. When he returned, she was playing three-handed bridge with the Dandridge cousins, her foot on an overturned wastebasket. In the next hour, she managed to escape from a porch chair. Since the officers had retired to their afternoon naps, Wade had Raleigh dust off his tracking skills. They found her in the gazebo, playing table tennis from the wheelchair with newlyweds Mr. and Mrs. Clarke and the Bradley's curly-haired daughter.

"Someone needs to keep a close eye on you, Miss Maybelle." And that someone would be him. Wade rolled her chair past the fountain.

"Do you have any crutches? I should be on my way."

"Always in a hurry." Wade shook his head, then consulted a paper. "Doc says—"

"This morning the doctor's instructions were on lined paper. And now they're on the back of a receipt." Keen powers of observation. "Mr. Alexander, are you pulling my leg?"

"Miss Maybelle, your lovely leg is already hurting. I'll not be pulling it." At least he'd do his best to avoid the temptation. He rolled her to room forty-seven. "You have a session in the swimming pool. And it won't do any good to tell me you don't swim as we have recently acquired a new invention called water wings. They're made by Yankees, so I'm sure you'll get along fine."

"I'm perfectly capable of swimming unaided." Of course she was. "But as I'm not on holiday, I didn't bring my bathing suit."

Whoa, Wade told his brain. "Miss Selina found one for you." After she cackled like an old hen. "I'll be back for you directly." He stopped by his cabin to change into his two-piece suit, navy with orange pinstripes in honor of his alma mater, then returned to room forty-seven.

Selina had decked Maybelle out in a purple swim dress, making her look like an advertisement for Roosevelt's strenuous life, strong and healthy. Dark stockings beneath the knee-length skirt displayed long, shapely legs. Short sleeves highlighted the contours of her arms. No doubt she could swim circles around him. Wade pressed his heart, trying to keep it from thumping in quick time. "Why, Miss Maybelle, I declare you're the prettiest girl to grace the Springs."

"Really," she said, her voice heavy with irony. Maybelle's wide mouth pulled in at the corners as if she couldn't decide whether to smile or frown. She may know chemistry and tennis, but she didn't know flirting - all the more fun for an expert like himself.

As she hopped into the wheelchair, she glanced back.

"Why Miss Maybelle, are you taking a gander at my legs? I'll be glad to let you give them a full going-over." He lifted his left limb beside the armrest and wiggled his ankle in a circle.

Maybelle pointed her nose to the sky. "Calm yourself, Mr. Alexander. Your legs are of no interest to me." Her blush belied her words.

"Whereas *your* legs, Miss Maybelle, are of considerable interest to me." Chuckling, Wade wheeled Maybelle to the finest pool in the state of Virginia.

The Wyethe girls popped out of the water and pushed dripping hair from their eyes. "Miss Easter! We're having an underwater tea party!"

"How grand!" She grinned, not raising a ruckus over the mangling of her name.

"Hi, Miss Maple!" called Hiram and Stewart Spencer. "We hit the tennis ball back and forth three times!"

"Good volley, gentlemen!" She waved back, then greeted the Dandridge cousins under their parasols, and said hello to the Clarkes and Bradleys. The Allertons motioned for her to join them in the shallows and gave rave reviews on the water temperature. Wait, when had she met them?

Maybelle fit in at Fauquier. Could she fit in with his life?

Mabel put her hand into Wade's strong one and lowered herself to the deck of the pool. "Thank you, Mr. Alexander."

"My pleasure, darling."

Darling, was it now? Hah. Sugar reduces to a mix of carbon, hydrogen, and oxygen. His job required friendliness and attentive service to his guests. But… had his hand lingered in hers? Had he leaned close for a kiss? Had his glance held a hint of admiration? Undoubtedly he was quite skilled with the ladies. And surely this time, she'd have the sense to keep her heart out of the equation. No, she mustn't dally with such a flirt. She'd only known him a day. They hadn't been properly introduced. And she had a research project to complete. She simply mustn't.

Wade ambled to the deep end of the pool. "Now you wait there, Miss Maybelle, and I'll catch you." He bent and jumped. His long body slipped into the water with barely a splash.

Oh, my.

Turning into a puddle of female mush would never do. Mabel pushed off the side and hoped the water would cool her ardor.

He popped up with a big grin. Unlike the rest of the world, dripping hair did not dim Wade's striking good looks. "Why, Miss Maybelle, you do know how to swim."

"I'm not swimming, I'm treading water." She wouldn't be doing any swimming in this bathing suit. As with most clothes, it didn't fit her. The shoulders and waist were too tight, the bust too loose. "This water is warmer than the springs."

"I keep the trees over the creek trimmed, so sunlight does the warming." He pointed up the slope.

"If the pool were painted a dark color, the sun would warm the water. You'd need a paint that wouldn't dissolve and wasn't toxic."

Hiram and Stewart swam toward them, churning the water as if they were made of dry ice. Mabel couldn't move out of the way fast enough and they drenched her.

"Now you boys leave Miss Maybelle be. She's here for the rest cure."

"Children are a lovely change from dusty scientists." And the perfect distraction to keep her focus off Wade. "Can you do a handstand underwater?" she asked the boys.

Both flailed about, unable to touch bottom, much less raise their feet.

"Dear me. I'd hoped their lack of prowess at tennis could be remedied by eyeglasses."

"Afraid not. Now watch," Wade said to the boys, while his gaze met hers. He disappeared beneath the surface. His legs shot up and held straight long enough for her to admire his well-muscled calves.

Mabel scooped water to her face. Her cheeks hadn't been this hot since scrawny Henry Shaftesbury had attempted a kiss in chemistry lab. She'd forgiven him for kissing like a catfish, but not for proposing the next day, less than twenty-four hours later, to a mousy domestic science major.

Wade popped up. "Miss Maybelle, are you all right?"

"I should cool off." If absence made the heart grow fonder, perhaps distance might keep desire from germinating. Mabel swam into the deep end.

"Miss Maple!" Hiram paddled toward her, then realized he was in over his head and sinking fast. He grabbed her sleeve. The seam ripped, baring her shoulder. With one arm, Mabel kept the boy's head above water and towed him to the side, with the other, she tried to stay decent.

Galloping hooves echoed across the resort. The rider called out a question, the aristocratic rhythm of his speech somehow familiar.

The Allertons pointed. The Dandridge cousins twirled their parasols and giggled. Wade vaulted out of the pool, then he glanced back at her, all trace of his grin gone.

The magnificent bay high-stepped across the lawn toward them. The rider was a stout man. With a thick mustache. Wearing a campaign hat and pince-nez. He waved and called, "Lieutenant Alexander!"

Wade saluted, "Colonel."

Mabel's heart sank faster than Hiram Spencer. This time, it wouldn't be a chemistry lab partner and mousy English major dashing her hopes. This time, it was a hotelier and none other than President Theodore Roosevelt.

CHAPTER THREE

Wade glanced at the pool. Maybelle held her sleeve up to hide her shoulder. She pushed wet hair from her eyes, peered at the approaching rider, and blinked. Her mouth opened and her cheeks lost their pink. Then she glanced at Wade, a trunk-load of hurt in her gaze.

Wade hurried across the lawn and reached for the horse's reins. "Mr. President."

Roosevelt dismounted and thumped him on the back. "Wade! Splendid place you've got here!"

"Thank you, sir." Wade pulled the bay's head around, steering him away from the pool. He pointed at the two story building with columns. "The President's cottage is ready for you."

"Many of my predecessors stopped by?"

"Madison, Monroe, Van Buren, and Tyler."

"Long overdue, then." He nodded at Miss Maybelle. "You seem to have the situation well in hand."

Drat. "Uh, you've met Miss Easterly?"

TR's grin showed an impossible number of teeth. "Washington is a small town."

Two detectives trotted up, clinging to their saddles like city boys. "Sir, you must wait for us," the older gasped, an absurd comment to the man who'd yelled "Follow me!" and charged San Juan Hill.

The livery's buggy arrived with a secretary and a

photographer. All three of Wade's grooms and two caddies took charge of the horses. Guests circled, gawking and vying for attention. Mother, on Robert E's arm, cut through the swath like a cavalry sword, then escorted their distinguished visitor inside. In the chaos, Wade caught Selina's eye and sent her to Maybelle. He dashed to his cabin to change clothes and grab the envelope from his last visit to the University.

Dressed appropriately, Wade returned to the President's cottage and waited for his eyes to adjust to the dimness. Mother served iced tea and shared memories of TR's mother. Robert E managed a civil conversation about his ship-building experience in Norfolk.

Wade pulled up a chair and tried not to fidget. He shouldn't have embarrassed Maybelle. No, not just embarrassed. Mortified. Here she was trying to be a scientist, to do some fancy research project, and he'd gotten her playing in the water, making her look foolish. She wouldn't meet with the president. She wouldn't show her face again. She'd slink back to Washington without another word. But… wasn't that what he wanted?

The screen door opened and Maybelle limped in wearing her tan shirtwaist and skirt. Her damp hair was pinned in a neat coil at her crown. Wait, where had she gotten that cane? Robert E crossed his arms and leaned back with a smile. Unfortunately Mother was too busy fluttering over the president to elbow him for smirking.

Wade stood and held his chair for her. She didn't look at him.

"Miss Easterly. Seems I went fishing for your father and you took the bait." TR explained to Mother, "I'd written to Miss Easterly's father, asking him to write up a report for the National Conservation Commission, not knowing Lewis had left for Hudson Bay." He pointed to Maybelle's foot. "Battle injury?"

"Twisted ankle. I'll be fit tomorrow." Maybelle handed him a thick envelope. "Mr. President, you asked for an inventory of our national resources. The springs of Virginia make health claims without any basis in science. They advertise various cures with no further proof than an 18th century tale of an Indian brave restored to health. For instance, this resort announced cures for everything from," she quoted from an 1882 booklet, "'Dyspepsia and Chronic Catarrh of the Stomach, to a prompt and permanent cure for Neurasthenia.' In support of their claims, they offer only a few letters from the 1830s."

Wade pulled a chair beside her. "Taking the waters has been considered an important aid to healthy living since biblical times and continues today throughout Europe." He had his speech memorized. "It's not just our water. The elevation and fresh air prevent cholera and yellow fever. Fauquier White Sulphur Springs also provides nutritional meals and recreational opportunities to restore and support good health."

Maybelle still wouldn't look at him. "The resident physician tells guests to drink six cups of spring water a day and bathe in it, yet no one knows what chemicals might taint it."

"The water was tested at the University of Virginia." Wade presented his own report for the president's scrutiny.

"The university is Mr. Alexander's alma mater," Miss Prim and Proper noted, "raising the question of a conflict of interest."

How dare she suggest— Well, his donation could be miscontrued in some circles. "None other than the Medical Association of Virginia endorsed our water. Doctors from New York, Philadelphia, Baltimore, and Atlanta recommend Fauquier." Yes, Wade had let the physicians stay for free. How else were they to evaluate the resort? It was the way business was done.

Roosevelt scowled his way through the university's analysis and Maybelle's newspaper clippings. Mother opened her mouth as if to fill the silence, then something, perhaps the president's bulldog frown, had her close it again. The room waited in the quiet of rustling papers and the creak of the wicker settee under the president.

Miss Maybelle sat with her hands in her lap, as composed as if she was at tea with a friend instead of meeting with the most important man in the country. She had to feel Wade's stare, but she didn't turn. He contented himself with a study of her ear, each whorl an excellent spot to plant a kiss.

As if, after this, Maybelle would let this bonehead within a country mile of her. No, she'd return to Washington with the president and he'd never see her again.

"Should have included mineral water in the Pure Food and Drug Act." TR's fierce expression should be filed in the dictionary under "browbeating." "The U.S. Geological Survey already tests mineral springs."

Maybelle answered with a steady voice. "The Department of Interior published a list of springs in 1886, labeled a preliminary study. A variety of sources, including springs' owners, provided the analyses. That list was entered, verbatim, into the 1903 Standard Medical Directory."

The presidential frown deepened, an expression that had a certain lieutenant shaking in his boots in 1898. "You decided against having the proprietors send you their water?"

Maybelle faced TR without blinking. "For integrity, absolute certainty of results, and consistent technique, the tests should be conducted by one researcher. As certain elements degrade or precipitate with time and temperature changes, testing at the site increases the accuracy."

"As recommended in Mason's *Examination of Water*." TR cleaned his eyeglasses. "The Department of Agriculture published a study on mineral water."

"In 1904." Maybelle nodded. "Chemists analyzed water

purchased in the Washington area and found numerous discrepancies. Bottlers claimed variations were due to minerals settling or attaching to the container, or city water being sold under their label."

The presidential moustache twitched. "Resorts which don't bottle their water weren't tested."

"Correct." Maybelle leaned forward, warming to her topic. "Previous analyses were reported in grains per gallon. The United States should join the international scientific community by using grams and parts per million."

"About time." TR snorted. "Quantitative or qualitative analysis?"

"Qualitative. Balance scales don't travel well."

"True." The opposition often referred to him as the cowboy-president, forgetting Roosevelt had attended Harvard and had a keen scientific mind. "So you'll use reagents and flame tests?"

"And reagent papers recently developed by a German company." Maybelle turned slightly toward Wade, focusing on his left shoe. "How was your analysis done?"

"I dropped a bottle off last time I was on campus."

"May I see the university's results?" Maybelle asked. "I'd like to compare them with mine."

Maybelle's test? Hadn't he derailed that train? Wade glanced over at his brother. Robert E's smirk spread into a full-fledged gloat. Mother still didn't notice and Selina wasn't here to threaten him with a belt.

"The university's results concur with yours," the president handed U.Va.'s analysis to Maybelle, then thumped his fist on his knee. "The health and safety of our citizens are at risk. Testing by an unbiased scientist is a project of considerable merit."

Mother gasped. "But Mr. President, it is hardly appropriate for a young lady to travel without a chaperone."

"Varmints," Robert E said. "Four- and two-legged."

Wade nodded. "The Blue Ridge mountains are home to black bears, mountain lions, copperheads, and timber rattlers."

The president straightened. "I should have brought my Winchester."

"I appreciate your concern, but I'll be fine," Maybelle said. "I traveled the Nile without incident."

"Not by yourself. You had your father and those Brits from Khartoum." Roosevelt waved over his secretary, who had been catching his breath in the corner. "Wade, I commission you to protect Miss Easterly."

"Wait a minute," Wade sputtered. This wasn't going well at all. "I've got a resort to run."

"Your mother reports you have a vacation coming up." The moustache widened.

Mother said, "I raised my sons to be gentlemen, to be honorable, and to protect the weaker sex."

Whose side was she on? Robert E's obviously. His brother resumed his usual blank expression, but he had to be kicking up his heels inside. With Wade out of the way, he'd have free rein at Fauquier, burning down buildings and driving off guests until nothing was left.

Dear Lord, my brother needs a lightning bolt to the head.

Roosevelt stood. "Raise your right hand. I, Theodore Roosevelt, president of these United States, commission you, Lieutenant Wade Hampton Alexander, to guard and protect the person and honor of Miss Mabel Easterly on her investigation of the springs of Virginia, on behalf of the people of this great nation." He returned the clippings to Maybelle. "I'll expect a full report on my desk by September."

The dinner bell rang.

"Mrs. Alexander, may I have the honor?" The president offered his arm to Mother. Robert E and the secretary trailed behind.

"I have no interest in traveling with you, either." Maybelle hobbled past, her head held high. "I hearby release you from your commission."

Wade had telegraphed President Roosevelt to try to uncover the truth about Miss Maybelle's water testing and get her out of his hair. In trying to send her safely home, he'd managed to destroy whatever small regard she had for him. Madder than a barn cat what missed the milking, Selina would say. But Maybelle couldn't rid herself of him that easily - he had orders from the president. This water testing nonsense had to stop and he was just the man to do it. The tension in Wade's jaw eased and he grinned.

Fauquier White Sulphur Springs's staff had President Roosevelt fed and pointed back in the direction of the capital city in no time. Wade headed into the kitchen, complimenting the cooks and waitresses.

"Don't you worry, none," Mrs. Fitzhugh told him. "I'll unplug all the lights and fans every night, double-check all the ovens, then lock up."

Apparently word of Wade's commission had raced through the staff. "You found a key? And it works?"

"Mama had it made when we had to hide the silver from the Yankees." She reached behind two cans of yeast and pulled out an ancient iron key and padlock. "I used it that summer the raccoons figured out how to work the latch."

"You kept track of that lock for near half a century." Wade grabbed the round woman in a hug. "Mrs. Fitzhugh, you surely amaze me."

She squeezed back with arms that had kneaded thousands of loaves of bread, then pushed him out the door. "Go on with you."

Wade stepped onto the porch and a cool, wet nose touched his palm. Wade rubbed the floppy ears. "Well, look at that, Raleigh. Sunset's turned the Shenandoahs navy blue and the sky orange, University of Virginia colors. Proof God loves Virginia best."

The hound followed him along the path. The sliver of a moon gave little light, but Wade didn't need to see. He knew every pebble, every leaf, every nail in every building. Fauquier White Sulphur Springs's water ran in his blood. Its rhythms kept his heart beating.

He started at Warrenton House. Clayton had swept the porch and pulled the rocking chairs close to the building, in case of rain.

Mother had rooms in the next cottage. Her windows were dark, which was no surprise - TR's energy had worn out many lesser hostesses.

The Tyler family rocked on their porch, watching the sunset and singing "Skye Boat Song" accompanied by a guitar. Maybe Wade would ask them to sing after supper tomorrow. No, tomorrow he'd be gone.

The next cottage held trouble in the name of Maybelle Easterly. She would have been a fond memory, the highlight of the summer, if his rotten brother hadn't suggested she needed an escort. Mother wanted Robert E to have his day in the manager's seat. Wade had planned to stay right here, ready to step in when Robert E fell on his face. Instead he'd be away for the first time in memory. Fortunately, running this resort had taught him many a way to deal with problems, especially those of the female sort. He'd be back at Fauquier in less than a week.

In the Monroe cottage, the officers still had their lights on, keeping Major Holston company as he partook of his medicinal whiskey.

Rowdy Hall stood empty as it had since the hotel burned.

When Papa ran Fauquier, bachelors packed the rooms to the rafters. Allowances were won and lost at the card table. Tips were traded about racehorses who hit their stride and girls who were willing to slip away from their chaperones. Boys competed with wild stories, silly pranks, and arm wrestling.

Many nights the bachelors stole into the swimming pool. Papa's death had left Wade with many difficult chores, the worst of which was clearing the pool at night. A puny thirteen-year-old with a squeaky voice tended to get dunked. Thankfully Colonel Vance had come to his rescue until Wade learned to wield his sense of humor to get what he wanted.

Tonight only a frog swam in the pool. Wade grabbed a bucket, scooped out the amphibian, and freed him beyond the fence. "Sorry to say Miss Maybelle won't be back to swim with you." And no one was sorrier than Wade.

Wade scanned the night sky, his gaze landing on the planet Venus. Yes, that's what Maybelle reminded him of, the statue of Venus de Milo, tall and curving. She'd felt just right when he carried her. Why couldn't she be a simple guest?

No, he'd never had a guest like Miss Maybelle. So much energy and life. Most of the unwed ladies who visited Fauquier had one thing on their minds: trapping some fellow into building them a gilded cage so they could recline on the couch and have vapors the rest of their days. Not Miss Maybelle. She made plans and had the vitality to carry them through. Unfortunately her plans, this water research, endangered his business. He had to stop her.

Wade strolled into the stables, and thanked the grooms and caddies for taking care of TR's entourage. They assured him the kerosene and gasoline were locked up. What a great staff. No doubt they could run this place without him… as long as Robert E kept out of their way.

He climbed into the loft and hunted through the collection of luggage guests had left behind. Not the nose-in-the-air imitation alligator suitcase - after all, he wasn't some son of a robber baron on a grand tour. The English Bellows model weighed more than ten pounds empty - no wonder it had been cast aside. Finally he found a plain cowhide case with working lock and catches, about the size of the one Miss Maybelle carried.

He climbed down and Raleigh left a damp nose print on the suitcase. "I surely don't know how that woman travels so light. Guess I'm about to find out."

Trailed by his hound, Wade returned to his cabin and lit the lamp on his dresser. He set the case on his bed, then pondered his clothes. Now what? He knew how to lug the luggage, but he didn't know how to stuff it. Last time he packed was during his Rough Rider days, serving under Colonel Roosevelt. He pulled his knapsack from under the bed, disturbing a ball of dog hair the size of a polecat. Let's see… a canteen might be handy, always enjoyed using field glasses, a bandanna or two…

The door flew open and the officers marched in bringing the smell of their after-supper pipe.

Colonel Vance saluted. "General, our battle plan is ready."

"We've got tactics and maneuvers." Major Holston unrolled a large scrap of wallpaper, pattern-side down, on the table. These West Point graduates had drawn a map of the resort, complete with topographic lines, and marked it like they were preparing for a Third Battle of Manassas.

Captain Drake lit the overhead lamp. "I'll stand watch in the crow's nest from reveille to dinner. The major will take dinner to taps. Raleigh can sleep in front of Robert E's door at night."

The dog raised his head upon hearing his name. Catching no scent of vittles, he plopped back to sleep.

"Gets mighty hot on that roof," Wade said. Not to mention what climbing those steps would do to the major's rheumatism.

"We'll set up a tent."

Clayton joined the group. "All the matches are locked in the safe."

Selina entered the room and closed the door on the night music of the cicadas and frogs. One look at the mess on his bed and she took over packing chores with a muttered, "Lord, give me strength."

"Won't be long," Wade assured them. "Shouldn't take more'n a week to convince Miss Maybelle to leave Virginia's water alone."

"Such a nice lady." Major Holston shook his head. "Too bad she's tangled in such nefarious business as science."

"Wade must go as a matter of honor." The colonel spoke so loudly Robert E surely heard their plans. "It's a commission from the president. His mother was a Bulloch from Georgia, you know."

Captain Drake reached under his jacket and pulled out a Colt Revolver that hadn't seen action since the surrender at Appomattox. "We're a bit short of ammunition, but we—"

Selina glanced up from matching socks. "Somebody gonna get hurt, you wave that thing around."

Wade gulped. These boys needed to be reined in—and now. "With all due respect, sirs, this is a resort, not a battlefield. You know the place these old buildings hold in my heart, but they're not worth an injury or loss of life. You wouldn't want to trouble the guests..." He paused to look each soldier in the eye. "Nor Mother."

"Lands, no." The men shook their heads. "Mustn't upset Miz Alexander."

"What about this?" Clayton unfolded a magazine advertisement for a sleeping draught. "We could knock Robert E out until you get back."

"I'm afraid Mother would notice his absence. Doc Daly says those remedies are snake oil sold by quacks, won't do any good and might could cause harm." Testing patent medicine would be a better use of Miss Maybelle's time. He'd suggest it.

"I'll give orders for the groundskeepers to clear the combustibles away from the cottages," the colonel said.

Now there's an idea. The groundskeepers could use an extra incentive to clear dead leaves from the underbrush. "Yessir."

The major tapped the map with his gnarled finger. "We'll station rain barrels and buckets at the northeast corner of each building. Every evening the troops, I mean, the caddies will fill them."

"I'll turn off the fountains at sunset, build up the water pressure," Clayton said. "And turn them back on first thing in the morning."

"And I'll track Robert E like a hound." Selina pulled a string with a silver whistle from under her shirtwaist. "We all know the signals."

"A brilliant plan," Wade said.

"Let us pray." The colonel rolled up the map. "Heavenly Father, who sees all and knows the intentions of every heart, preserve this, your acre of heaven on the Rappahannock. We'd be ever so grateful if you'd see fit to send regular rain showers - only at night, of course. And traveling mercies for this young officer as he carries out his duties. Amen."

"Thank you kindly." Wade shook hands all around. "It surely eases my mind to know the resort's in your good hands."

"If your father were here, he'd be bursting his buttons." Clayton patted his back. "You make him proud, every day of your life, Wade."

The three soldiers saluted, then the men filed out into the night.

Selina whipped a pair of scissors from her apron. "Sit yourself down and no wiggling. I'm not sending you out in the world looking like some old ragamuffin child nobody loves." She trimmed the hair curling behind his ears, then blew on his neck. "Now you mind yourself out there. I won't be able to keep an eye on you, but Jesus will."

"Yes'm." He pulled the resort's keyring from his pocket and handed it to her.

She grabbed him in a fierce hug. "Less worrying, more praying."

"Always." He grinned.

Selina narrowed her eyes. "Might could warn Miss Maybelle about you."

His grin widened. "More fun for me if you don't."

CHAPTER FOUR

Morning ought to be shrouded in low clouds and drizzle, but instead Virginia did its best to impress with a cloudless sky and gentle breezes infused with the perfume of summer flowers.

Mabel slumped in the seat of the train's passenger car, her sore foot elevated on her suitcase and her aching head propped against the window. Foolish pride. She ought to know better. An amazon like her had no business letting her heart hope. In spite of the progress women had made in education and employment, females were primarily judged by their beauty. Gibson girls were allowed to bike and swim, but a Boston study had decided the perfect American woman was five foot, three inches tall. Mabel had zoomed past that height in fourth grade.

When teachers paired up the students to learn the Virginia reel, Mabel had been relegated to the role of the caller, to keep her from squashing another child. A few years later, when the students paired themselves for romance, she'd been the odd one out every time. Even in college, when some boys finally caught up to her height, they still preferred dainty girls like Wade's mother. Petite versus huge. With her bones, she'd never win that battle.

"You'll bump your head, soon as this train gets going."

Oh, no, not— Who else but Wade Hampton Alexander? He slung his suitcase and slouch hat onto the luggage rack. His khaki jacket and riding breeches hinted at broad shoulders and muscular thighs. Mabel didn't need any more hints - the image of this man in a swimsuit was imprinted on her foolish brain.

She straightened and tried to muster indignation. "What are you doing?"

"Mr. Johnson?" He addressed the porter. "Might you have a pillow for Miss Easterly?"

"Yes sir, Mr. Wade. Here you go."

Wade took the seat beside her, propped the pillow on his shoulder, and patted it. "There, that'll be a lot more comfortable."

Put her head on his shoulder? When lead turns to gold. "I released you from any obligation to me."

"You're outranked. TR was my commanding officer and now he's my president."

"You served under—" Mabel pressed the aching spot between her eyebrows. "That's why he raced down here."

"Up. The heights of Fauquier range up to a thousand feet, while Washington's pretty much at sea level."

How could she rid herself of him? "The elevation here is 340 feet."

"I'm certain you noticed the ride to the resort was uphill all the way." He arched an eyebrow. "Only one way to shed me."

And rid her heart of its reckless attraction? "Fine," she huffed as she gathered her satchel. "The first time I defy my father, I sprain my ankle, get caught in a lie, and encounter someone who has the president at his beck and call. May as well go back to Washington."

If she were an ordinary girl, she could slip past him. But at this size, her clodhoppers had no place to step except on Mr. Wade Hampton Alexander. She hesitated a moment to consider doing just that. And then the train lurched out of the station, throwing her back into the seat with a graceless plop.

"Too late." Wade said with excessive cheerfulness. "Although to tell the truth, I telegraphed TR to find out if you were part of the National Conservation Commission. I had no idea he would show up here."

"To tell the truth?" Mabel echoed. "If you want to tell the truth, admit your water doesn't cure dropsy, dyspepsia, diabetes, and neurasthenia."

"Ah, you've read our brochure from 1882. We no longer make those claims." Wade leaned back in his seat. "I was raised by a woman who doesn't suffer liars, who can fire a shoe around a corner and slap the back of my head."

"That's exactly what I'm talking about." Mabel shook her head. "I cannot imagine your mother ever throwing a shoe."

"I'm talking about Selina. She said you didn't drink your water this morning." He handed her a canteen, its canvas marked "U.S." When she hesitated, he said, "C'mon, now. It's been tested more recently than any water I know of."

Unless ridiculous amounts of crying had led to dehydration, this water wouldn't cure what ailed her. Mabel pulled the cork and took a sip. "Your water is safe. You don't need to—" Flirt? His denial would trample her heart further. "Butter me up."

"Why Miss Maybelle, the more butter the better. That goes for sugar, too." Even if he didn't lie, Wade laced his conversation with flattery and nonsense, as embellished as a mineral spring's advertisement.

Wade jumped out of his seat to help a diminutive woman stow her bag. "Be still my heart, if it isn't the yellow rose of Roanoke. Are you leaving town without visiting the springs, Mrs. Davis?"

Mabel closed her eyes, wishing she could as easily shut her ears to Wade's chitchat. But he insisted on introducing her, announcing where she was from and what she was here for to the lady across the aisle, the family sitting ahead of them, and the resort guests behind them. Most responded with a narrow-

41

eyed gaze. Was it because she was a Yankee or because she was a scientist? Either way, Mabel found Southerners more suspicious than hospitable.

At the Calverton junction, Wade helped her off the train. He hefted her bags and headed for the main line while greeting other travelers and railroad employees. He must know everyone for miles about - everyone and his dog.

When he paused for a breath, she said, "I am capable of carrying my own bags." Of course, her ankle appreciated the relief, even if her prickly mood wouldn't let her admit it.

"Now Miss Maybelle." His grin indicated he found her claim amusing. "I'd be no gentleman at all if'n I let you tote your own poke. Word would get back to Miss Selina and she'd whoop me into next week."

Wade greeted an ancient man curled in the corner of the platform. "Mr. Absalom, heads or tails, sir?"

Clouded eyes turned toward Wade's voice. "Oh, Mr. Wade, I believe tails this morning."

Wade tossed the quarter, caught it with a slap of his palm, then pressed it into the man's bony hand. "Tails it is. Mr. Absalom, you sure can call them." Then he handed over a package from his pocket. "And Mrs. Fitzhugh has another recipe for you to try. Next time I'm through, you'll tell me what you think."

"Thank you kindly, sir. Traveling mercies, sir."

"Appreciate your prayers, Mr. Absalom." Wade handed Mabel into the southbound passenger car. She sat by the window and he settled next to her, stretching out his long legs.

Mabel watched through the coal-dusted window as the elderly man shuffled up the street. One hand clutched a sack, the other tapped a walking stick. "Did you give away your lunch?"

"Reckon he needs it more than I do. Absalom worked at Fauquier all his life. When his eyes started to fail, his daughter moved him in with her and her always-hungry sons." Wade frowned over her shoulder. "Taking those biscuits home, likely he'll end up with only the crumbs."

The train pulled away from the station. Wade strolled to the back of the car to chat with the other passengers. Snatches of conversation drifted over the rattle of the passenger car.

"Did you see the legs on—"

"—descended from fast—"

"—with a chest like that, won't get winded—"

Were they speculating on horse racing or gossiping about women? The others disembarked at Culpepper and Wade returned to his seat.

A barefoot boy slipped onto the seat across the aisle and set his wicker hamper beside him.

"Meow."

"Excuse me, young sir," Wade said to the boy. "Your picnic just said 'meow.'"

"Ain't no picnic." The kid flipped open the lid and pulled out a wiggling ball of striped fur.

The kitten filled Wade's hands. Tiny teeth tried to gnaw his knuckle. "Sorry little fellow, already gave away my lunch."

"That there's a girl cat."

"Sure enough, it is. And a mighty fine one she is." Wade set the kitten in Mabel's lap. "Just what you need to keep you company, Miss Maybelle. You could name her Dixie."

Quickly, before she could become attached, the cat went back in the boy. "I'm sorry. She's a very nice cat, but with my traveling schedule, I couldn't possibly care for a pet." Mabel narrowed her eyes at Wade and he grinned. What wouldn't he do to derail her research?

The conductor announced Charlottesville.

"Shall I take you on a tour, Miss Maybelle? You'd enjoy the University of Virginia and Jefferson's Monticello."

She wouldn't be detered from her mission that easily. "No thank you. But feel free to tip your hat, bow, genuflect, or pay your respects as you must."

"Well, if your Yankee sensibilities won't be offended." Wade stood and saluted toward the university. He helped an elderly lady stow her valise, then returned to his seat. "Now North Garden, the next stop, is near the Roosevelts' country place, a little old cabin back in the pines. Believe it has a spring. If you'd like to test the presidential waters, they'd surely appreciate it."

The train rolled past a closed mill and two humble farm houses. Would the numerous and wealthy Roosevelts squeeze into a backwoods cabin? Not likely. "The president would have directed me to test his spring if he'd so desired."

Wade was a troublemaker with a capital "T."

He stretched, brushing against her shoulder. "So, where to? God blessed Virginia with an abundance of springs. I hear The Homestead's nice. You have the pamphlet for Rockbridge Alum Springs. I'm guessing you have a plan, maps, and such."

"My plans are no concern of yours."

"Your plans are my only concern at the moment." He pulled out the map from her pocket. "Ah, here we go."

"Careful." If he ripped it, she'd be hard-pressed to find a replacement.

Ward unfolded it. "Miss Maybelle, you've been swindled - we don't have this many roads in Virginia."

"It's a topographic map from the United States Geological Survey. The contour lines show differences in elevation. Closer lines indicate steeper slopes. Don't they teach anything—" She caught a glimpse of his mouth quirking up.

"Oh, Miss Maybelle, how you say those big words."

Her traitorous body vibrated to the purr of his voice. She pointed to a dot in the southwest corner. "Washington Springs is my first stop." Maybe he wouldn't want to be so far away from his resort.

"To give your ankle more time to heal. If only you'd taken advantage of your opportunity to heal at Fauquier." He leaned close to examine the map. "Way down there? You're certain it's not in Tennessee or North Carolina?"

Ignore him. Except he smelled delicious, like a rain-washed forest.

He followed her pencil lines. "Then looks like Wyrick is next. Make sure they're not bottling and selling poison. Montgomery has the distinction of being destroyed not only by fire, but by flood. We don't need to stop there."

We is it now? "I'm commissioned to survey all the springs that have made health claims. What if someone tried to reopen the resort?"

"Not with the devil sending all those calamities."

Mabel blinked. If there was a devil, she was looking at him, a handsome one at that. "You attribute disasters to an evil spirit? Were you haunted by the ghost of Edgar Allan Poe during your time at the university?"

"Only in print." The side of his mouth tipped up. "No, the guests believe the devil's behind Montgomery's misfortunes. Once rumors set in, may as well close up for good."

Perhaps she could take advantage of his knowledge. "So what do you know about these other resorts? Which ones have you visited?"

"Visited?" He leaned back in the seat, finally giving her some space. "Running a resort is no vacation. I can't remember when I last had a day off, much less time to explore."

"Oh." Mabel and her father traveled between every semester, mixing research with sightseeing. She'd been down the Nile, the Amazon, a host of rivers in Russia with unpronounable names, and the Yangtze. Her favorite was the Danube. "What do you do when your resort is closed?"

"Off-season. Never speak of the resort being closed - that's my nightmare." He shuddered. "Plan for the next season. Repair the buildings. Hire and train staff. I'm probably more of a grind than you."

"So who is running Fauquier while you're gone?"

"Robert E." His jaw clenched and he shrank down in the seat for a moment, then he bounced back to full size and full-force personality. "Not to worry. My staff knows what to do."

Mabel considered the long hours she'd spent in the laboratory, classroom, and library against the fact Wade seemed to spend an inordinate amount of time lounging about. "Well, you've finally gotten a vacation now. You won't have any duties while I complete my research."

"Not unless you count me fishing you out of our springs." He studied her, his smile growing. "Which was too much fun to count as a duty."

CHAPTER FIVE

Wade had made it his life's business to see that his guests enjoyed themselves. So while Miss Maybelle started the day in a temper - no doubt his own fault - a few jokes and smiles should smooth the frown from her face. Then all he had to do was sit back and the beauty of Virginia would make her forget this silliness about water testing.

"Excuse me," Miss Maybelle interrupted his recounting of Hiram and Stuart's misadventures with the honey tree. "Did the conductor announce Lynchburg?"

Wade shook his head. "Can you guess how many bee stings —"

The man in the seat in front of them turned. "Yes'm. Next stop Lynchburg."

"I'm changing trains here." Maybelle shooed him out of the seat.

"Are you sure?" Wade took her bags. "This train seems mighty fine."

Her frown returned, accompanied by a narrow-eyed glare. "I studied the schedule and mapped out the route." Of course she did.

The train crossed the James River and stopped at the two-story brick depot.

Wade got a move on. "Well, would you look at that." He pointed out the narrow waterway on the city-side of the tracks.

"The James River Canal. George Washington surveyed and planned it all out."

"Notable," she murmured without stopping to admire it. She hurried into the depot.

Wade followed her to the restaurant. The staff rushed around with the fierce efficiency characteristic of Yankees. A waiter took Maybelle's order before she even settled in her seat, then turned to Wade.

"Good afternoon, my good man. Don't suppose you have a specialty—"

"He'll have the same," Maybelle said and the waiter raced off before Wade could contradict her.

"Wait a minute—"

"There's no minute in the schedule." She compared the watch pinned to her shirtwaist with the large clock on the back wall.

"No wonder so many of Fauquier's guests come to us with digestive complaints."

The waiter returned so quickly, he must have grabbed some old food sitting around. He dropped sandwiches and iced teas on the counter, then disappeared again. Wade peeked under the bread, finding a slice of ham without any mayonnaise, butter, or mustard. And the tea - he took a sip - lacked an adequate amount of sweetness. He waved to catch the waiter's attention. "This food isn't fresh."

Miss Maybelle finished the first half of her sandwich.

Wade found a sugar bowl on an empty table and set his tea to rights. "Is this how people eat in the city?" He pointed to a glass case as a waiter dashed past. "Two slices of chocolate cake, please."

Maybelle shook her head and pointed to the clock.

"You've got to make time for dessert. Doesn't the Bible say to consider the lilies?"

"That verse is about worry, not hurry." As fast as she downed her food, dyspepsia would be her next worry.

"Seems like much the same." The cake arrived with as little ceremony as the sandwiches. Wade pushed her plate and fork closer, then sampled his. A dense, smooth burst of dark chocolate swirled over his tongue. He waved a forkful under her nose. "Hmm, hmm, hmm. Miss Maybelle, you have got to try this. This restaurant may not do anything else right, but they've got one humdinger of a cook."

She leaned away from him. "Bring it with you."

"Oh Miss Maybelle, the restaurant would miss their plates." Not likely. The manager had chosen plain dishware, a nickel a piece.

"Wade." Maybelle stood. What sort of self-control did this woman have that she could resist chocolate cake?

He took another bite. "This could be the answer for Fauquier White Sulphur Springs, if I can hire away their cook."

"The next train—" She tried to step around him.

"Let me talk to the kitchen. Maybe they'll share the recipe."

"I'm boarding." Back as straight as a soldier's, she marched for the door.

"I'll bring your tote, soon as I—"

With a gasp, she executed an about-face and reached for her suitcase.

"No, allow me. Don't want to injure your ankle. I'll be along."

She tugged on the handle, but he wouldn't let go. Then she grabbed the satchel's strap hanging on his shoulder, giving up her suitcase of clothes for her scientific paraphenalia. Brows lowered over flashing eyes. "Let go of my satchel."

"See now, I believe that Bible verse was right. Your hurry's turned into worry."

"I never said the Bible verse was wrong," she said through clenched teeth. "I said your reference was incorrect. And I wouldn't have a worry if I was boarding. Let me—"

"Miss Maybelle, your face is as pink as a mountain laurel blossom just before it blooms."

She yanked, pulling him within reach of her lips, and raised her chin. Such a temptation. "Mr. Alexander—"

Outside, a whistle blew and a bell rang. They both looked up in time to see the westbound train huff and rattle pass the window.

Maybelle muttered in a foreign language, then covered her mouth.

She might call him a louse, but resort owners would be calling him a hero when he stopped her.

"We'll catch the next one, don't you worry." Wade pushed her plate closer. "There, now, Miss Maybelle, you can have dessert. You have plenty of time."

"But no appetite." She moved to an empty table, opened her map and the Southern Railway schedule. After a moment, she folded her papers and spoke to the clock behind him. "Mr. Alexander, in seven minutes you will leave on the northbound train." She snatched up her luggage and limped out of the restaurant.

"Aw, Miss Maybelle..." Wade picked up his bags and hurried after her. He scanned the waiting room. A six-foot tall woman with a worse-for-wear straw hat perched on her chestnut hair shouldn't be difficult to find. But she wasn't there. He stepped out onto the platform and watched the northbound passengers board. No, Miss Maybelle wouldn't give up and go home, that much was for certain. He studied the timetable and tried to picture her map. Westbound, toward Roanoke, he decided. Keeping a sharp eye out, he hiked around to the other tracks.

"Wade Hampton Alexander!" A flurry of ruffles and curls cornered him. "I declare, you are a sight for sore eyes."

Horrible timing, but he couldn't afford to offend a hotel guest. Wade shook the extended gloved hand. "Miss Hopkins. Your eyes are too pretty to be sore." Although as fast as her lashes fluttered, it was hard to see what condition her eyes were in.

The young lady giggled and pulled his hand far too close to her bosom for propriety. "As well as we know each other, you ought to call me by my given name. Unless…" She brought her head within inches of his shoulder, nearly suffocating him with attar of roses perfume, "…you've forgotten."

"You, Miss Florence, are unforgettable." He had to get rid of her, so he could watch for Maybelle. *Lord, have mercy.* As badly as Wade behaved today, he couldn't expect help from above.

"How fortunate to bump into you when I'm in need of assistance of a gentleman such as yourself."

This damsel in permanent distress had worn out her welcome years ago. "I only have a moment, until the next train."

"Well surely you wouldn't mind helping a little bitty thing like me with her luggage." Florence tucked his hand under her elbow and strolled toward the depot. If she wanted to play antebellum South, she ought to travel with a chaperone and a servant.

The westbound whistled and chugged around the curve of the river, braking to a stop. Serve him right if he missed the train and Maybelle. Florence dangling from his arm, Wade double-timed it to the baggage room. "Good afternoon, sir," he called to the nearest porter. "Might could you help this lady with her luggage?"

"Well, I never." Florence huffed and puffed as loudly as the steam engine.

"Nice seeing you again." Wade disengaged his arm and hurried away. "All the best to your folks."

He still hadn't spotted Maybelle. And sure as shooting, he hoped she hadn't seen Florence digging her claws into him. He hefted his bag and ran for the train as the conductor called "all aboard."

Maybelle's voice carried over the murmur of the other travelers. "No, you may not sit here."

"Aw, you think you too good for the likes of me?" A man tried to tuck his grubby carcass onto Maybelle's seat. He spaced his syllables with care as if he'd imbibed overly much. "You a mite plain, you ask me."

"Which she didn't." Wade jabbed his thumb over his shoulder. "This lady is accompanied. Find another seat."

"Well…" Bleary eyes turned his way and rose to meet his gaze. "Don't mind if I do." The drunk swayed toward the back end of the car.

Maybelle glared at them both. Wade's shenanigans and being pestered by an old coot had got her in quite a lather. "And here I thought wildlife was the worry."

"You don't think that fellow was a bit wild?"

"Almost as wild as your lady friend." She gestured toward the receding depot.

Did he hear a touch of jealousy in Miss Maybelle's voice? "Hotel guest," Wade said in a soothing tone. He reached for her satchel, to move it off the seat. She snatched the bag up and clutched it on her lap with both hands. He slid onto the seat beside her. Now, time to make Miss Maybelle forget about water testing.

Lord in Heaven, I didn't ask to have my patience tried. Mabel fought to hold in a scream as the warehouses of Lynchburg slid past the passenger car window. Father would have drawn and quartered any expedition member who caused as much trouble as Wade had. Mabel had dismissed the man twice, but still he turned up, as unwelcome as mold spores in a petri dish. "Mr. Alexander—"

"I declare, you sound like a teacher." Wade braced his head with two fingertips at his temple and studied her. "If I say 'ain't,' you gonna whack me with a ruler?"

"Hardly worth the effort as I suspect you're beyond redemption." *Don't look at him. Do not look at him.* "However I may use my Coddington magnifier to try to find your brain."

"Many a teacher searched for my brain or suggested where I should look for it, all to no effect. I've been switched, belted, and whupped with a shoe, but never magnified." Wade's low chuckle set off an oscillation deep within her. "The Geophysical Lab hasn't been open all that long. Where'd you teach afore that?"

"The Friends School."

His grin widened. "The Friends School. I highly recommend making friends at school."

Mabel uncrossed her legs, pivoted toward him, and tried to spear him with a glance, but her heart took the piercing. "I'll have you know the Friends School was started by the Quakers, has been in business for twenty- five years, and is considered one of the best schools in the nation. The president's youngest son attends, and the president himself gave the commencement address last year. It has both chemistry and physical laboratories. And, unlike your archaic University of Virginia, it's coeducational."

"Well sure that's where Archie gets his schooling, seeing as how it's so close to the White House."

Of course, President Roosevelt's old Rough Rider buddy knew all about the Friends School but pretended ignorance to make a fool out of her. Mabel turned to peer over the back of her seat. "I'd prefer to travel with a more affable companion. Where is that inebriated man?"

"D'you suppose the engineer might could harness the steam coming out of your ears, we'd get there a mite sooner."

"Mr. Alexander—"

"Good teacher trick, using the surname. Gonna send a note 'round to my mama?"

"I will complete my research with or without your

cooperation."

He raised his hands. "I'm cooperating. We're headed in the right direction, aren't we? Can't get more cooperative than that."

"You could stop talking."

"Aw, Miss Maybelle, we're just passing the time. We'll be in Roanoke in two shakes of a beagle's tail."

She checked the watch pinned to her shirtwaist. "If you can be quiet for an hour, I'll give you a lemon drop."

"What age students did you teach?"

"A range. I learned to adapt my lessons to any level. Even yours."

He grinned and she nearly smiled in response. "So what would you teach me?"

"Honesty."

"Honesty?" Wade pressed his hand over his heart. "Miss Maybelle, you wound me. I'm as honest as the train tracks are long. Even with your best microscope, you won't find a dishonest bone in my body."

Never mind his bones. It was his tongue, all his sweet words, leading her heart astray. She reached in her satchel and brought forth a small brown bag. "Take one."

He pulled out a lemon drop. "Don't mind if I do."

Even quiet, Wade managed to rattle her. He leaned across her, enveloping her in his pine scent, to point out the Peaks of Otter. He brushed against her elbow or knee every time he shifted position. And, in spite of the pleasant vistas, he spent most of the ride watching her.

The silent interlude ended when an ancient fellow took the seat across from them at the Bedford stop.

Wade pointed to the narrow wooden box on his lap. "Good afternoon, sir. Might that be a dulcimer?"

The old man brightened. "Yessiree. Not many city folks

recognize 'em."

"I'm from the hills of Fauquier County. If you've a mind to play us a tune, I'd surely appreciate it."

"Be glad to. Whatcha ya wanna hear?"

"Do you know 'School Days?' I'm traveling with a teacher."

"You go ahead sing it and I'll follow along." Gnarled fingers reached into his overalls' pocket and pulled out a quill. He strummed the feather across the strings, then twisted a knob to bring the D into tune. "Go on."

"'School days, school days, Dear old Golden Rule days,'" Wade sang in a rich baritone.

Mabel groaned.

"Sing along, Miss Maybelle." Wade nudged her. "'Reading, 'riting, and 'rithmetic, taught to the tune of a hickory stick.'"

"If only I had a hickory stick," Mabel muttered.

Wade leaned closer. "'You were my queen in calico. I was your bashful, barefoot beau.'"

She plastered her body to the window. "I doubt you've ever been bashful."

He changed the lyrics to avoid mention of love. "'You wrote on my slate, "Wade is great," when we were a couple of kids.'"

"You still a couple of kids." The old man cackled. "Now I'll play you one of mine." His repetoire included an assortment of old time and Celtic tunes. Mabel couldn't make out his words through his thick drawl, but her toes tapped of their own volition.

The dulcimer player started in on "The Cat Came Back."

"You know this one, the chorus at least." Wade gave her hand a pat, his touch warm and entirely too friendly. "C'mon, Miss Maybelle. Ornery don't get us there any faster."

The old fellow made some encouraging noise and she joined in. He segued into "When the Roll is Called up Yonder," and she added the harmony. He ended their concert with "Keep on the Sunny Side."

"Trust our Savior always," the song counseled. Yes, Mabel would trust Jesus, but not the scoundrel next to her.

Wade had just started to sweeten Maybelle's mood - thanks to the dulcimer player - when she announced she was disembarking.

The sign on the little white depot read "Dublin." "Your first stop is Washington Springs."

He finally got her to look at him, but it wasn't with the affection he hoped for. Far from it. In fact, he'd swear fire shot from her dark eyes. "It was. Until you ruined my schedule." Clutching her satchel, Maybelle disembarked.

"I'll make it up to you by showing you how a Virginia gentleman treats a lady." Wade gathered their suitcases and followed her to the platform. "All my fault. I'm genuinely sorry."

"I find that difficult to believe." She stood with crossed arms, surveying the cluster of buildings huddled by the train tracks, all closed for the night, and not even a hound dog to greet them. Farms stretched across the foothills. The land rose into a ridge forested with pines and maples. "A different world from the northern part of the state."

"And a whole different brand of people down here," Wade said. "If you think I'm a hillbilly…"

"You don't want to know what I think of you."

Wade's stomach growled. "We should have stopped in Roanoke. I hear they have some nice restaurants."

"If you'd spend less time talking and more eating…"

"You're right, Miss Maybelle. Absolutely right." Being agreeable worked with most women. "We'd best be finding a place to stay. Don't want to wander these mountains in the dark."

"Summer solstice was last week. It's only ten miles." Maybelle checked the watch pinned to her shirtwaist and started up the road. "We'll arrive before dark."

"A fur piece for a sore ankle."

"Someone will come along and pick us up."

"Have much experience riding in a manure wagon, Miss Easterly?"

"Do you have another idea, Mr. Alexander?" She glanced over her shoulder, then stopped and stared. "Oh, for heaven's sake. Pulaski Alum Springs has a telephone. Right behind you."

Wade opened the door of the closet and lifted the handset. The voice on the other end promised to send a buggy directly, which could be a while. He plopped down on the bench, stretched out his legs, and patted the spot beside him. "Phone connection's a great idea. We could do that at Fauquier." He said another prayer that his staff would keep Robert E at bay.

Miss Starchy-Drawers perched as far away as possible. The evening sun get her hair aglow. "Perhaps this could be a research expedition for you, too."

After all the stumbling blocks he'd thrown in her way, she gave him a helpful suggestion? Or was she just trying to keep him out of her way? "Reckon so."

A wagonette raced down the hill. The driver braked to a stop in front of them and asked, "Looking for a ride up to Pulaski Alum Springs?"

CHAPTER SIX

A young woman with white-blonde hair, creamy complexion, and an hourglass figure celebrated by her eyelet dress held the wagonette's reins. "Looking for a ride up to Pulaski Alum Springs?"

Someone new for Wade to flirt with so Mabel could concentrate on her research. But instead of relief, a sinking sensation weighted her steps. Mabel reached for the back seat, but Wade surprised her by handing her up to the front.

"That all y'all got for luggage?" The driver eyed their suitcases. "Wish I could travel so light."

"That's all." Wade hopped into the second seat, then leaned forward, bringing his face close to the princess's. "I'm Wade and this here is Maybelle."

"Pleased to meet you. I'm Destamonia." No ordinary name for this beauty. She shook the reins and they trotted out of town. "Sorry I look such a fright. Y'all called just as I got out of the bath, so I didn't have time to pin up my hair nor put on shoes."

Through the magic that favored pretty girls, her dainty feet were still clean.

"Any rooms available?" Wade crossed his arms on the seat back, probably to keep from running his hands through Destamonia's tresses.

"Yep." She clucked to the horse. "Hold on. I'm going to make sure y'all get to supper. We've got us a dance band coming across the mountain from Pumpkin Center!"

Wade and Destamonia chattered on about music, dances, and resorts as they raced past farms, splashed through a creek, and then climbed a ridge whose sides had been raked by a giant's fingers. Her heart fluttered about Wade, and now her brain had gone fanciful. Mabel shook her head.

Wade nudged her shoulder. "What you shaking your head 'no' for?"

Mabel collected herself and pointed to a specimen with drooping branches laced with white flowers. "No, I've never seen a tree like that."

"Sourwood," Destamonia said. "That there's the makings of the best honey in all Virginia. Think it's pretty now, y'all come back in the fall when its leaves turn red. And it sparked a fine song, too." She belted out the ballad, sliding in and out of notes. Wade kept time tapping his feet and joined in on the "hi-ho fiddle-di-day" lines.

When the tune ended Wade said, "Good way to keep your guests entertained on the long ride from the train. My resort is about the same distance from the depot and our guests fret about the distance."

Destamonia nodded. "Ours come from Atlanta and Charleston, so what's ten more miles?"

"Our guests travel from Washington, Baltimore and Philadephia mostly."

Mabel wasn't sure if it was the ride - Destamonia barely slowed for switchbacks - or the scenic views that took her breath away. They crossed the ridge and descended into a high valley. Cattle grazed in meadows beside a burbling creek.

By the time they arrived at the resort, long shadows stretched through the pines and summer's heat had eased. The buildings had been built in the same style as Fauquier's, with two stories and wide porches.

Destamonia jumped down, not waiting for Wade's Virginia-speed manners, then grabbed their bags. Mabel let her take the satchel. "Y'all eat supper. I'll put your bags in twenty-eight."

"We'll need two rooms." Mabel enjoyed Wade's assist in dismounting.

Cornflower blue eyes blinked, then widened. "You're not married." She looked Wade over with a gleam in her eye. "Room twenty-nine and I'll see *you* at the dance."

"Uh-oh," Wade muttered.

"What's wrong?" Mabel asked. Didn't he want to dance with the perfect Miss Destamonia?

"It's wood frame. Fire trap." His frown deepened. "Make sure your window opens. Know where the exits and staircases are. And fill your pitcher with water before going to bed."

Since when did Mr. Happy-Go-Lucky worry about safety? No doubt another attempt to distract her. Mabel headed for the dining hall at a brisk clip.

Wade caught up to her and wrapped his hand around her elbow. "No running away."

"You'll have a wonderful time dancing while I work on my report."

"Your report isn't due until September, dancing partner."

"I have a sore ankle, remember?"

"I'll never forget." He flashed a grin. "But you're walking just fine, Miss Maybelle. More than fine."

The kitchen staff seated them and brought out platters of fried chicken.

Mabel scanned the diners finishing their meals. Women outnumbered men two to one. "It's not as though Destamonia won't have plenty of competition."

"You'd desert me in my moment of need."

"For your own safety."

"I suppose you left a trail of broken hearts up north."

"More like broken toes, if I had danced."

A violin tuned outside.

"You didn't dance? Ever?" Wade forked his cornbread and raised it like a scepter. "Well, Miss Maybelle, it's high time you got out on the dance floor."

A mandolin and a guitar added their voices. Then a banjo joined in. The guests drifted out, each female giving Wade her most inviting smile.

Mabel dug in her figurative heels. She'd be an ungainly elephant among these gazelles. "I'd hate to have to report to President Roosevelt that you'd been injured in the line of duty," she said.

"Sip of spring water will set me right." Wade pulled back the tablecloth and peered beneath. Oh, well, he'd seen her big feet when she sprained her ankle. Neither the local stores nor the Sears catalog sold women's shoes larger than size eight. And the latest style - pointy-toed horrors - pinched and made her feet look even larger. So a shoemaker had made Mabel pair of comfortable, but frumpy boots.

Wade slid his leg close and pressed his leather boot next to hers. His extended a good inch, maybe even two past hers. His smile grew slowly, heating her cheeks. He let the tablecloth drop and put his open hand in front of her. "Let's be brave."

Seeing no way around it, she put her hand in his. His fingers closed around hers with a comfortable fit, warm, strong, and dry. Dancing with Wade meant holding hands, and that could only lead to heartbreak. "Promise to stop if I step on you."

They stood up together and he led her outside. "If you promise to save me from Destamonia," he muttered from the side of his mouth.

"But she's lovely."

"Like porcelain," he said as if there was something wrong with fine china.

They joined a set of five couples. Without a doubt, Wade was the most handsome man in the line: broad shouldered, thick copper-brown hair, and a full-of-mischief smile. The rest of the women in the set fluttered their eyelashes at him. Mabel wished — once again — that she could attract the heart of someone as delightful as Wade. And that he wasn't so opposed to her fieldwork.

"All hands around!" A barrel-chested man climbed on a crate beside the band and drawled something that might have referenced the Virginia Reel.

Mabel winced. "I won't be able to understand his calls."

"That's all right." Wade nodded. "I will."

The music started. With hand-signals and tips of his head, Wade kept her from making any disastrous mistakes. They sailed through the turns and the do-si-dos. Wade's innate sense of rhythm and nimble moves made her feel light on her feet. Why had she resisted this so? Dancing was fun.

As the head man turned her around, Mabel caught a whiff of body odor - if he'd bathed in Pulaski Alum Springs water, he'd forgotten to use soap. Fortunately the field of thyme beneath their feet and the cool breeze off the mountain kept the air fresh. With the next turn, he spun her back to Wade and his clean spring trees scent.

The head couple cast off, then formed an arch. The other pairs joined hands and passed below their raised arms. Oh, no — Mabel wouldn't fit. She would clobber the arch. The head woman glanced over her shoulder, eyes wide. She went up on tiptoes, loosening hold of her partner, and inched backwards. Wade met Mabel at the bottom of the set. He reached, but instead of taking her hand, he grasped her elbow and guided her ahead of him. She popped through the arch and he followed. He slid his hand forward into hers and they finished the dance.

"We did it." He grinned as they returned to their places.

"All toes intact." One heart, however, do-si-doed itself silly.

Wade had hired his share of local musicians, so he knew bands could be hit-or-miss. Fortunately the Pumpkin Center group came through. Various performers sat in, spelling the first bunch, but every one stayed in tune and in time. For the grand finale, all the musicians played together, including an ancient fellow on the washboard and Destamonia on spoons for a rousing performance of "Dixie." Then they dove into an a cappella "Carry me Back to Ol' Virginny," and Wade figured it was time to make their exit. Once Maybelle heard those lyrics, she'd give him no end of trouble.

"A perfect night." Wade tucked Miss Maybelle's arm under his, and strolled with her down the gravel path to the edge of the resort. If he were the kind of fellow who had a plan, this evening went according to it. He and Maybelle had danced every dance, even though she kept trying to escape to her room on one flimsy excuse or another. He got her to relax and smile for a change. Unlike most of the girls he knew, she never got winded and had to sit out a set. With Maybelle on his arm, the aquisitive girls stayed away - he didn't end the night facing down an angry pappy armed with a shotgun and a preacher.

"No toes were harmed," Maybelle said.

"And now the perfect ending: stargazing."

"Aren't you exhausted from evading all that female ardor?"

"Are you worn out from defending my honor?" He stole a glance at her. She'd lost her smile again, so he stroked the back of her hand with his thumb. "What if I'm taking advantage of traveling with a scientist? I'm guessing you know the names of all these stars." The ridge blocked any lights from civilization, so the stars shone their best.

Maybelle stopped trying to wiggle away and gasped. "Almost

as clear as the Sahara." She rattled off the names of several constellations while he admired her profile: a straight nose, strong jaw, full lips. Curls tumbled down her neck due to her hairpins loosening while dancing. "That's all I can recall. I'm a chemist, not an astronomer." There she went, running herself down because she didn't know everything. Who likes a wisenheimer anyway?

Hands on the back of her arms, he aimed her toward Arcturus and the other stars forming the Herdsman constellation, and stretched out his drawl. "Now I'll tell you the true story behind all these stars. That 'V' first appeared in the sky in 1583 and guided Sir Walter Raleigh to the colony of Virginia." He stepped closer, so the heat of his body would soften her like candle wax, and turned her south toward Hercules. From this position, her cheek was in range of his kiss, but his cheek was out of range of her slap. He whispered, aiming his breath into the elegant curve of her ear. "That one's the Cavalier, hung in the sky in 1825 by none other than Thomas Jefferson to celebrate the founding of the University of Virginia." He couldn't resist running his finger along the soft curve of her neck.

Maybelle stiffened and stepped away. Uh-oh, he'd moved too fast. She raised a shaking hand toward the north. "I suppose you're going to tell me Cassiopeia's 'W' stands for your athletes, the 'Wahoos.'" She crossed her arms, clasping her elbows. "Enough of your silliness. No one's watching. You can stop now."

"Stop?"

"Stop trying to finagle me into giving up my research." She marched back to the hotel, leaving Wade alone in the dark.

"Actually," he whispered to her retreating back, "I was going to say Cassiopeia is beautiful and grand, just like you, Miss Maybelle."

CHAPTER SEVEN

Sunrise hit Wade's face and he jumped out of bed. Wait— This wasn't his cabin. This wasn't Fauquier White Sulphur Springs. Instead of starting the ovens for the bakers, turning on the fountains, and making sure his staff showed up for work, all he had to do today was keep track of - as his grandfather would say - one bonny lass.

Wade pressed his ear to the wall. No sound on the other side. He expected Miss Maybelle was sleeping in, after all her frolicking about last night.

He dressed then peeked out the window. Morning haze gave the Blue Ridge Mountains their famous color. A few shreds of clouds crossed the sky - nothing to interfere with anyone's vacation. The lawn spread green and empty, recovered from the dancers' trampling, all the way to the dining hall. Too early for breakfast, then.

What should he do now? His minister recommended morning prayers, but Wade had never had time before.

Dear Jesus, Please help me get Miss Maybelle headed back to Washington. And please help Fauquier's staff keep Robert E from setting any fires.

Fire. Last night, Pulaski Alum Springs had lit their dance floor with torches and lanterns hung in the trees. Fauquier had a set of those torches in the basement of... was it the Fairfax or the Monroe cottage?

Just in case he didn't get home today, Wade grabbed a sheet of stationery and dashed off a note to Captain Drake, asking him to lock up the torches. Robert E could cause a lot of trouble if he got ahold of one. He sealed the letter, then headed to the kitchen for a cup of coffee. When Miss Maybelle woke, he'd be ready.

Whoever had built these bathrooms must have been four-foot tall, Mabel decided. The mirror reflected the second button of her shirtwaist. Bending in any direction bumped her against the walls. She rolled up her gloves and tucked them under the bottom edge of the mirror, tilting until the outline of her head came into view. Dawn's light through the narrow window revealed a body large enough for a man.

"Plain as the nose on your face," she said as she brushed, braided, and pinned her hair while pummeling the walls with her elbows. "A nose which must be kept to the grindstone to avoid Mr. Wade Hampton Alexander's nonsense."

Mabel returned her gloves to her pocket and caught a glimpse of her watch. Late. Virginia weaved its southern tendrils around her Yankee work habits. She grabbed the doorknob and it came off in her hand.

Don't even think of being on time, Pulaski Alum Springs seemed to say.

Mabel stuck the knob back into the hole and jiggled, but it failed to engage. She sat on the toilet and peered into the mechanism. Impossibly dark. Further study of the knob showed the spindle had worn through. This was why she preferred chemistry. Reactions either work or they don't. They don't wear out like mechanical parts. If she had a screwdriver, she could pop the latch. Perhaps the mirror— No, its plaster frame would crumble.

Footsteps echoed on the wooden floorboards.

Mabel knocked. "Hello? Can you open this door please?" She hoped it wasn't Wade on the other side. He didn't need another rescue to tease her about.

"Why—" An elderly lady freed her. Her eyes widened at the knob in Mabel's hand. "Lord a'mercy, give me that. Of all the — I hope you weren't shut in all night."

"Only a few minutes. Thank you for releasing me." Mabel retrieved her bags and hurried downstairs to breakfast. To her relief, Wade wasn't in the dining room. Well if he wasn't ready on time, she'd leave him behind. That's how Father ran his expeditions. Her work would proceed more smoothly without his silver-tongued distraction.

Destamonia took the seat across from her, looking as fresh and radiant as the new day. No doubt she hoped to find Wade. "Where's your… friend this morning?"

"I have no idea." Mabel unfolded her map. "Have you ever heard of Kimberling Spring?"

"Do believe I—" The girl's quick intake of breath was echoed by every other female in the room. Mabel knew without looking up, Wade had entered the dining room.

He took the chair next to her. "What are you two girls in cahoots over this fine morning?"

It would serve him right if she had conspired against him, but she didn't have a conniving bone in her skeleton. Mabel focused the map on the table. She couldn't look at him - not after nearly succumbing to his wooing last night. When would she learn? "We're consulting on today's route."

The kitchen staff noticed Wade's arrival - who wouldn't? Within seconds three waitresses called him "Sugar" and served him fried eggs and ham, a cornbread they called pone, a full cup of coffee, and a side-dish of new strawberries. No one else in the dining room had fruit. Wade thanked them and they hovered like electrons around their atom's nucleus.

A tiny man, his face as wrinkled as a dried up apple, tottered up to the table and joined them.

"Ah, the washboard player." Wade shook the man's hand. "Fine job last night."

Destamonia introduced the old fellow. "This here's my great-grandpappy on my mama's side. He runs the dairy, milking the cows, making cheese, and such."

The man said something, but between his thick accent and his lack of teeth, Mabel couldn't understand a word.

Destamonia interpreted. "He heard you're asking about Kimberling Spring."

The grandfather preached a lengthy sermon, complete with pointing, head shaking, and stroking his chin wisps. When he paused for breath, his great-granddaughter said "no."

"No?" Mabel looked from one pair of sky-blue eyes to the other. All his words condensed to one word—no?

Destamonia elaborated, "The resort's been gone well nigh thirty years. Afore the War, they had tournaments with knights and ladies, and dances, fancier than ours last night."

"Let me guess," Wade said to the elderly man. "You played Merlin the Wizard."

A gnarled hand grabbed a table knife, swished it through the air, then jabbed. Wade raised his arms in surrender. Granpappy cackled.

"He weren't so old as he is now. He played Sir Galahad and ran off with Maid Marian."

"Maid Marian?" Wade met Mabel's gaze and winked, the rascal. "Didn't Robin Hood object?"

Granpappy pushed up his sleeve and showed off a tennis-ball-sized bulge of a biceps, then pointed at Mabel.

"He says he could run off with your woman without breathing hard."

Before Wade could deny she was his woman, Mabel asked,

"Where is the spring?"

The elder jabbed an arthritic finger at a spot in the map thick with contour lines. Hogback Ridge topped three thousand feet.

Destamonia continued, "Hotel big enough for five hundred guests."

Wade set down his coffee with a thud. "Let me guess - it burned down."

The girl shuddered, "Thankfully no. Hauled off piece by piece. Houses for lumberjacks, I suspect. Once the lumber company took the trees and left, road went to ruin. You couldn't get a wagon in there nowadays. Nor a horse. 'Bout the only ones into that wilderness is hunters."

Wade pointed to a town on the map. "Hey, I had a classmate from Hicksville. His name was Skeeter."

The University of Virginia admitted Skeeter from Hicksville, but declined to admit women? Mabel squinted at Wade, but for once he didn't seem to be kidding. "Well, if no one drinks from Kimberling Springs, I'll skip that one and go on." She stood.

"I'll bring the wagon around." Destamonia hurried out.

"Meet you out front," Wade said as he picked up Mabel's suitcase. "Try not to get stuck again."

Her face heated. *Stop - scientists do not blush!* "For a place with only one telephone line, gossip certainly spreads quickly."

"Most notable event in Pulaski Alum Springs since Granpappy ran off with Robin Hood's girlfriend." He reached for her satchel, but she wouldn't let go. "Too bad you won't have time to test the water here."

"Already done. At sunrise."

His gaze narrowed for a fraction of a second - aha, the stinker *had* planned to interfere with her research - then his grin returned. "Without me guarding you? Oh, Miss Maybelle, it's a wonder some bear didn't eat you for breakfast."

"I'll take my chances." Mabel considered Wade a greater

threat - to her research and her heart - than any wildlife.

CHAPTER EIGHT

On the train south, clever Miss Maybelle had found an empty seat next to a woman, leaving Wade to sit with a loquacious former classmate. But once they disembarked at Glade Spring she couldn't avoid him any longer. Wade emerged from the livery with a two-wheeled cart known hereabouts as a one-hoss shay, and a lively mare. "Miss Maybelle, may I present Miss Dixie."

The scientist tipped her head toward his classmate lounging on the porch of the local hotel. "You're welcome to stay and visit with your friend."

"As Selina would say, I'd rather clean a chicken coop." Wade nodded at the bovine-filled fields surrounding the town. "Otis has gone from foolish about football to batty about beef. Is there anything, anything at all, you'd like to know about the cattle industry hereabouts? No, I'll come along with you."

"All right, then. If you promise to behave." Which of course, he never promised. She stowed her satchel beneath her seat, grabbed the handle, and put her foot on the step. Wade took the opportunity to give her a boost and she didn't take the opportunity to kick him for his effort, which he counted as a thawing in their relationship. She faced straight ahead and said, "Thank you, but my ankle is fully restored."

"I'm here to help," he said, earning a back-of-her-throat "huh." Wade joined her on the seat and giddy-upped to Dixie.

71

A block later, he stopped the horse and put on the brake.

"Now what?"

Wade hopped down and studied the wheel.

Maybelle leaned over the rail. Dark brows lowered over darker eyes. "Drag your feet all you want, but I will complete my research. You cannot stop me. I'm perfectly capable of going on without you."

"We'll be both dragging our feet when this spoke gives way."

"Well, I'll just see about that." She slid across the seat. Before she could jump down, Wade lifted her again, easing her to the street. She spun out of his grasp and bent to examine the wheel, spotting the problem even faster than he had. One spoke rattled in the hub. A spot of dried glue showed where someone had tried to shim it tight. Heavy wear marred the rest of the spokes. She stepped back and took a breath. "You're right. This wheel is ready to fail."

"C'mon, Dixie." Wade grabbed the mare's bridle and walked her back to the livery.

"Further delay will not be tolerated." Maybelle walked on the other side of the horse. "Did you deliberately ask for the most decrepit buggy? Do you intend to try every junk carriage in town? Must I check this horse for soundness?"

Dixie tossed her head with an emphatic no.

The stableman must have heard them coming, as he quickly swapped the old chaise for a new runabout with staggered spokes. He promised this one wouldn't fail. Wade helped Miss Maybelle again - he dearly loved the firm feel of her waist. Then they headed out of the village.

She folded her hands in her lap. "I'm sorry I questioned you."

"Suppose I can understand you being a bit wary." Seated this close, he could enjoy every shift of pink in her cheeks. "Miss Maybelle, I'm truly sorry about messing up your schedule."

She gave a dramatic exhale, complete with shuddering. "Mr.

Alexander, why are you impeding my research? Your water tests concur with mine." She didn't weep or wail, which he surely appreciated, but her ramrod straight posture and clenched hands showed her frustration.

"Mineral spring water is useless for curing illness - isn't that your notion?" No, he shouldn't talk like a hillbilly around this Yankee scientist. "Isn't that your hypothesis? But Fauquier's guests won't read the fine print saying my test is honest. They'll just hear spring water is no good, giving them one more reason to spend their summer elsewhere. And investors will have one more reason to say no to rebuilding my hotel."

"I'm not saying your water is worthless. I'm saying there is no scientific basis for claims of cures." She crossed her arms. "None other than your beloved President Jefferson recommended this research. He proposed having physicians at every spring to explore the best use of each in the fight against illness. Now, in the twentieth century, science has progressed to allow accurate water analysis in the field, the first step in learning if mineral water is beneficial."

"The first step? Then what?"

"I'm not exactly certain." She relaxed enough to tap her fingers against her chin. "Perhaps biochemists will study the effects on cells and microbes, or compare distilled water with mineral water using a short-lived species, such as mice."

"Have some mice drink city water, and other mice drink water from each mineral spring? The Fauquier mice need a golf course, swimming pool, tennis court, hearty meals—"

"Not to mention a hotel manager making sure they're having a good time." A hint of a smile crossed her lips.

"I have plenty of experience trapping mice. Guess I can take up entertaining them, if Fauquier shuts down." He brushed away that gloomy thought with another prayer for the resort.

Finally she turned her overly-intelligent gaze his way. "I'm asking for honesty in advertising, not trying to put resorts out of business."

Resorts had been going out of business - or burning down - for the past twenty years. Wade sighed. "All right, Miss Maybelle."

They approached a fork in the road.

"Wait, let me consult my map."

"It's in your satchel, but unnecessary. Lost guests don't pay." Wade nodded to a sign. He eased up on the reins and the horse made the turn of her own accord. "And I'm guessing Miss Dixie's made this trip a time or two."

"Should be easy to find, then." Being a careful sort, she checked her map anyway.

Wade pointed over his shoulder. "Ol' Chub at the livery said this resort was started by a doctor with poor health. He found the cure in these waters."

"Hardly."

"Someone must agree. The hotel has forty-six rooms and guest cottages."

A second sign directed them to the left into the heavily wooded mountains.

Maybelle sighed. "If beautiful scenery could cure, this would be the place."

"That's what I'm trying to tell you. It's not just the water, it's the scenery, fresh air, square dancing, stargazing…"

Maybelle's cheeks turned as pink as a ripe peach. She needed to relax and he was the man to help her.

The blue flowers bordering the gravel lane would help guests find their way at night. The proprietor needed to prune the rhododendrons and maple trees framing the hotel. Seven windows on each of its three floors overlooked the valley.

"Wood frame construction. How soon before it burns down?" Wade dug out his field glasses. "Tennis court, croquet lawn, dance pavilion, bowling alley. But not many guests."

"You can check out the attractions while I take a sample."

"I'd better come along, make sure Dixie doesn't wander off without you," he said, earning a roll of Maybelle's molasses brown eyes. He parked the rig. "Are you planning to announce yourself?"

"This isn't a social visit." She slung her satchel over her shoulder and started to dismount.

Wade raced around in time to help her to the ground.

"Honestly, I'm not an invalid."

"But I am a Southern gentleman." A man who never missed a chance to get his hands on a beautiful woman. A man who knew how his touch affected women.

She marched across the lawn. Just before reaching the spring house, she jumped backwards and gave a clearly female shriek. "Snake!"

Wade yanked her backwards and got the varmint in his sights. "You woke a copperhead."

"You have a pistol," she squeaked. Her legs wobbled and she leaned into him.

"Why, yes, Miss Easterly. What kind of soldier would I be without a firearm?" Keeping an arm around her, he bent and inspected her boot. "Fortunately you made an intelligent choice in footwear. And fortunately you got only a warning nip from a little one."

"Little? It had to be three feet long and as thick as my wrist."

"Expect all springs have their share of reptilian residents."

"Are still trying to get me to quit?" Maybelle stepped out of his embrace, er, grasp.

A short man charged up and beat the grass with his spade. "Rotten copperheads ruining business," he growled.

So much for taking samples on the sly.

"I'll do the talking. Mountain people are wary of outsiders,"

Wade said quietly. He stepped up to the man and spoke with a thick drawl. "Howdy, sir. We'd be ever so grateful if you'd let us take a sip of your fine water."

The man stopped burying the snake and shook his head. "Can't understand a word they say here," the man said in a New England accent.

Miss Maybelle interrupted and made the appropriate introductions. The spade-wielding man turned out to be Dr. Edmund Longley of Maine, the proprietor of the resort.

He squinted up at Wade. "Heard of you. Run a resort up north. You're here to keep an eye on her." He pointed at Maybelle.

"Keep her honest." Wade grinned.

"Ayuh. Long as you don't tell anyone about the snakes, you can have the water all you want." He pointed out seven different springs, offered the dance hall for use as a laboratory, and loaned Wade his shovel, then skedaddled back to the hotel.

"You're welcome to go with him." Maybelle started toward the chalybeate spring.

"What kind of guard would I be, leaving you alone with the snakes?"

She gave him a sidelong glance, eyebrows lowered, head tilted.

He took off his hat and pointed to his hair. "Go on and say it, Miss Maybelle. Won't be the first time I've been called a 'copperhead.'"

"I suppose we have one thing in common."

He hadn't thought of her as a redhead, seeing as how her hair was a shade darker than his. "Virginians are known for courtly manners. You won't be finding any bullies in this state." And if she did, he'd cut them down to size.

Maybelle motioned him ahead. "All right, lieutenant. Patrol, reconnaissance, reconnoiter, as ordered. Just do not interfere with testing procedures."

He saluted, then, holding the shovel at the ready, inspected the path. "All clear!"

"Back away. Further." Keeping a sharp eye out, Maybelle approached the gazebo. She uncurled a string tied to her satchel and dropped a thermometer in the stream, then wrote in a notebook. She pulled a glass bottle from her satchel. "Not one step closer."

Only teacher eyes could spot him sneaking up behind her. "But this is the part I like best."

"There's no creek to fall into, no moss-covered rocks to slip on." She waved him away. "Get started on the sulphur spring."

But he didn't. Instead he sprawled on the grass, leaning back on his elbows, and watched her. If that fancy laboratory bottle broke, as glass often did during travels, would she stop?

Maybelle stared at him for several seconds, then filled her bottle. "What did Colonel Roosevelt say about your inability to follow orders?"

"It was a short war. Don't believe he had time to notice."

Inside her satchel, a wood frame held a miniature chemistry laboratory. Her kit assembled like a puzzle, everything tightly fitted to save space and prevent rattling and breaking. Maybelle filled each test tube from the flask. Moving quickly, she dipped a paper strip in one, an eye dropper of something in the next, and on down the line. She lit a small alcohol burner, dunked a loop of wire into the water and held it in over the lamp, making the flame change from yellow to red.

Miss Maybelle had a certain grace, purposeful without being fluttery. Wade had no idea what she was doing, but she sure was an expert in it. As she worked, her tongue flicked between her teeth to touch her top lip. She focused on her task to the exclusion of everything around her. Including him. That would never do.

"What's that you're doing?" he asked to see if he could sidetrack her.

"Reagents." She didn't look up. "Chemicals that change color in the presence of other chemicals."

After each step, all down the row of tubes, Maybelle recorded the results in her notebook. Her notebook. Ah, now there's a thought. Wade sat up. She couldn't finish her research without it. All he had to do was get his hands on that notebook. Or maybe it would slip out of her satchel into a creek. All sorts of trouble could befall a notebook.

Maybelle emptied out the test tubes and set her kit to rights, then gave him a triumphant smile. "Next?"

Wade swished through the grass to the next spring. It would be a lot easier to stop Miss Maybelle if she wasn't so excited about her research, if her face didn't glow while she worked. "So how'd you get interested in— Uh-oh."

She came up behind him and read the sign, "The Arsenic Springs."

"Dr. Longley put rat poison in his spring?"

Maybelle set her satchel on the bench and started testing as if nothing were wrong. "It's naturally occurring. The water runs through rock embedded with arsenic."

Wade sat beside her. "He must know what it is."

"Of course. Arsenic has been notorious as a poison since ancient times. I believe the Roman Emperor Nero used it against a rival."

"Anyone who fiddles during a fire is a first-class scoundrel, not to mention plumb crazy." Wade shifted, brushing his knee against hers. "I don't see why anyone'd drink poison."

"At this dilution, it's fairly innocuous." Maybelle held up a long strip with a dot of color on the end.

"But what if the water wore through the limestone to a rock full of arsenic? Could the concentration increase to a dangerous level?"

Those molasses dark eyes flashed his way. "Another reason to analyze the water."

"Why would anyone mess with arsenic?"

"Some believe drinking or washing in it improves the complexion."

"I hope that's not what Mother is taking. Much of the time she looks like death eating a cracker."

"Arsenic is used in medications to treat several diseases. What is your mother's affliction?"

"Neurasthenia."

"Nervous exhaustion? I'd think your resort would be the last place anyone would develop that."

"She'd make a full recovery if Fauquier had a hotel again." He hoped. Thinking about Mother led to fretting about Robert E. Best think about something else, anything else, especially the fascinating female next to him. "Good thing your complexion doesn't need any improving, Miss Maybelle."

Her cheeks bloomed as she wrote in her notebook. "In the mountains of Austria-Hungary, there are people who deliberately consume arsenic, in small amounts, of course. They say it increases their vigor."

Wade's knee again pressed hers. He made a purring sound deep in his throat. "I believe I'm vigorous enough, thank you."

She jumped, scooting six inches down the bench. "Arsenic is often found in the company of a number of chemicals, including sulphur. I was surprised your springs don't contain any."

"Perish the thought." He prodded her with his elbow and got a sidelong glance for his effort. She got his joke, but she had no intentions of laughing.

"Arsenic is also found with cobalt." She retreated into science when flustered. Good to know. "When I taught, I drew stems and leaves with India ink, then added invisible flowers with a cobalt solution. Held over heat, the flowers bloomed. The students loved it."

He stared at her long enough to make her squirm. "And you loved teaching. Why did you leave it?"

Her spine straightened and she looked down her noble nose at him. "I'll have you know, I received the highest scores in every chemistry class I took. I am perfectly capable of doing my job."

Wade raised his arms in surrender. "I'm last one who'd question your skill as a chemist. I'm just puzzling over why you'd leave teaching."

She focused on packing up her kit. "Father found me a position at the Geophysical Laboratory. They conduct significant research."

"Which is so much less fun you ran away."

"I'm not running away." She spoke so quickly, he had to have hit a sore spot. "I'm conducting fieldwork." She raced off to the next spring without waiting for him to check for snakes. So... whatever happened at the Geophysical Laboratory worried her more than any copperhead. Oh Miss Maybelle...

Maybelle finished analyzing all seven springs and Dixie got them back to Glade Spring minutes before the train was due.

Wade dropped Miss Maybelle at the depot, returned the buggy to the livery, then ran for the train. As he climbed the platform steps, he heard a pair of loudmouths spouting off. "Get a load of that, will you? How tall d'ya suppose she is? Could pick my apples without a ladder."

Maybelle stood with her back to them, shoulders tight, clutching her satchel with white knuckles.

"How's the weather up there?" they yelled. "She's not talking. Maybe she really is a giraffe."

"Better than being a jackass." Wade marched across the platform and set the suitcases beside her.

"Ignore them," she whispered without moving a muscle.

Instead, Wade ignored her. He faced the bums, hands on hips, fury heating his blood. "I don't know where you boys hail from, but here in Virginia, we treat ladies with respect. You understand me?"

A muttered apology heralded the arrival of the northbound train.

"Sorry you had to hear that." Wade handed her into the passenger car.

"It's nothing I haven't heard before." Maybelle took a seat in the first row with extra room for their legs.

"Well, no more. No one's going to discomfit you while I'm around." No one but Wade Hampton Alexander himself.

Lord, I am in a mess of trouble here.

CHAPTER NINE

Mabel did not understand Wade. She expected he'd want to finish the research quickly so he could get back to his beloved resort. But instead he threatened her with trout fishing at Wyrick Springs and hiking at Grayson Sulphur. At the town of Pulaski, he dawdled over their meal, chatting up not only their waitress, but everyone else in the restaurant.

As departure time approached, Mabel picked up her bags and crossed the dirt street to the granite depot. She had research to conduct. She couldn't let his dilly-dallying slow her down. The march of progress, the advance of science must continue.

As she reached the depot's entrance, an arm shot around her and opened the door. "Miss Easterly, are you trying to ditch me?"

"Mr. Alexander, losing you was not my intention, but it might be the result if you do not keep up." A ridiculous relief eased her breathing. Despite his opposition to her research, she enjoyed his company. She settled onto the passenger car seat and they rode northeast together.

The rail stop nearest Yellow Sulphur Springs didn't have a livery or a telephone line, but it was only a short walk to the resort.

Wade hefted their suitcases and started up the winding gravel road. "Miss Maybelle, I wish you'd let me tote your poke. It's just not right for a lady to carry anything when she's traveling with a healthy man."

The healthiest specimum Mabel had the pleasure of observing. "Your arms are full."

"I'm perfectly capable of carrying your satchel. I've been hauling trunks around Fauquier since I was a young 'un. Just loop that strap over my head."

And never see it again. "No, thank you."

"I saved you from a drunk on the train, from poisonous snakes at Washington Springs, and from those two armed ruffians at Grayson Springs."

"Tweedledee and Tweedledum? Their guns weren't even loaded."

"You didn't know that when they came roaring up on us." He turned in front of her, trying to get her to look him in the eye. "What are you worried about, Miss Maybelle? Don't you trust me?"

"As far as I could throw you." She stepped around him and turned left between two gateposts. They entered a narrow valley filled with large trees. Cottage ranges, rows of one-story cabins with long porches, circled a three-story hotel.

"One stray spark away from disaster," Wade said.

"Enchanting. Like a secret fairy tale world." Since scientists didn't indulge in fanciful ideas, Mabel added, "The hill and the trees dampen the railroad noise."

"But make it impossible to stop a fire."

Mabel nodded at the creek beside the drive. "I don't even have to measure the flow - it's obviously insufficient for firefighting."

The water trickled from a pipe beneath an Italiante gazebo.

Mabel ran her tests. "Fifty-four degrees. Iron, calcium, magnesium, copper. Not enough sulphur to generate a smell."

"Did you say my water stinks?" Wade peered from beneath his hat. He'd stretched out on the chaise longue while she worked. A 1904 Roosevelt campaign bandanna graced his neck. A small brown dog had positioned itself under his hand for an ear-scratching.

"As Fauquier's water has twice the sulphur as this, the odor is to be expected." She packed her testing kit and stood, but Wade didn't move. "You could rest here while I test Montgomery Springs."

He pushed his hat higher, revealing one mischievous blue eye. "Beautiful afternoon for a nap."

"Beautiful afternoon for a ride."

"You've tested Pulaski Alum, Washington, Wyrick, and Grayson Springs, and found nary a molecule to fret over. Why not take the afternoon off, enjoy the day God's given us."

"I can enjoy it on horseback."

He rolled upright and planted his legs on either side of the footrest, scaring the dog back into the woods. "Now, Miss Maybelle, I surely recollect telling you the Montgomery is no more. Flood, fire, and financial woes brought an end to its glory. Not a trace left, like that other place near the West Virginia border."

"Yes, but Montgomery's location is known and in close proximity to the towns of Blacksburg and Christiansburg. People could consume the water." Mabel showed him the map and checked her watch. "It's only five miles from here."

Teasing blue eyes slid her way. "Or we could wait until morning and try out the bowling alley now."

"Tomorrow's Sunday. I'd like to attend church." Help from the Higher Power proved essential in dealing with Wade.

"Bowling this evening, then. Let me reserve two rooms and tell them we'll be back for supper."

By the time Mabel returned from the ladies' restroom, Wade had filled his canteen and rented a pair of sorrel geldings, Romulus and Remus. He reached for her satchel. "Allow me—"

"No thank you." She secured the bag to the saddle. He stopped talking and stepped away. Mabel found she rather enjoyed the sound of his voice, so she asked, "Is this Romulus or Remus?"

"Don't matter. They answer to both names." Wade tucked a cluster of purple flowers into her hat band, then helped her mount. "Named for the twins who founded Rome. Don't suppose you had time to learn about them while you were busy studying chemistry."

"Romulus and Remus were mentioned in Bullfinch's *Mythology*, but not to any great detail. Seeing their sculpture in Rome led me to read their complete account." She glanced at Wade. Poor fellow, his travels had been so limited. But he did enjoy a bit of joshing. "A story about being raised by a wolf must be an enormous consolation to you Wahoos."

He chuckled, refusing to be offended. "You'd be right about that, Miss Maybelle."

Wade broke into a gallop, leaving her horse half a length behind. They passed the old hotel and cottages, then turned east. Rows of corn covered most of flat lands. Small houses backed into the surrounding hills. Each yard contained a milk cow and a dozen red chickens.

Instead of following the road through the valley, Wade turned onto a trail up the mountain. The horses slowed to accomodate the steep grade. "The desk clerk told me about this shortcut."

"Are you sure of these directions? I didn't see any signs."

"Now, Miss Maybelle, a vanished resort doesn't post signs." Wade turned in his saddle, riding as effortlessly as he danced. "This trail was established by none other than General Jubal Early of the Confederate Army."

"I've heard the name."

He held a low branch out of her way. "Good bit of history here. During the war, Montgomery Springs served as a meeting place for Jeff Davis and his generals and later as a hospital for the wounded."

"All of them cured by the water, I suppose."

His grin faded. "Unfortunately Montgomery Springs was no match for smallpox."

The trail leveled at a high meadow, then followed a ridge through a stand of cedars. The trees thinned and the horses' shoes clattered on outcroppings of… was that schist or gniess? Metamorphic rock had been Mabel's nemesis in geology class. Below them spread a narrow valley bordered by tall mountains, almost a canyon. A roofless silo next to a collapsed barn showed farming hadn't been any more successful than the resort.

"None other than Varina Davis, the only child to be born in the Confederate White House, summered here. The hotel accomodated a thousand guests, but there's no trace of it now."

Mabel kept the gelding to a walk and let him pick his way down the hill. "Did the desk clerk have any advice on the location of the springs?"

"None at all." Wade didn't sound worried. "We'll look for a creek, then trace it back to the source."

A faint odor of woodsmoke reached Mabel's nose, yet she didn't see any houses. "Do you—"

"Maybelle. Stop." Wade's voice lowered and sharpened to a hiss. "Turn your horse around."

A trio of men stepped into their path. They wore homemade overalls, denim shirts, and slouch hats, all coated with a layer of grime, yet their firearms gleamed new and spotless. No doubt they were engaged in criminal activity.

Firearms? Wade carried a pistol. If he took it into his head to brandish it, he'd be wounded or worse. Her heart clenched and she said a quick prayer for safety.

The one with the drooping mustache motioned with his gun. "Git."

"Went for a ride and got lost," Wade said. "Yellow Sulphur Springs is back that way? Come along, Dear."

This scientist didn't answer to "Dear." She had research to conduct. And she had to keep these moonshiners from shooting Wade. "Good afternoon, gentlemen." Mabel dismounted. "I'm testing mineral water. Perhaps you might know the location of the springs?"

"'Course they know," Wade muttered. "That's why they're here."

"Don't know nothing." The mustache twitched, then his finger twitched over the trigger. "Git on out of here."

Leaves rustled as Wade's mount backed into the underbrush. "Fine idea. Thank you kindly. Let's go, Sweetheart."

"Sweetheart" is it now? "Impurities in water can affect its taste, impart turbidity, and even cause illness. Particulate matter can produce scale in pipes and boilers, reducing their efficiency."

Wade murmured, "None of which is a concern to these here folks."

With a fair share of scowling and pointing, the three men engaged in a brief consultation. The youngest scurried off into the underbrush. The mustached one stepped forward. "Gone fetch you some water."

"Thank you, but testing at the source is necessary for accurate results." She hefted her test kit onto her shoulder. "Is the spring far?"

Wade groaned. "Have mercy."

The remaining two engaged in further debate. The mustached one nodded at Mabel. "C'mon." Then he pointed his gun at Wade. "You stay."

Wade raised his arms. "Miss Maybelle, you should skip this one."

"This water is being consumed."

"Water's the safest ingredient in the recipe."

The moonshiner led Mabel into a thicket as dense as the Amazon jungle. Leaves overhead formed a shady tunnel, too dark to spot snakes. Vines and underbrush caught at her skirts. Perspiration broke out on her brow. Flies and mosquitos fought over her blood, and other insects sawed a loud rhythm. Within a half-dozen steps, she lost her way.

These men, these moonshiners, could kill her - or worse - and her body would never be found. And what would they do to Wade, especially if he attempted any foolish heroism?

The man climbed down some boulders, moving fast enough for Mabel's breath to quicken. He stopped and waited for her to catch up, staring with narrowed eyes until she dropped her gaze. Wade was right - she should have run from these lawbreakers. No one would have missed Montgomery Springs' results. No one except herself. She was her father's daughter. She was a scientist. She was conducting research for the benefit of the country.

Mabel lifted her chin and hoped her voice didn't betray her fear. "Is it much farther?"

"Nope." He pointed right. Water seeped into a pool then trickled down the hill. She would have heard the burble if her heart hadn't been beating her blood to a froth.

Mabel inched around the perimeter of the spring, not taking any chance of falling. Wade had rescued her in Fauquier, but she couldn't expect gallantry from a moonshiner. She completed her tests with utmost expediency and then announced, "No danger drinking from this sulphur spring, although it contains enough calcium to cause scale, a white deposit. Where are the others?"

The man led her through a nearly-dry creek and across a weed-choked field. Mabel would never find her way back if he lost her. What was Wade doing back with the other hillbilly? And where had the third one gone?

"Here ya are."

The next spring flowed from a pipe at the base of the mountain. Mabel set her test kit on the dressed stone blocks forming a semi-circle around the spring. Could this be all that was left of the great Montgomery White Sulphur Springs? "This is the chalybeate," she told the moonshiner. "You'll notice a brown deposit, similar to rust."

The mustached one grunted and led her to three other springs. Wisps of smoke spiraled through the air, but Mabel kept her eyes on the ground - she didn't want to trip nor glimpse their operation. She paused again to catch her breath. How long had they been wandering through the forest?

"C'mon."

Mabel followed the man on hands and knees through a prickly bush. They ended up on the trail next to Remus and Romulus. Perhaps the moonshiners didn't intend to kill them after all. Mabel managed a full breath.

Wade sat crosslegged on the ground with the other two men. They played a game moving pebbles in and out of shallow concavities in the dirt, similar to something Mabel had seen in Egypt. He glanced up and a smile stretched across his face. "Why Miss Maybelle."

"Mr. Wade."

"She says," Mustache announced, "third spring is the best. First and second, stuff in the water chokes the pipes."

"See," said one of the boys. "Not my fault."

The other slapped him on the shoulder. "You lazy about cleaning."

"Back to work." Mustache motioned the boys through the pricker bush. Within seconds, Wade and Mabel were alone.

Mabel returned her kit to her saddle to keep from showing how relieved she was to see Wade in one piece. "Gambling again? How much did you lose this time?"

"Forty-two cents." Wade ran his fingers through his hair. "You foolish girl, almost getting killed. Selina would slap some sense into you if she were here. What was I going to tell TR? Sorry, I lost your scientist to moonshiners? What were you thinking?"

"I was thinking of Father's expedition to the Amazon. He faced warriors armed with poison darts with the philosophy 'never give them a chance to shoot you in the back.'" Mabel mounted before Wade could help her. "And now I'm thinking, let's not be late for Yellow Sulphur's supper."

"Yeah, I hear they make a make a mighty fine strawberry pie." He settled on his horse with a relieved sigh. "Miss Maybelle, you're one lollapalooza of a scientist. And I'm right proud to be your side-kick."

"And I appreciate your entertaining the moonshiners and not getting yourself shot." She glanced over her shoulder, pleased to see his grin restored. "And, for a man who's never roamed further than Cuba, you are one lollapalooza of a traveler."

The bulk of Yellow Sulphur Springs' guests were families, so the kitchen staff placed the sundries at one table. Wade did the same at Fauquier. Unfortunately it meant he and Maybelle were tossed in with a young couple on their honeymoon. The Mr. and Mrs. gave a replay of the wedding and reception, which, considering they both descended from First Families of Virginia, rivaled a circus. The new bride babbled so much she barely stopped to eat, explaining why she was big around as a toothpick. Not that the groom had much more in the way of muscles. He supervised a Norfolk and Southern office. His bride had been one of his typists.

Maybelle let her ear be bent, saying "oh my" and "oh dear" at all the right moments. She should be given a prize for listening to all this drivel. And Wade would see that she did.

He set aside his strawberry pie, not half as good as Fauquier's, and addressed the couple. "Say, would you two like to try a little bowling?"

The honeymooners exchanged glances. They probably had better things to do, make that *bedder* things to do, but it wouldn't be polite to say so. "I suppose we could manage a game," the new husband offered.

Maybelle opened her mouth, probably to make some excuse involving the report TR wouldn't expect for months.

"It's Saturday night," he said. "You can *spare* the time."

Maybelle's lips squirmed between a smile and a frown. "Another pun like that and I'll *strike*."

"Oh, you two are so funny." The new bride giggled. "You should be on stage. Don't you think so, Ralph?"

"Right up their *alley*, dear." The groom held her chair and the foursome punned their way across the lawn. Maybelle's sharp mind provided a comeback to every joke.

The resort had four new rubber balls. Wade handed one to Maybelle and took the other for himself. The spindly bride passed on those and picked the lightest ball, a softball-sized wooden one likely used in duckpins, and Ralph chose the second lightest.

Alice's first throw bounced out of the gutter and sent the pin boy and the brown dog chasing it into a flower bed. Ralph managed to keep his ball on the lane, but missed all the pins. Maybelle knocked over half with her first, then cleaned up with her second. *Way to show them how it's done, Miss Maybelle.* Wade did the same.

On the next round, Maybelle's perfect form earned her a strike. Wade watched her closely - his favorite pastime these days. She adjusted her stance left and hooked wide to the right, finding the lane's sweetspot. Brilliant Miss Maybelle had decoded the maple.

"Oh, you two are such good bowlers." Alice giggled. How old

was she anyway? Didn't Virginia have a law against children getting married?

"It's the ball." Maybelle held out hers. "Here, try this one."

"Have mercy!" Alice staggered and nearly dropped it on her toes. Her groom had to save her from it. "I don't know how you can lift such a thing."

Maybelle turned red and seemed to shrink into herself, slouching and crossing her arms over her waist.

Ralph tried the heavier ball and managed a spare. Alice kept hers in the gutter. Maybelle used the duckpin ball and only knocked over two. "It's the ball," she said again.

"What'd you do that for?" Wade whispered. "Now we're behind."

She shrugged and studied the floor.

But in the next round, after the honeymooners missed more than they hit, Maybelle started missing, too.

"After all your talk about honesty, don't you dare throw the game," he hissed after his strike.

"I don't want them to feel bad." Maybelle rushed to the other lane to coach Alice.

When she returned, Wade handed her the heavy ball. "Do your best."

She sent a worried glance at the couple, who took advantage of a dark corner to snuggle. The breeze off the mountain cooled the temperature to perfect for kissing and hugging. Unfortunately Wade wouldn't be doing any of that.

"Go on, Miss Maybelle. They won't notice."

Maybelle resumed competitive play. The game ended with Alice giggling her way to a spare. Ralph broke a hundred. Maybelle tied with Wade for high score.

"You're improving so quickly," Maybelle said to the bride. "Would you like a rematch?"

"We're pretty tired." Alice faked a yawn. "Bowling's

exhausting."

Ralph rubbed his skinny wrist. "We'd better turn in."

The honeymooners skipped off to the real reason they were visiting the resort.

Wade pointed to the lane. "You and I have a tie to break Miss Maybelle. No more of this holding back."

The pin boy perked up and the brown dog gave an encouraging woof.

"I'm sorry, but—"

"I mean it." He handed her the heavy ball. "Be proud. And don't apologize."

"But, Wade—"

He grinned, liking the sound of his name from her lips. "Play your best, or else…" None of Selina's threats - to take a switch to him, to go upside his head, to slap some sense into him - fit this situation. "If you don't play your best, I'll giggle."

"You wouldn't." Molasses brown eyes widened in mock horror then she rolled a strike. After ten frames, the delightful Miss Maybelle won by a point.

CHAPTER TEN

The white-frame church was plain, with the door on the gable end and windows on its long sides, built from the same plan as that used for country schools. A wealthy parishioner must have left a bequest. The church boasted a new steeple.

"Good morning, fine day, God bless you." An elderly man decked out in a suit and tie greeted them. "Mighty thin service this morning. Our preacher's down with the catarrh, him and his whole family. No sermon and no singing, lest one of you can plink the piano."

"Surely someone could rush them some spring water," Mabel muttered as she smoothed her skirt.

"Pardon?" The elder pushed his ear toward her.

"Surely someone in your congregation plays piano." Traveling had kept Mabel from regular lessons, but most of her acquaintances could stumble through simple tunes.

"No, ma'am. There's only thirty of us. Miss Winnie passed on shortly after the war. Miss Stella played until rheumatism hit that hard winter. Miss Luella only knows 'Twinkle, Twinkle,' on account of she's six."

A voice behind her said, "It'd be my pleasure to assist you."

Mabel turned to Wade. "Indeed?"

He removed his hat and introduced himself to the older gentleman. "On occasion of the weather being uncooperative, I've led worship in our hotel, giving a message agreeable enough to accommodate most any denominational palate."

"Very fine. God provides. C'mon in then."

A gentle breeze crossed through the six open windows. The elder led them down the aisle, their footsteps loud on the pine floor, to the first pew. Mabel didn't have a Sunday dress, so she had done the best she could with her hair and hoped her traveling suit was presentable. Although with her height, she'd never be inconspicuous.

The elder found a hymnal and fan from a Blacksburg funeral home for Mabel, then introduced their guest preacher. Wade sat at the upright and played "Shall We Gather at the River." With his strong voice and mastery of the instrument, he easily led the hymn and kept the sopranos in tune.

Wade stood and used the piano as a lectern. "Working at a hotel with mineral springs beside the Rappahannock River, I think quite a bit about water. Who can tell me which book of the Bible first mentions water? You, sir?" he asked a gangly-legged boy in the second row.

The kid thought for a moment then guessed, "Genesis?"

"Right. I figured you had some Bible experts in this congregation. The first chapter talks about the Spirit of God moving over the water, dividing it from land, and filling it with life. What's alive in the water?" he asked the first boy's younger brother, who propped his bare feet on a blue-tick hound.

"Frogs!"

"Another expert. You're raising smart children." He nodded to the parents. "When God built this world, He started with water. Can't do without water." Wade moved down a pew and enlisted a family of towheads in reviewing Noah and the flood. Two ancient women in black told of the infant Moses hiding beside the Nile and the Red Sea parting to help the Israelites escape Egypt. The elder and his family covered Jesus' baptism. A teenage boy recounted His walking on water. Others chimed in with the woman at the well, water into wine, and Jesus calming stormy water. No one snoozed through this sermon.

Wade meandered back to the piano. "This summer I've been thinking of water in a different way. This lovely lady here," he nodded at Mabel, making her face heat, "is traversing our fine Commonwealth of Virginia, serving our nation by testing the waters at our mineral springs. It has been my privilege to guard Miss Easterly as she completes her work. I've learned minerals can change the water, sometimes making it healthier and sometimes making it dangerous. The amount might be so small, you couldn't taste it. Maybe you'd even feel better at first. But if there's too much of the wrong chemical, you'd fall sick and not know why. You could have lasting damage. You might die.

"It's like that with our spiritual life. Maybe you've been diving into untested waters. The change seems refreshing at first and you might not know anything's wrong. Maybe you wouldn't notice that you're drifting away from God. You might be soul-sick and not know why. Just like Miss Easterly tests the waters, we need to test whatever we're taking in, to make sure it's healthy for our souls. Are we growing the fruit of the Spirit? Are we working for justice and showing mercy? Are we sharing our faith?"

Wade sat and played, "It is Well With My Soul."

The elder thanked him and gave a closing prayer.

A man who could sing, play piano, and preach a decent sermon at the drop of a hat. Mabel sighed and bowed her head. *But, Lord, didn't you hear me? I'm trying not to fall in love!*

Wade thought Maybelle would be proud of all the attention coming her way, instead she seemed embarrassed. The elder invited them over for Sunday dinner - fried chicken, of course - then he got her to test the mineral spring on his land. Maybelle was back in her element.

"So's this good water?" the elder asked.

"It's good for drinking, but the high iron content could turn your laundry yellow."

"What'd I tell you?" The wife gave him the elbow. "I use the rain barrel or haul water up from the crick. It's a fur piece, but my clothes are cleaner for it."

"And it may stain your dishes and p—" Maybelle glanced around. Wade suspected she'd been about to mention plumbing and just realized the best they had was a pump in the front yard and an outhouse in back. "Potatoes."

"Should I cook with crick water then?" the misses asked.

"Not unless you boil it for five minutes first. It could be contaminated, carrying germs, and make you sick."

"Might could test the crick," the elder suggested.

"I don't have the right equipment." Maybelle's gaze traced the water's path upstream. "The test results would be of no use. Creek water changes constantly. Any events upstream - recent rain, cattle crossing, someone building a bridge over it - all change the water."

The wife nodded. "I told Adelia not to let her children play in the crick on wash day. Leastways, not in the morning."

They traded thanks and returned to the buggy. Maybelle went back into her Yankee mode, checking her watch, and hurrying him back to the train station. And she still wouldn't let him lay a finger on her satchel. Smart girl.

They hopped off the Norfolk and Western at Shawsville, another small town with a general store held together with Coca-Cola signs. The livery rented a buggy and a sorrel gelding named Ajax, who pulled them down a road blessed by the soft music of the Roanoke River.

"Thank you for your sermon this morning," Maybelle said.

"It wasn't a sermon. More like a Sunday school class."

"Now who's holding back? Do I have to giggle?"

"Can you?"

She considered a moment. "I suppose not."

Well, now, there's a challenge. Get Miss Maybelle to giggle.

She had already moved on to the next item on her agenda. "Turn here for Alleghany Springs."

"The hotel burned down a few years ago."

"They're still bottling water."

"And golfing," Wade said as the resort came into view. "The cottages are occupied. Wow— Now that's what I'd call a humdinger of a gazebo."

He stopped the buggy at an octagonal pavilion with a two-tiered roof. The gate had been made of fencing, but knobbed and twisted branches formed the pickets and roof brackets.

"It looks like something made by fairies." Maybelle blushed and covered her mouth.

"With the help of elves."

Maybelle shot him a glance. "You read fairy tales?"

"Well, I wasn't always an old fellow." He hurried to help her climb down. "A good imagination came in handy when the season's over and the guests leave.

"So what type of wood is this?" Maybelle ran her fingers over a gnarled post.

"Laurel or rhododendron. The supports are cedar."

"Was the hotel built like this?"

"Too much work. I heard it was the usual wood-frame, with cedar logs for the porch supports to give it a rustic feel."

Maybelle stepped inside the gazebo, looking up to marvel at the construction. "Fantastic."

"Quite the challenge, getting all these pieces to fit together." And making sure they stayed together. "Keep an eye out for the goblin. Or is it a troll?"

She laughed, not quite the giggle he was going for, but he'd take it. "As long as there are no copperheads."

"No copperheads, just an old hound." Ears dragging, the dog ambled into the gazebo.

While Maybelle ran her tests, Wade accompanied the dog on her rounds. The resort had long passed the day when a thousand guests stayed all season. Now they were lucky to have a hundred, most staying only a week. The prized asset here was the surrounding mountains, more wild and rugged than Fauquier's gentle foothills. The cottages climbed the mountain like a giant's stairsteps, the roof of one level with the porch of the next.

Keeping an eye out so he didn't get hit, Wade and the hound skirted the edge of the golf course. One of the duffers puffed on a stogie, fouling the air with a barnyard reek. A female player worked her fan and the men coughed, but the old guy didn't get the message. Where was the resort manager?

"See a ball around here?" he asked the hound.

She snuffled through the grass a moment, then looked up with a soft harumpf, a ball between her splayed feet.

"Smart dog." A Goodrich Pneu-matic. Perfect. Wade put on his grandfather's Scottish accent and marched onto the battlefield. "How's the game, lads and lassie? What ball might you be using? Haskell's very fine. Very fine indeed. What might you be thinking of Goodrich?"

"A Scotsman, eh?" The duffer peered through his smoke. "Think you own the game, eh? Join us for the rest of the course. We'll show you how Americans play, then you can treat us all to your fine whiskey."

Wade had to get back to Miss Maybelle. "Wouldn't dare interfere in your game. How about the longest drive? Your cigar for my quarter?"

He puffed furiously. "Stingy Scot. All right, you're on. You need to warm up?"

If he did, Maybelle might get a notion to move on to the next springs without him. "Ach, no. Go ahead, do your best."

Smoking hadn't done the old guy's game any good. He whacked, sending the Haskell halfway to the next hole. One of the other players held out a nice iron, but Wade figured, for fairness, he should use the duffer's. His hands stuck on the grip. Yuck. Hope the Allegheny spring water could wash that off. He lined up and hit the Goodrich so it landed a foot past the Haskell. No need to shame the man as long as the smoking stopped.

"Goodrich, did you say? Let me try that."

"I'll be trying your cigar now." Wade gestured for him to drop it on the ground.

The man held it out. "What, you're not going to smoke it? I thought Scots were supposed to be careful with their money."

Careful not to burn up our cash. A swing of the iron sent the butt sailing into the nearest pond.

The hound barked and the other golfers clapped. "Well done."

"G'day, lads." Wade tipped his head, gave the dog one last pat, then sprinted for the spring house. He couldn't stop being a resort manager, not even when he was supposed to be guarding Miss Maybelle. Lord only knew what he'd do if Fauquier ever shut down. Wade hoped he never found out. He washed off the nicotine, then joined Miss Maybelle in the buggy. "Sorry for the delay."

"You're a Christian," she said quietly, "but you gamble."

Uh-oh. No praise for clearing the air over the golf course or accurate hitting. "Thirty-nine cents to old timers on the train, forty-two cents to the moonshiners, a quarter here."

"Which you didn't lose."

Ah, she did notice. He turned the buggy onto the road beside the Roanoke River. "Which commandment did I violate?"

She squirmed. "I don't know."

"How about that one in First Corinthians that says all things are lawful, but I will not be brought under the power of any."

Maybelle pondered a moment. He liked that about her - she didn't blurt out the first thing she thought of or spout whatever she'd heard from someone else. "It's all right to gamble, then?"

"Selina and I've gone 'round and 'round about this. I know gambling has ruined plenty of lives, especially when it's tangled up with alcohol or when it leads to stealing. Maybe the country would be better off if it was illegal. But it's not prohibited in the Bible." He waved at the mountains curving down to the burbling river. Red-winged blackbirds sang from fences around small farms. "It's too nice of a day to be so solemn. So is Crockett Springs any relation to Davy Crockett?"

"None that I know of. This is one with an Indian legend," Maybelle said. "A warrior drank the spring water and was cured of whatever ailed him. Their advertisement claims cures for skin diseases, rheumatism, kidney ailments, insomnia, and nervousness."

"Nothing to be nervous about around here. Unless you object to being chewed on by a bear."

"According to the advertisements, whatever the water doesn't cure, the physician can have a go at with electrical apparatuses."

Wade scanned the skies. "No electric wires. Must have to wait for a lightning storm."

"Would be quite a shock."

"At least a jolt." He met her gaze and got a jolt of his own - Miss Maybelle had a dazzling smile.

The two-and-a-half story Crockett Springs hotel seemed tucked into the mountainside. The building looked to be about twenty years old and some of the cottages were older, but the paint was fresh and the shingles recently repaired. A fiddler played "Soldier's Joy" on the wide first-floor porch. A couple of gray-haired men pitched horseshoes for an audience of robins and a half-dozen younger guests enjoyed the swimming pool.

The horse made a beeline for the livery stable.

"Ajax isn't worried about wood-frame construction," Maybelle said.

"Horse sense is overrated."

Still no giggle.

Maybelle checked the water and Wade secured their rooms for the night.

"Arsenic, magnesium, bromide, and lithium," she told him on his return. "So, yes, this water might ease a minor case of nerves."

"I've got something even better for your nerves," Wade said. "Styles Falls is a short walk from here." Because he knew Miss Maybelle needed an adventure.

The mountains formed a steep-walled canyon. At some places the trail was wide enough to walk side by side. Holding hands would be good, but he doubted she'd allow it. Maybelle stepped out from the trees and paused at the creek bank.

"What's wrong?"

"These boots claim to keep socks dry. And of course I waterproofed them…"

"Of course." Opportunity awaited. Wade slipped past her and jumped to the first stepping-stone. "Here, take my hand."

And she did. With a good firm grip. She let go when they reached the other bank but took it again for the other crossings.

"I hear the waterfall." Maybelle hurried toward the roaring water. A plume tumbled fifty feet down a cliff. "It's so beautiful…"

The falls weren't half as beautiful as she was. Wade gave them a glance, then went back to admiring Miss Maybelle's noble profile. Her high forehead, strong brow, and straight nose attested to her strength and intelligence. Her long neck revealed her elegant side. But those full lips were meant for kissing. Was she interested in kissing him? Because suddenly kissing Miss Maybelle was all he could think about. Should he? Usually Wade could predict how his kiss would be received. But Miss Maybelle was no ordinary woman.

"But why is it getting dark?" Maybelle consulted her watch.

"Uh-oh. Looks like a thunderstorm. We'd better run for it."

"Why not? It's downhill." And off she went.

And he distinctly heard not just a giggle, but a *whee!*

CHAPTER ELEVEN

Mabel had forgotten how snug a gig could be. Taking the streetcar in Washington brought her within inches of hundreds of people, but being alone with Wade, his knee brushing her skirt, his elbow bouncing against hers, seemed entirely too cozy.

Belting out "In the Good Old Summer Time," Wade leaned on her shoulder as he sang "your tootie-wootsie," and a heat beyond the ambient temperature shot through her.

None of that, Mabel resolved, sliding as far as possible from Wade. Focus on research. Immersing herself in work kept heartache away before. Wade must have sensed her mood as he didn't argue when they stopped in Salem to test Johnston's Springs, even though the hotel had burned down in 1892.

A winding road up the mountain brought them to a half dozen cottages clustered around Bennett Springs. They parked on the road and followed the path through the wildflowers.

Mabel took a deep breath. "I love the smell of the forest."

Wade picked a yellow flower and slid it under her hat's ribbon.

A door slapped open. A ratchet clacked twice. Mabel found herself on the ground, wrapped in Wade's arms. A shotgun boomed, destroying whatever romance the moment might have had. Leaves ripped from the trees overhead.

"These shoot-first boys give hillbillies a bad name," Wade muttered, his mouth inches from her ear.

"Someone shot at us." *Wade's holding me.* Mabel's heart galloped. Her head rested on Wade's shoulder, her back against his front, his warm and muscular— Oh, for heaven's sakes, this was not the time for sordid thoughts. She rolled out of his arms and tried to peek through the fence. "Perhaps if I explained about the water testing."

"Keep down." Wade planted his hand on her head. "Miss Maybelle, you're a Yankee, a citified flat-lander, and a trespasser. Most likely his next shot won't miss."

"But—"

A voice called from an inert figure on a hammock, "Lewella Moomaw, leave off shooting. You're disturbing my nap."

"No 'count yallar dogs," a high-pitched voice yelled. "Trying to steal my baby."

"Lewella, your baby's all growed up and working for the railroad," said the first voice. Then after a pause, "It's only salt, folks. You can out run it."

Wade found a pellet on the ground and rolled it between his fingers. "Rock salt." He made a zigzag motion with his pistol. "When I say go, run like a rabbit. Stay low."

"What are you going to do?"

"I'll play hound dog to your cottontail." He crouched, then helped her onto her feet. "Go."

Mabel darted up. Three steps left, four right. At any moment, she expected to feel the sting of shot on her back. But no, Wade ran right behind her, shielding her. When they reached the gig, he tossed her in, and jumped up behind her. Instead of his usual loose grasp of the reins, letting the horse choose her own way, Wade cracked the buggy whip beside the mare and shook the reins. They raced away from Bennett Springs.

"Easy, Miss Lucy. Good horse." He stuffed the pistol in its holster, stowed her satchel under the seat, then turned toward her. "You all right?"

"Thanks to you. I hope I didn't hurt your arm when I landed on it."

"Oh, Miss Maybelle. If only it didn't take getting shot at to bring you into my arms." He tipped his head toward her and unleashed his grin. A grin that, for the female portion of the population, must be the main attraction of Fauquier White Sulphur Springs.

Mabel hid behind the map. "Turn left at the bottom of the hill." If only she didn't want his embrace so desperately that being shot at seemed like a small price to pay.

Over one ridge, through a valley of orchards and grazing fields, and up another mountain brought them to Red Sulphur Springs. The hotel was built with a portico supported by columns running from the ground floor to the gable. Additional two-story cottages had been tucked into the evergreens. A gazebo decorated with elaborate ironwork and flowers contained the spring. A sheepdog greeted Wade with a lazy swing of her white tail. Mabel set up her testing equipment on the nearby stone wall.

"Miss Maybelle." His voice didn't warn of snakes, moonshiners, or gun-toting brothers. How many ways could he distract her? "Miss Maybelle, you'll want to take a look." With a warm hand on her shoulder, distraction enough, he pivoted her around.

From this height, close to the summit of the mountain, the lawn of the resort sloped down to a broad pastoral valley. Two tree-covered ridges showed in the distance.

"Spectacular." Mabel's deep sigh released the last bit of tension from the shooting. "What a beautiful view. So many shades of green."

"The Catawba Valley," Wade announced, proud as if he'd built it himself. He glanced around the grounds. "Seems safe enough. I'm going to see what they're building." He and the sheepdog hiked off in the direction of hammering. By the time she finished, he returned, his expression grim.

"What's wrong?"

"The resort's been sold to the state. It's going to be a tuberculosis sanitorium." He gave the sheepdog a pat then helped Mabel into the gig. "They're building pavilions and tents for the patients."

Mabel recalled Red Sulphur's advertisement. "The proprietor promoted the water as the cure for lung diseases. Although the cool, dry air might be the essential agent of recovery. The map says the elevation is 1890 feet."

Their next stop stood on level ground amid peach and apple orchards. Buildings from the former Botetourt Springs had been incorporated into Hollins Institute, a women's college. A groundskeeper directed them past a hotel building now used as a dormitory. Mabel squeezed between a pyracanthus bush and a musky boxwood to reach the squat limestone springhouse. Inside the temperature dropped twenty degrees. "I can see why the colonists stored butter and cheese here."

"Cheese? Let's find a place to eat."

Did the man have a hollow leg? Or was his constant need to eat another way to block her research?

Mabel gathered her sample, stepped out in the sunlight, and set her satchel on the steps. As she filled the test tubes, Wade reached for her lab notes. She seized his wrist with her free hand, but his strength far exceeded hers. He could drop her notebook into the algae-ridden pool and there wasn't a thing she could do about it. "No."

"Just trying to be helpful and do some sharpening for you." His free hand grabbed her pencil. He raised an eyebrow and gave her one of his heart-stopping grins, his face just inches from hers. "What did you think I was doing?"

Heart racing, she let go and looked away. If he absconded

with her pencil, perhaps the college would give her another.

Scrape, scrape, scrape. "There you go, Miss Maybelle." He held out the pencil, but forced her to tug it from his fingers. "Are you ever going to trust me?" Did his eyes show a molecule of hurt or was that another attempt to wrap her around his finger?

"I'll trust you when your priority, your most important concern, is pleasing God, not keeping your resort open."

Wade blinked. He opened his mouth to say something, then looked down. "Keep testing. I'll stay out of your way."

Out of her way? A country mile would be too close.

Coyner Spring's creek had been straightened and graded until it resembled a drainage ditch.

Wade peeked into one of the unoccupied rooms. "Who decorated this place? The walls, furniture, and linens are all white. The best you can say about this place, is it's convenient to the train."

"And the worst you can say is have a glass of water." Mabel held up a test tube with yellow sludge in the bottom. "Look at the precipitate. The arsenic levels are high at all four springs."

Wade looked over her shoulder. "Too high to be safe?"

"Unfortunately, science has not yet settled on a safe level."

Mabel located the proprietor who assured them he was well aware of the saturation levels. He'd been hoping the state would choose his resort for the tubucular asylum. Since they chose Red Sulphur, he planned to close.

As they left, Wade glanced over his shoulder. "Poor grouser probably can't afford fire insurance."

"Do you know why your hotel caught on fire?"

"I have my suspicions." He shook off his gloom as they boarded the train and gave her a wink. "Can't worry about that on such a great day with such an attractive traveling companion."

Wade could tell her anything and she'd believe it. And wasn't that the problem? Mabel smiled in spite of herself. "As much blarney as you come up with, you must have been to Ireland."

"Well, no I haven't, but if you need to test their water, I'd be glad to accompany you."

"I'll keep you in mind." Mabel couldn't think of anyone she'd rather take to Ireland. Or anywhere else for that matter. No, no. Concentrate on work. How should she organize her test results into a report for the Conservation Commission?

A short ride northeast up a wide green valley brought them to Blue Ridge Springs. The view from the depot showed an elaborate fountain, large cottages, and landscaped grounds with several gazebos - how many springs did this resort have? A covered walkway led into a fancy four-story hotel. Uh-oh, it had been built with wood. What would Wade say?

"Plenty of guests." Wade nodded at the traffic on the bridle paths and wide porches. "At least they're still a going concern."

"Won't fewer resorts mean more guests for Fauquier?" Mabel asked.

"There's a grand summer tradition in the South of making a circuit of the mineral springs resorts. We're losing that ritual." He shook his head. "So what's their big brag here?"

"The advertisement says 'Drink the celebrated Blue Ridge Virginia spring water for indigestion.'"

Wade stopped to read their sign. "'The celebrated dyspepsia water.'" His mouth quirked in an ironic smile. "Told you we should have eaten supper in Roanoke."

CHAPTER TWELVE

Wade had never heard of Dagger's Springs, so Maybelle asked the slick-haired agent at the Roanoke depot.

"Doesn't ring a bell, hon." The man shook his head. "But then I just moved here from Baltimore."

Maybelle turned and surveyed the other passengers milling about the platform. Wade held his peace, waiting to see how she'd solve this problem. Even Yankee women considered raising their voices and speaking to strangers to be dreadfully poor form.

Maybelle made a beeline for a frail man hunched on the bench. "Sir?" she said loudly. "Do you know anything about Dagger's Springs?"

The man raised his ear trumpet and said, "No, I don't sing. Can't hear no more."

"DAGGER'S SPRINGS," she yelled, attracting the attention of every man, woman, and child in the waiting room. "Is DAGGER'S SPRINGS still open?"

A man in a three-piece suit doffed his homburg. "Miss, perhaps I might be of assistance. I grew up in the Eagle Rock area. The resort closed years ago. I'm not sure I could find the springs anymore, so overgrown and wild it's gotten up there."

Maybelle thanked both men and they boarded the train.

"Miss Maybelle, your cleverness continues to astound me."

Her cheeks bloomed like a summer sunrise. "The last

newspaper mention of Dagger's was in 1886, so I suspected it was closed."

"Even University of Virginia boys know, got to advertise at least once a decade."

As the train picked up steam, a quartet of gents bearing field glasses took seats across the aisle. They argued about "black-throated blues" and "blue yellow-backs." The men whistled and chirped, then tossed Latin names at each other.

One brandished his notebook like a pistol. "It was a nesting pair, I tell you."

His opponent parried with a copy of a *Catalogue of the Birds of the Virginias.* "Dr. Rivas says they're migrants and rare at that."

The other two shook their heads, "Probably was a white-throated—"

The conductor called the next stop and the men got off.

Wade exchanged a wry smile with Miss Maybelle. "Bird watchers," he said at the same time she said, "Ornithologists." They laughed together. He liked a woman who could laugh, who wasn't so tightly corseted that a titter was all she could manage.

"Loud as they are, it's surprising they find any specimens." Maybelle shook her head. "And what does it say for humanity, when men fight over birds?"

"Aw, Miss Maybelle, the end of the day will find those boys still friends, celebrating their finds over a glass of beer."

"The ornithologist on our Nile trip rose early every morning and used up all the hot water. He never did understand why the rest of the explorers were so irritated with him."

"Instead of a worm, your early bird got the bath." What interest would a world-traveler like Maybelle have with a homebody like him? "You got to see the pyramids and the Sphinx?"

She winced. "From a distance. Father said we weren't tourists, so he didn't put those attractions on the itinerary. Some day I'd like to revisit all those places and explore… see the things that interest me." She turned toward the window and moaned. "Oh, how awful."

The mountains hereabouts had been stripped of trees to feed iron furnaces and lime kilns. Huge bites had been taken from the rock. Piles of rubble, logs, and rough-built tipples littered the valley floor.

Maybelle twisted her fingers together. "I suppose you think I should investigate water used by mines instead of resorts."

"You've only found one resort with questionable water." Wade leaned back in the corner of the seat, the better to admire his beautiful traveling companion. "My guess is water polluted by mining affects a lot more people than my few guests."

"Water analysis should be continuous near any excavation. Mining companies must be required to prevent pollution and to restore the land afterwards." Maybelle's luxuriant lips pressed together as she turned to Wade. "How well do you know the president?"

He shrugged. "We invaded Cuba together. Why?"

"In May, he gave a speech about conservation, but he seemed more concerned with using national resources for material prosperity than with preservation."

Wade removed TR's 1904 campaign bandanna from his neck and held it so Maybelle could read its slogan: "Protection to American Industries," it read. Wade retied the bandanna. "Mining provides jobs, but it harms the miners, everyone who lives downstream, and the land. It's a dilemma." Like the dilemma of a too-serious traveling companion.

"You don't want the countryside around Fauquier all torn up like this."

"No, but I do want fast trains for my guests, low-cost building materials for my hotel, a warm house in winter. What's the answer?" he asked rhetorically, but Maybelle had a reply ready.

"Stewardship. Responsible use. Setting aside parks for all."

"You've got my vote, Miss Maybelle."

She expelled her breath in a frustrated rush. "I wish."

The train turned south into an untouched wilderness, mountainsides dense with trees. Miles passed with no evidence of inhabitation.

Unlike most city women, who lowered their eyes to half mast and sighed at the tedium of it all, Maybelle greeted every day with wide-eyed wonder. She marveled over the cuts through the mountains, speculating on the types of rocks exposed and the engineering challenges represented, using words like orogenesis and stratified. She delighted in the vistas of the Blue Ridge Mountains, admired the apple groves, and asked questions he couldn't answer about coalfields and iron ore. And she seemed reasonably interested in his stories about his guests at the resort.

Wade had made the mistake of questioning their route this morning. Now he had to formulate an apology. "Glad we didn't attempt to ride up here. We could have made it on Fauquier horses, but not with that stable queen we had yesterday."

Ever the conciliator, Maybelle said, "You were prepared to camp out, hack a trail through the forest, fight off bears and mountain lions..."

"It's the mosquitos I'm worried about." He pulled his sleeve back. Red circles dotted his wrist. "Give me a hotel with screens on the windows any night."

"The spring water didn't cure those bites?"

A deep bubble of laugh burst out. Wade laughed hard enough that Maybelle joined in. Never mind her being a Yankee. Didn't matter that she was a scientist sounding the death knell of mineral springs resorts. Miss Maybelle Easterly didn't deserve his sort of nonsense. He held out his hand. "Truce? I'll admit spring water isn't a cure-all."

"And I'll admit that the clean water, clean air, and recreation activities at resorts might have a beneficial effect on a person's health." She put her hand in his and shook.

He should let go. He'd held her hand before, assisting her in and out of buggies and across streams. He knew it was almost the size of his and that she had a strong grip. But he hadn't noticed her skin… soft, a bit cooler than his. He ran his thumb across the back of her hand. Maybelle pulled in a little breath. Her eyes widened and lips parted. Selina would tell her to slap some sense into him. He *should* let go—

"Craig City!" the conductor announced. Wade released his hold and reached for her satchel.

She clutched it with both arms. "No."

"What happened to our truce?"

Those brown eyes studied him as if decoding a chemical reaction. "A truce does not constitute a surrender."

Ouch. He picked up their suitcases and followed her off the train.

The branch line ended at a red and white depot. Wade rented the first ladies of the livery, Dolly Madison and Elizabeth Monroe, and a curricle. Their route through New Castle took them past an old three story hotel - all brick! - then wound along a twisting mountain track bounded on one side by limestone outcroppings and the other by a steep drop-off.

"What a glorious day!" Maybelle lifted her face to the clear sky, something no lady who fussed about freckles would ever do. "John Muir is right. City dwellers must escape to nature. Have you read anything of his?"

"We have some of his books in our library. Hard to see how any world traveler who claimed to love nature could skip Virginia."

Maybelle looked around, then faced him with a smile. "I'd have to agree."

"God sure made a beautiful world." Wade glanced at his fetching companion. He gave her a nudge since he couldn't miss any opportunity to touch her. "What? Don't you think chemistry is beautiful?" As alluring as the smile on her face.

"Oh, yes. All the colors and crystals, especially from copper. Experiments and equations can be beautiful, too, when they work out."

He pointed to one of the clouds decorating the sky. "Will you look at that."

"A cumulus cloud?"

"Look again."

"A scalene triangle?"

"Scalene? Now there's a word from distant memory. No, it's the great state of Virginia. Yet another reminder, Miss Maybelle, that God is a Virginian." He got her laughing again.

A rusty mailbox leaned toward the road, but they saw no house or even a path. Coming around the corner, they startled a white-tailed buck munching his greens. He sauntered off into the underbrush. A meadow held an abandoned shack; had someone tried to herd sheep up here? How did anyone make a living, much less survive, so far from civilization?

"They say George Washington slept here, but I have no idea how he found the place. Can't imagine how the proprietor coaxes guests out here or where he finds his workers. I root around Warrenton for groundskeepers and scour nearby farms for my kitchen staff. Then they marry each other and quit." Wade looked around for any evidence of civilization. "We've got a spirited team and this curricle rides well, but feels like we ought to be in West Virginia by now."

They slowed to rest the mares and Maybelle handed him the map. "Two miles inside the border."

The contour lines were so close together, Wade figured they'd need mountain climbing equipment. "And after this? Sweet

Springs and Sweet Chalybeate?"

She shook her head. "They're nearby as the crow flies, but as the horse trots, another matter."

"Blue Healing Springs?"

"Another closed resort. We'll return to Craig."

The tunnel of oaks and hickories opened to a wide valley with one lonely farm house. A herd of horses and cows grazed in a field punctuated by stumps. A new rail fence ran for miles. Another green tunnel finally brought them to a two-story hotel with wide porches, a spring house, and several construction projects.

All Healing Springs the sign read.

"Now there's a claim."

Wade checked for snakes, watered the horses, then stretched out on the grass.

"What are you doing?" Wade peeked from beneath his hat. A young girl, all ringlets and ruffles, peered over Maybelle's shoulder.

"I'm testing the water, to make sure there's nothing in it that will make you sick."

"Do you mean like bugs? My brother swallowed a beetle once."

"Ugh." Maybelle held up her sampling bottle. "What I'm looking for is smaller than bugs. What do you see?"

"Just water."

"It's much more than just water. Here, I'll show you." Maybelle dumped out her bottle and started all over again, showing every step, answering every question, as if she had all the time in the world.

Miss Maybelle was one humdinger of a teacher.

"How do you know all this?" Big blue eyes widened in admiration.

"I studied chemistry in college."

"And now you can tell people if their water is safe to drink and keep them from getting sick. Hooray!"

Maybelle beamed. "What would you like to do when you grow up?"

"Besides marry a stinky boy?"

"They're not all stinky, but yes, what else? What do you like to do best?"

The girl chewed on a fingernail while Maybelle packed her kit, then she whispered, "I would like to be a photographer."

"A wonderful profession. Composing pictures uses the artistic part of your brain and developing them uses the scientific part, specifically chemistry."

"My brother has a Brownie, but he only photographs automobiles."

"What would you photograph?"

"My friends Minta, Annie Maude, and Agatha. And my dog Blackie. The Fourth of July parade. The mean old iron mining company."

"Maybe you'll be the one to get them to clean up their mess."

"Maybe I will." The girl shook Maybelle's hand, then marched back to the hotel.

Miss Maybelle would make one humdinger of a mother. Her children would be strong, healthy, and smart - just like her.

Wade rolled upright. Hundreds of female guests had stayed at Fauquier, yet none held his interest like Maybelle. Did he have a chance with her? Declaring their truce didn't amount to a surrender might have been her way of telling him to keep his distance. "So, am I a stinky boy or a not so stinky boy?"

Miss Maybelle's grin set his heart a quivering. "Nothing that a good dose of spring water won't cure."

CHAPTER THIRTEEN

"You got your wish for a brick hotel." Miss Maybelle said as Wade escorted her from Covington's Intermont Hotel into the morning's fog.

"Standpipes to the roof, fire escapes, gas lights. Couldn't be safer." Could be quieter, though. He hadn't slept a wink. A hundred coal trains passed through this boomtown every hour, 'round the clock. Whoever had declared the Intermont was the finest hotel between Washington and Cincinnati must have been deaf.

Wade hurried up the stairs - this fast-walking Yankee wouldn't wait for any slow Southern gentleman - and opened the door of the fancy new Chesapeake and Ohio depot. He managed to get the door to the platform, too.

"I picked up the railroad's publication about the resort." Maybelle settled into the seat, then hid her perfect nose into a booklet.

The train passed a tannery, an iron furnance, and a paper factory with their related stenches. The world needed coal, leather, iron, and paper. And people needed jobs. But industry sure roughed up the land and plopped dirty towns on it. He hoped it never came to this in Fauquier.

Maybelle gasped. Wade jerked out of his doze. The train chugged beside a river. Forested ridges rose steeply on either side, their tops lost in the clouds. Pretty scenery, but nothing warranting a gasp. He turned to his lovely charge.

"Listen to this," she read from the list of conditions the hot springs might cure, everything from obesity to prostration, diabetes to heart trouble.

"It's advertising," Wade said. "People know it's all ballyhoo."

"No, they take it as a promise, a guarantee. But if they're not cured, they don't get a refund."

"Course not. They have to pay for their hotel stay." The train went around a curve, leaning Wade into Miss Maybelle, to his delight.

"It concludes with this note, 'The company will not be responsible for the effects of baths on the system.'" Her eyes flashed. "So, responsible or not responsible? How can it be both?"

Wade read over her shoulder. "It says to consult the resident physician."

"Who will say whatever necessary to keep his job."

The tracks curved back the other direction, sending Miss Maybelle his way. Now if he could keep her this close… "Does it say how much arsensic is in their water?"

"None."

"Most likely won't kill anybody then." Wade breathed in Maybelle's sweet-as-pie smell as he read aloud. "'General bathing hours in the pleasure pool with music by the hotel orchestra.' I wish you'd brought your swim dress," he said, making her cheeks turn as pink as a dogwood petal. He still wanted to kiss her. And it was still a bad idea. "So did the Indians discover this one, too?"

"Yes. George Washington slept here. And Thomas Jefferson took the waters." She handed him the booklet and wiggled away.

"Their springs are naturally 106 degrees. Some resorts have all the luck." The C&O hadn't spared any expense on this booklet, using high quality paper and dozens of photographs. "You won't even have to find the springs for testing since the water is delivered right to the bathtub with all of its 'health giving properties.'"

"For scientific integrity the test must be conducted at the source."

"Scientific integrity" must be Maybelle's middle name.

Her eyes lost focus. "Maybe I should test both at the source and from the faucet. It would be interesting to see what contaminants are introduced in transit. I wonder if they're using chestnut or lead pipes."

The back of the title page boasted a photograph of Falling Springs waterfall. "None other than Thomas Jefferson rated this waterfall the best."

"It's not on the schedule."

"People could drink it."

"No one makes health claims about it."

The train popped out of the cloud into a blue-sky day. Mists laced the peaks, turning their leafy-green into the color that gave name to the Blue Ridge Mountains.

The booklet bragged the New Homestead could accomodate seven hundred guests. Seven hundred? How could any hotel proprietor keep track of that many people?

The train slowed for another curve, went through a gap, then braked to a stop. The hotel, red brick with white trim, glowed against the green mountains. Plantings of rhododendrons, laurels, azaleas, and dogwoods decorated the grounds. "As majestic as my old alma mater," he said just to hear Maybelle say, "Hardly."

A squad of men in dark green suits trimmed the grass, swept the walks, and carried golf bags. Fauquier's staff would walk out on him if he ever tried to truss them up in summer's heat. "J.P. Morgan built a nice resort."

Maybelle fussed with her hair for the first time on this trip. "I thought the Chesapeake and Ohio was behind it."

"Morgan owns the railroad. Wish I could get a railroad interested in rebuilding Fauquier." He grabbed their suitcases and reached for her satchel. "Fancy place like this, don't you think I should—"

"No." She gave him a dark look as she shouldered her bag. "No thank you."

They stepped off the train. "Their hotel burned in 1901, same as ours."

"The brochure said they have a slate roof and fire walls."

"So did Fauquier."

In spite of being on vacation, male guests wore three-piece suits, the women and girls were dolled up in pastel dresses and enormous hats, and boys sported sailor suits. A troop of porters marched the luggage - tons of it - across the street and past the bathhouse.

"May I carry those for you, sir?"

"If you're strong enough." Wade squeezed the porter's bicep. Yep, he was sweating under that outfit. "What did you have for breakfast this morning?"

He grinned. "Grits and bacon, sir, and a healthy glass of spring water."

"Good man." Wade handed over their bags and offered his arm to Maybelle who'd again refused to relinquish her satchel. They trailed the man into a colonaded lobby lit by electric sconces and hanging lamps. Waiters served tea to guests seated in wicker chairs. He spotted the ambassador to Belgium, a New York cotton broker, and one of Robert E. Lee's daughters. The air even smelled of money. *Dear Lord, help me find a millionaire or two to rebuild Fauquier.*

The desk clerk looked up their reservations. "Ah, yes. Your trunks are in your rooms."

"Trunks?" he whispered to Maybelle as they followed the porter down the carpeted wide hall. "What trunks?"

"I'm ready for a change of clothes, aren't you?" The lady scientist had a few holes in her social skills repetoire, but she had no trouble pulling off an enigmatic smile.

The porter entered the elevator. Of course Maybelle been in one of these before. Wade took a gulp of air and stepped into the car. The porter pushed the buttons. The doors closed, locking them into a paneled box with a too-close resemblance to a coffin. A rumbling noise vibrated up through his shoes. Were they moving?

"I'd like to conduct my tests first," Miss Maybelle continued, all casual and relaxed, "shall we meet in the lobby for dinner at six?"

The rumble stopped and the doors opened. Ah, air.

"I'm not letting you wander about without me." He didn't want to miss a moment of Maybelle in action. "What would TR say?"

"It's perfectly safe here." Her sigh ended with a smile. Probably flattered himself, but he rather thought she enjoyed his attention.

The porter set their suitcases in their rooms, then pointed up. "Yes, sir. Perfectly safe here. Sprinkler system throughout the building. If fire ever broke out, the lead chain on the fire doors would melt and close them."

Wade studied the design. "Smart."

"All right," Maybelle said. "I'll test the springs near the hotel, then we'll meet at the livery in an hour."

"Until then." Wade gave her a salute and entered his room.

The accomodations were as luxurious as the rest of the place. The dresser and desk were made of cherry. Wallpaper, drapes, rugs, an upholstered chair went together in restful shades of blue. The room even boasted a telephone. And - the reason for

Maybelle's smile - his small trunk. Inside he found his black socks and shoes, and a note from Selina. Fauquier's staff was surviving Robert E's reign. Mother continued to enjoy ill health. Raleigh had tangled with a skunk. Phew. Glad he'd missed that. And, of course, Selina reminded him to say his prayers.

The Homestead staff had hung up his dinner jacket, waistcoat, matching trousers, and white shirt with winged collar and bow tie. Hmm. If the folks here found out how broke he was, maybe they'd let him serve dinner.

Out in the hall, a door clicked. Miss Maybelle. If she got away, Wade would never find her in this maze. He threw open the door. No sign of her in either direction, but he knew she was headed for the springs. He grabbed the map of the resort off the nightstand. Springs? Springs! Mercy, there were twelve of them. If he knew Maybelle - and he'd come to know her pretty well - she'd start at the one furthest from the livery.

He set a brisk pace, taking the stairs since they seemed safer. In the main hall, he got caught behind a group carrying on about politics. The rotund fellow in the middle turned out to be none other than Secretary of War and presidential candidate, Judge William Howard Taft. No way to squeeze past, so Wade changed direction at the next hallway. For crying out loud, was that a broker's office? And they called this a vacation spot. Wade snorted, quietly, so as not to disturb the nabobs. He passed a jeweler's, a souvenir shop, and a notions store. The Homestead had everything.

"Wade Hampton, are you working here now?" asked a bow-tied dandy.

Wade flipped through his mental hotel register. "Mr. Homer Allston of Charleston, South Carolina. How do you do, sir? No, I'm on special assignment." With a special woman. "Are you vacationing at the Homestead now?"

The fellow glanced away, then leaned close. "I'll be back as soon as your hotel reopens. How is the rebuilding coming along?"

"Still hunting for investors. Are you looking for a good project for your millions?"

Allston's laugh rang hollow. His daughter hadn't married well and his silver mine had played out. The man wagged a finger, then hurried off. "I'll keep you in mind."

In his mind's back drawer of Lost Causes, no doubt. Enough gloom. Time to find the delightful Miss Maybelle.

A shortcut through the Golf Club House took him past a squash court, ping-pong tables, the ladies' badmitton court, and a billiards' room. All full of guests. Guests who hadn't chosen Fauquier.

Outside, a group of noisy tennis players - so many white shoes - nearly trampled Wade. He followed a white path - they used ground marble for paving? - and started checking off springs. Six gazebos later he was wondering how well did he know Miss Maybelle. She couldn't be that far ahead of him. Sure, she'd gotten faster with her testing - still careful, but more efficient. But the test still took— Hey, there she was. Maybelle sat under a gazebo, her apparatus and notebook at her side. Some gent in white loomed over her, one hand on his hip, the other leaning on a golf club. The city boy had parted his hair in the middle and glued it to his head so it didn't move in the breeze.

Wade knew it. Soon as he left Maybelle alone a moment some other guy would swoop in and snatch her away.

Not without a fight.

Wade loped past a row of wood-frame cottages, cut across the lawn, ducked under a locust tree, and jumped a creek. He shook out his hands and loosened his shoulders, ready for battle. But before he was close enough to hear what they were saying, the gent twirled his golf club and sauntered off.

Maybelle slumped, head in hand, like someone had let the

starch out of her.

Wade broke into a run. "What's wrong? I'll shoot that man if you want."

She didn't even look up to see if he was joking. "Thank you, but I'm in enough trouble already."

"I knew I shouldn't have left you alone. Who was that?"

"The director of the Geophysical Laboratory."

Uh-oh. "He should be thrilled. You're researching for Roosevelt, working, taking intiative."

"Without his permission."

Wade plopped onto the gazebo step beside her. "Miss Maybelle, I haven't know you too long, but you seem awful smart about following rules. Why didn't you ask your boss about your project?"

"He'd left for the summer."

"And his second in command?"

"Gone. They had all left on fieldwork or vacation. Except for me and the janitor."

What was he missing here? "I know the city's miserable in the summer, but why would you risk a job with the Geophysical Lab? All the important research you do—"

"The men do. The women… One is a stenographer, and the other—" She pointed to herself, "—is charged with cleaning test-tubes and flasks."

Uh-oh. "Reckon cleanliness is important for accurate research." He caught her glare.

"How many of your dishwashers have a college degree, Mr. Alexander?"

"Now don't get your dander up, Miss Maybelle." He raised his hands. "I'm on your side."

His oath of loyalty earned him a skeptical glare. "When the letter came from President Roosevelt, about the National Conservation Commission, I thought it was an answer to prayer." Maybelle glanced around, but no other guests were nearby. "I should have known someone would recognize me."

"Washingtonians ought to go to Fauquier." If he had a fancy hotel with a dozen hot springs, maybe they would.

She packed her kit. "What time does the next train leave?"

"You are not quitting." Wade grabbed her hands, her noble hands, gentle enough to control a medicine dropper, strong enough to rein in a rowdy horse. "Miss Maybelle, you will not give up. President Roosevelt himself authorized your project."

She nodded toward the direction her boss had gone. "He's going to call Father."

"Didn't you say your father is up by the North Pole? You're here in your father's stead because you can't reach him by phone."

"He'll send a telegram." She bit her lip, the very lip he'd like to kiss.

"Which will take a good long while to find him. And then Professor Easterly will wrap up whatever he's doing and meander on back, when? September, at the earliest?" He squeezed her hands and she finally met his gaze. "By then your report will be on the desk of the president. You've made a great start, gathered lots of numbers. Finish the research. You can do it."

"I suppose I must." Her eyes watered, but his brave girl didn't give in to tears. "Since I no longer have a job."

On expeditions, Mabel had served as her father's deputy, organizing details of travel and dealing with problems as they cropped up. In school, male students assigned her recording duties during experiments. She had to return to the lab at night to gain actual experience. With friends, Mabel listened to their woes, brought soup to the ill, delivered flowers to their weddings. She never had anyone act as her assistant, someone to support and encourage her.

Until now.

"Come too far to quit now." Wade got her to her feet and marched her to the next spring. "Miss Maybelle, your papa will be mighty proud of you."

Glancing at Wade led to molecular rearrangements within her heart, so Mabel focused on her work. "He expected me to stay in Washington, but I didn't."

"Anybody with a lick of sense leaves the city in the summer. The newspaper said it's been over a hundred degrees there this week." He tapped his hat on his leg. "Rotten boss. You don't want to work with that tyrant anyway. Boring job. Waste of your talent."

As she completed her tests, his rant changed direction. "Why, when TR sees your work, who knows where you'll go? Head of water testing for the entire United States. Is there such a position?"

"There should be. A few states and larger municipalities check their water but most don't. If a problem is found, they'd have the expense of cleaning the water and most don't have the funds."

"Cheaper to poison their citizens. Instead of 'Let them eat cake,' it's 'let them drink Dr. Pepper.'"

"I wonder how many companies test the water they use to produce beverages." What an interesting study that would make. "Biological contaminants are a concern, too, especially in non-alcoholic liquids."

"Let them drink whiskey, then."

"Don't let Carrie Nation hear you." Mabel hurried to record her final results as a waiter approached. Would he demand her test results? Drag her off to the resort manager?

The waiter bowed. "Will mister and missus be joining us for tea this afternoon?"

Tea? The last time she'd partaken, she'd been seven. Her playmate Violetta had received a new china tea set. Cinderella's carriage graced the teapot. Goldilocks skipped across the sugar bowl and a fairy fluttered on the creamer. Over giggles they sipped Earl Gray, fed their dolls, and pretended to be royalty.

The disaster came when Mabel tried to stand. Her hips caught on the arms of the chair. She bumped into the table. The teapot tipped, rolled off the table, and crashed to the floor. Violetta's screams brought the entire household running. The mother glared, the cook "tsk, tsked," and the housekeeper muttered about an elephant in a china shop. One of the footmen managed to pry the chair off Mabel, then hurried her home. Violetta had never returned Mabel's doll.

"Miss Maybelle?" Wade touched her arm, bringing her back to 1908 and the Homestead.

Mabel blinked. "No tea, thank you."

The waiter bowed again and left.

Wade's hand slid up to her shoulder. "Are you all right? I'd say you'd seen a ghost if it wasn't broad daylight."

"It's nothing." A ridiculous, humiliating ghost of a memory. Mabel turned her heated face to her satchel. "Let's find a conveyance."

The livery was two-stories with a gambrel roof like a barn.

"Of course the stables are as fancy as the rest of the Homestead," Wade said. "Hope they'll have some good horses." He emerged minutes later with a pair of bay geldings and a surrey. "Castor and Pollux, stars of the livery."

"Twins again? I didn't know horses had twins so often."

"They don't. These are matched pairs." He grinned and boosted her onto the seat. "Do I know more about horses than you, Miss Maybelle?"

"I expect there are many topics on which you're better informed. For instance, business." The business of flirtation, especially.

A quick ride south, two and a half miles according the brochure, brought them to the closed Healing Springs.

Wade frowned at the small white hotel. "General Lee took the waters here and it was used as a girls' school."

"I like the way the mountains cradle it." Uh-oh. Single women should avoid "cradle" or any other baby-related term. Mabel walked past the hemlocks and boxwood, downhill to the spring and bath house. "The claim is the water 'strengthens the nervous system,' but I'd give the scenery credit." Her test showed lithium, which had some use in the treatment of gout and mania, but the concentration was too low to be beneficial. "General Lee must have been a Spartan. The water's only 68 degrees."

They rode a short distance south to Little Healing Springs, where Mabel almost gushed about the "embrace" of the mountains. "Funny story about this place."

Wade gasped. "Miss Maybelle knows a funny story?"

Mabel crossed her arms and pretended to be offended. "Perhaps I should keep it to myself."

"Nope. Blurt away. You've got my full attention." He flapped his ears. "Don't leave me in suspense."

"Well, all right. Jakey Rubino from New York bought land down here."

"Wait, a Virginian sold land to someone named Jakey Rubino? Had to be a yegg with a name like that."

"He was a stock trader from New York."

"A Yankee grifter."

"Anyway, Mr. Rubino built a nice house." Mabel pointed out a modern Italianate mansion, limestone with buff brick and wrought iron. "Supposedly he has an indoor swimming pool."

"Filled with champagne?"

Mabel gave him her best "would you like to rephrase that?"

face.

Wade slapped his forehead. "Spring water, of course."

"Of course. So anyway, when Mr. Rubino began a bottling operation, the Hot Springs Company took him to court. They said Rubino's water had no curative properties so he couldn't call it 'healing.' And yet the Hot Springs water, which is nearly identical in chemical composition, supposedly accounts for all sorts of cures."

"That is funny - funny business." Wade turned the rig around, then helped her down. "Test quickly, Miss Maybelle. With a name like Jakey Rubino, he'll be gunning for us."

Mabel dropped in the thermometer and took her sample. People made assumptions about her based on her size, guessing she was older or asking if she played basketball, so she tended to be sensitive to this issue. "You've formed an opinion about the man based on his name and hometown?"

"Same way Yankees reckon my intelligence by my home state and accent." When Mabel raised her eyebrows, he continued. "You should hear them talking slow and loud, waving their arms. 'Do-you-have-a-room-for-tonight?'"

She recorded her results. "What do you say to that?"

His shoulders slumped. He turned, facing the Homestead, and murmured. "Ain't got no hotel."

He'd been so good about cheering her up, Mabel should find a way to elevate his spirits. "Let's go."

"Off to Warm Springs?"

"No, back to the Homestead. Take the waters, eat a meal prepared by a French chef, and relax. If you're up to it?"

He grinned and boosted her into the surrey. "Why Miss Maybelle, now you're talking like a Virginian."

CHAPTER FOURTEEN

Upon returning from the livery, Wade found the normally staid hotel all abuzz.

"What's all the excitement?" he asked a guest hurrying past.

"The Republicans challenged the newspapermen to a baseball game."

Wade followed him to the field. The yellow clay was slick from a recent rain and the players' white duck pants showed streaks from sliding. The politicians were older and more sedentary than the newsmen, but they had recruited skilled substitutes from the local population.

A member of the House of Representatives went up to bat. He stepped in front of the pitched ball, got hit, and was allowed to take first base. The man on third took advantage of the moment to run for home.

"Safe!" yelled the umpire. "Tie score!"

The spectators booed.

"Hey, I've been promised a job!" the official yelled back.

"What? Who promised?"

"Not saying." The ump grinned and motioned for play to resume.

Wade wished Maybelle hadn't gone to take the waters. Everything was more fun with her around. And she could chat with the politicians about funding her water testing plan.

Judge Taft shrugged out of his coat and lumbered to bat.

The kid playing shortstop motioned for the fielders to back up.

"That's Charlie Taft," one of the onlookers noted. "The candidate's son."

The judge fouled the first ball, but hit the second. His son caught it and fired it to first base. His father and a senator were out. The rest of the politicians had better luck, earning three runs to finish the game 14 to 11. The teams headed to the clubhouse to celebrate.

Mrs. Taft grabbed her son by the ear. "That's the second pair of shoes you've ruined since we arrived."

Wade chuckled. One baseball game like this and Fauquier would be back in full swing.

Mabel stepped into the spout stream. Within moments the aches and pains from a week of traveling were eased away by the drumming of warm water. If water had any healing power, it must be found here. She gave herself a thorough scrubbing, then emerged, relaxed and refreshed, and donned her drawers and chemise. A chaise lounge in the sun beckoned and she stretched out.

"Miss?" A uniformed woman touched her shoulder. "I'll help you with your hair."

"Thank you, but it's really quite impossible." Mabel squeezed it, finding it nearly dry. How long had she napped?

"Oh, no, miss. It's right pretty." The maid started combing out the tangles. "Now you drink your tea - it's made with our spring water - and I'll have you ready in two shakes of a lamb's tail."

Mabel figured it was easier to take her hair down when she returned to her room than argue with the woman.

"There you go, miss. Come see in the mirror."

Mabel gasped. She'd never dared such a large pompadour,

figuring it would only make her look even more portly. But somehow the roll around her head made her look more - well, delicate would never apply to her strong features - but perhaps she looked more womanly.

"And the steam in here took out the wrinkles." The maid held out Mabel's gown.

Fashion dictated young women wear white with ruffles and poufs, which Mabel thought would look silly in her size. After considerable negotiations with her seamstress, they'd settled on pale periwinkle cambric, with a wide ruffle at the knee, and a matching ruffle at the elbow of the narrow sleeve.

The dress had never fit correctly - the seamstress's revenge, Mabel figured. But today the corset laced without a fight, the petticoat dropped into place, and the gown slipped on easily. Apparently fieldwork benefitted her body as much as her mind.

At the Lab, Mabel pulled her hair out of the way and wore a rubber apron over a plain skirt and shirtwaist. For the past week on fieldwork, she'd worn what Father called her safari suit and kept her braid under a straw hat. But tonight... Mabel analyzed the image in the mirror.

But tonight, she was a woman. A woman who might be attractive enough to turn Wade's head. Just for tonight she would enjoy being part of a couple.

Wade frowned at the mirror as he shaved. His hair was due for a trim. No doubt the Homestead's barber charged a lot more than Selina and wouldn't catch him up on all the staff gossip either. He picked Raleigh's fur off his suit - should have gotten a black dog to match his tuxedo - then dressed. Fortunately running around Fauquier kept him from growing out of his clothes. And men's fashions hadn't changed much in the past twelve years. No one would guess Wade was the penniless manager of a cash-strapped resort.

Wade knocked on Maybelle's door. She stepped into the hall - whoa! She wore her hair in a crown, her skin glowed, and her dress curved out and in and out. Her neckline scooped making her neck look even more elegant and revealing two soft amazing assets. Wade's mouth went dry. "Miss Maybelle!"

Her glow brightened. "My, aren't you handsome."

"You, too." He gulped. Handsome is what you called women who weren't pretty, which didn't fit tonight.

One eyebrow arched. "Passable for a scientist?"

"All dolled up!"

She winced. "Dolls don't come in this size."

Third try and he'd better get it right. "Miss Maybelle, you are glorious and gorgeous!" And irresistible. How would he survive the evening?

"Thank you kindly." She took his arm and they strolled down the hall. "How did you spend your afternoon?"

"Watched the politicians and the newspaper correspondants attempt to play baseball. And tried out the Pleasure Pool. It wasn't half so pleasurable as swimming with you, Miss Maybelle."

"But it was warm."

"Eighty-two degrees, as promised." Promise? That's why he must not kiss Miss Maybelle, because she'd think he was promising more, promising marriage. And he had nothing to offer a woman who was brilliant in every way. Wade looked up at the ceiling, the electric lights, the other guests. If he could keep from staring, he might have a chance. "And you?"

"I took a spout bath. You must try it, Wade." She shifted her shoulders, giving a glimpse of the lacey edge of her chemise, a manuever Wade would have guessed Miss Maybelle didn't know. "Warm fingers of water knead your body all over. I feel hmm…" Where did she learn to moan like that? "Revitalized. Stimulated. Exhilarated."

GILDING THE WATERS

Fortunately they arrived at the dining room. Wade noted its features - anything to keep from staring at the temptation beside him. The coffered ceiling curved down to fanlights - a double set that shouted "spare no expense!" - above tall windows. Massive columns - if he'd paid attention in Ancient Greece class, he'd know what type - bordered the room. They took up a lot of space, but also provided a place for servers to safely set their tray stands. Linen and fancy china dressed tables in a variety of shapes and sizes. He would have gone with lower flower arrangements, though, to keep guests from having to lean to see around them.

The maître d' seated them at a rectangular table between two other young couples. Miss Maybelle ended up across from him, so Wade inspected the silverware - spotless - and assessed the vittles - presentation and taste excellent. Throughout courses of fish, beef, and lamb, the new bride plagued them with her wedding story - did anyone marry nowadays without bedlam and catastrophe?

The new groom worked for Coca-Cola. Maybelle tried to talk water with him, but he sidestepped with a patronizing smile and the line about mixing business and pleasure. For Maybelle, talking water was pleasure.

The couple on their other side turned out to be some sort of minor league British royalty - at least he was. The Baroness originated with the New York Astors. Baron Something Hyphen Something didn't mind talking water. In fact, he asked so many questions about plumbing, roping both of them into the discussion, Wade knew where Miss Astor's dowry would be spent. Wade wanted to suggest they invest in Fauquier instead, but indoor toilets would make a nice addition to their castle.

The Baron asked a question about the best material for pipes and cisterns. Wade got lost in Maybelle's complicated answer.

If you're looking for complicated, try love. Love? Where had that come from? Was he falling in love with Miss Maybelle? Well, he liked her. She met each day with enthusiasm, ready for about anything. Water testing was her quest, but not her only interest. And even though she was a good bit smarter than him, she was easy to talk to.

But he couldn't fall in love with her. She blazed trails at the Geophysical Laboratory in DC. He whitewashed buildings and account books at a needy resort in the hills of Fauquier County. He shouldn't even flirt with her - she'd take it as seriously as she did everything else.

The dessert was called Baba au Rhum, but tasted like sponge cake. Finger bowls appeared and the orchestra tuned. If he danced with Miss Maybelle, if he took her in his arms, he'd fall head over heels and blurt out a proposal. Wade glanced across the table. His radiant, alluring Miss Maybelle.

The Coca-Cola bride missed her groom's signal to avoid talking water. She leaned toward Maybelle. "So how many more springs must you test?"

Maybelle recited a list of over a dozen places. She met Wade's gaze. Instead of the warm glances she'd given him all evening, her eyebrows creased and she pressed her lips together, almost as if pained. "Another week should do it."

Only a week? This had been the best summer of his life. It couldn't end so soon.

The Baron helped Maybelle out of her chair. The other couples headed for the ballroom. The last rays of sunset lit clerestory windows as the orchestra began a waltz.

Dear Lord, help me control myself. God should be all over that prayer in a heartbeat. "Shall we?"

Maybelle took his arm. "We both had something to contribute to that conversation. Wasn't that delightful?"

"You, Miss Maybelle, are always delightful," he said, meaning it with all his heart.

She sent him one of her "you've got to be kidding" glances, but then they arrived in the ballroom. Not pausing to study the architecture, not checking out the orchestra, not giving his dance partner a chance to warn him about stepping on his toes, he swept Miss Maybelle onto the floor. She held her arms stiff, swiveled her head to avoid bumping into other dancers, and counted under her breath, "One, two, three."

That will never do. Wade snugged her closer - oh, the wonder of her strength, her warmth, and her peach-sweet fragrance. "Look at me," he whispered. She gave his Adam's apple such a stare, he figured he'd forgotten his tie. "Look in my eyes, Miss Maybelle. I've kept you safe all week. I'm not stopping now."

Warm brown eyes travelled up his chin, paused at his lips, and finally met his gaze. *Have mercy.* This was his pleasure pool, right here in her arms. She studied him as if she wanted to ask a question. Her lips parted and her breathing quickened. Did she want to kiss him as much as he wanted to kiss her?

The orchestra changed keys, changed tempos, and played four ruffles and flourishes, then "Hail to the Chief." The dancers moved out of the way as Judge Taft and his wife took the floor.

"Oh." Maybelle blinked and squirmed out of his arms. They'd circled the room, ending up by the entrance. She hurried into the hall and said to the carpet, "We have a lot to do tomorrow. We should turn in."

"Let's stay another day." Wade reached for her arm, but she moved too fast for him. "We could ride out to Falling Springs. And try out the clay tennis courts. We could take on the British royal family."

"Add a diplomatic faux pas to my list of indiscretions?" Maybelle raced away from the ballroom. "Besides, neither of us has appropriate attire. No. I must finish the research before Father returns."

She didn't speak again until they reached her room. "Thank

you for the lovely evening," she said briskly and dashed inside. The door closed with a firm click.

Well. He'd managed to avoid kissing Maybelle. So why'd he feel lower than a toad in a dry well?

CHAPTER FIFTEEN

Wade strolled into the dining room at breakfast, turning heads of females young and old, and heating Mabel's cheeks. If she had thrown herself at him last night, she very possibly would have succumbed to spontaneous combustion this morning. Fortunately she'd decided against such foolishness. Establishing a professional relationship and earning his respect had been an uphill battle. Much as she enjoyed his appreciative glances last night, nothing must endanger her research.

"Miss Maybelle, you outshine the sun this morning." Wade grabbed a handful of raspberries from her bowl. "Good news. We don't have to backtrack through Covington. Before the C&O built their spur line, the Homestead's guests got off north of here at Millboro and took a stagecoach through the mountains. The resort has a carriage that can take us to Millboro."

"What about my tests?"

"Already talked to the driver. Since we're the only passengers, he'll stop wherever you want. Got your luggage loaded and we're checked out."

"My satchel?" She shot out of her chair, a giant fist clenching her heart.

"Easy, now. Every element and atom is intact."

"We'll just see about that." Mabel raced through the lobby out to the circular drive. Loss of her notebook would mean starting over. Loss of the reagent strips would mean ordering more from Germany, missing the deadline for the National Conservation Commission, and losing any chance to improve her lot at the Geophysical Lab. *Oh dear Lord, please, please, please...*

A lone carriage waited. Without a word to the driver, Mabel pulled her satchel from beneath the seat and opened it. Test tubes, reagent bottles, alcohol lamp, notebook. Nothing damaged, nothing missing. The fist released her heart and she exhaled. *Thank you, Lord.* She glanced at her traveling companion. Had she misjudged him? Was he trustworthy? "Thank you, Wade."

"Miss Maybelle, I'm no scientist, but I will do what I can to help you finish your research," he said, his expression as serious as she'd ever seen. "I've never seen anyone work so hard."

Foolish tears. Scientists do not cry. But she'd never had a champion before. "You're no slouch. Waking early, arranging transportation..."

"Habit from running a resort. Get a jump on the latest crisis." Wade assisted her onto the tufted seat and introduced the driver, Archibald McDowell. Mabel had heard southern whites treated coloreds with contempt, but Wade gave everyone he met an equal dose of respect. They headed north up the valley through a misty morning.

"Most of the places we've stopped seem so peaceful," Mabel said. "It's hard to imagine any crisis here."

"Ah, success." He sprawled in the corner. One arm rested on the back of the seat, his hand by her shoulder. His feet angled toward hers. "Every hotelier strives for that illusion of tranquility. Never let the guests know you ran out of eggs, the head cook overslept, some fool scared a skunk under the porch."

"Really? You think other resorts have such problems?"

"I know it. Last night the Homestead staff moved several dozen wheelbarrows of dirt, replaced porch boards, and scrubbed everything down with vinegar. The head cook overslept at Blue Ridge, but they had a big enough staff to cover. And our pin boy at Yellow Sulphur Springs made a morning run to the nearest farm for extra cackleberries."

"I had no idea."

"Always something going on. That's what makes it fun." He spent the rest of the ride entertaining her and the driver with stories of mishaps at Fauquier. Mr. McDowell offered a few stories of his own.

"So the hotelier creates the illusion all is well," Mabel concluded.

"An illusion? No." Wade's lips moving into kissing position for the last word. "We work to make all well, so guests enjoy their vacation."

They passed through the small town of Warm Springs, then turned off the road to a collection of white wooden buildings.

"Nearly a hundred years old and overshadowed by its younger cousin down the road." Wade studied the hotel. "Sad to lose the history, but at least no one's staying in that firetrap."

Mr. McDowell pointed out two cottages off to the side. "Artist in that one and author in the other. They like the quiet."

"Reminds me of Mount Vernon," Mabel said as they pulled off the road.

"Same cupola." Wade strode to an octagonal board-and-batten structure, the men's bathhouse. He stepped inside and emerged a moment later. "The coast is clear. So how did all these hot springs end up here and how can I get one for Fauquier?"

Mabel inhaled the distinctive whiff of sulphur. Inside, changing rooms and a narrow boardwalk circled the still pool. The peak of the roof had been left open. Sunlight through the triangles gave the rocks on the bottom an emerald hue. "They used to think the heat came from chemical reactions, but none of the concentrations are adequate for that. More likely the water is warmed by the core of the earth." Mabel could relate to heating at the core and it wasn't just due to the humidity inside the bathhouse. She fanned herself with her notebook.

"No chance of getting a hot spring at Fauquier, then." He bent over her testing kit. "Hey, you restocked."

"The Homestead is approximately halfway—"

"And you were having your dress shipped down anyway. Miss Maybelle, you are amazing in too many ways to count."

Unfortunately her boss held the opposite opinion.

Wade tapped on the boards bracing the walls. "This is the oldest spa building in the United States, built in 1761. Thomas Jefferson sang its praises."

"I didn't know he could sing." She set up her test.

"Well, I sure can." He burst into a jaunty "Keep on the Sunny Side."

Mabel had been out of sorts this morning, but Wade knew just how to cheer her up.

When he finished the song, she thanked him.

"Music for research. Just part of the service."

"Of course." How had she forgotten? And how fortunate she hadn't attempted a kiss. He might have gone along, as "part of the service."

And she would have enjoyed it anyway.

Wade took her elbow as they walked the rough planks to the larger, round building. This too stood empty. "The women's bath house was built in 1836. The windlass was used to help Mrs. Robert E. Lee in and out of the water. Rheumatism afflicted her something awful."

"The warmth of the water would be soothing."

As Mabel worked, Wade serenaded her with "You're a Yankee Doodle Dandy," changing the word "sweetheart" to "chemist." Of course.

Test finished, they headed east.

To keep Wade from adapting more songs, Mabel shared what little she'd read about the water. "During treatment at Warm Springs, Jefferson initially reported improvement in his rheumatism, but he developed boils in an uncomfortable place."

"Especially uncomfortable for the long ride back to Monticello."

"Ah, so you know about his problem. Required study at your university?"

"Presidential Rumps. Essential course in the history department."

Laughter bubbled up within her. She couldn't stay grumpy around Wade.

He noticed. "Just because you're doing serious work, doesn't mean you have to be serious."

"Doesn't it? Scientists seem to frown continually."

"You'd think they'd be happier than hogs in wallow, getting to see God's great work up close and personal."

So why weren't they happy? And would she ever be happy at the Geophysical Lab?

The road zig-zagged over the mountain, giving views of long rows of ridges in every direction. Squares of farm fields partitioned the valleys.

Mabel counted four church steeples. "I've seen many churches but few schools."

"The state's been short on funds for schools since The War," Wade said. "We're catching up."

"Never had public schools," the driver informed her. "White folks don't want to pay to educate colored children."

"How awful!" So backward. "An informed citizenry is essential for modern life. To calculate an interest rate, or to read a label to see if a product is a cough medicine or a polishing compound-"

"Or pass a literacy test to vote," the driver said.

"In the last election, my head groundskeeper was asked to name all the judges for the state of Virginia," Wade said. "Fortunately I was behind him in line. I confessed I couldn't list them all either, but I did know several judges who'd been guests of the resort. We were allowed to vote."

"Have you been kept out of the polls, Mr. McDowell?" Mabel asked.

"Depends on who's working." Dark brown eyes met hers. "Suspect you'd like to vote, too."

She returned his smile. "That I would."

"You both should," Wade said. "This country needs you."

Mr. McDowell parked at Bath Alum, then gave Wade a tour of the brick hotel while she tested the five springs.

"Robert E. Lee and Stonewall Jackson slept here," Wade reported on his return. "They've got a ballroom, plus fireplaces and wire-woven mattresses in every room. The big draw seems to be lower rates than the Homestead, yet close enough to visit Warm and Hot Springs."

An eight mile ride took them to Wallawhatoola Springs which consisted of a giant elm tree, a two-story hotel, and a bottling plant.

"This is one of my favorite ads." Mabel held out the newspaper clipping.

"'You deserve to have indigestion the rest of your days,'" Wade read. "Got my attention. 'If after hearing of the wonderful, quick, and lasting cures effected by the Wallawhatoola Water, you do not give it a try, you deserve to have indigestion the rest of your days.' There you go - it's all your fault."

While Mabel tested, Wade found one of their bottles. He studied the drawing of King Powhatan on the label. "I thought Powhatan lived down by Jamestown."

Mabel ran her tests. "Maybe he came here for a cure."

"From the expression on his face, I'd say he had the same problem as Jefferson."

Mabel glanced up from recording the sulphate of alumina. "He does look rather distressed. Poor Powhatan."

"And poor proprietor of this hotel, having to stand in the dining hall and say 'Welcome to Wallawhatoola Springs,' to guests three times a day."

"Fauquier isn't easy to say."

Wade stared northeast, as if he could see all the way to his resort. "It is if you've been saying it all your life."

After testing Millboro Springs, they said goodbye to Mr. McDowell and ate lunch.

Wade took a bite of his ham sandwich. "Where to next?"

"Cold Sulphur Springs."

"No." Wade's face lost all color. He pushed his food away. "It burned down a couple of months ago, the hotel and most all outbuildings. It'll be awful... the smell, everything gone."

"But it's so close to Goshen—"

"It would be like a funeral, a death." His hands tightened on the edge of the table and finally he met her gaze. "Please."

"I haven't heard of any plans to rebuild, so I suppose we could omit it." Once again, Mabel wondered about the fire that had taken Fauquier's hotel. "Is that why you send a letter every day, to warn your staff about fire safety?"

"Not much gets by you, Miss Maybelle." Wade's grin passed as quickly as an iodine-zinc reaction. "No, I'm just sending reminders. Mrs. Bland prefers tea over coffee. The Burwell family always brings their own pillows, so the staff should put ours away. Meet Mrs. Graves's carriage with a wheelchair."

"All things Robert E wouldn't know. In most families, the oldest brother inherits the business. Why—"

"You've met him. You know better." A grimace mixed into his

grin. "Now Miss Maybelle, let's enjoy our beautiful Virginia day."

The livery sent them out with a grey gelding and a buggy.

"His name is Traveller," Wade told her. "Direct descendant of Robert E. Lee's horse."

"That sounds as suspicious as the advertisements for this resort," Mabel said.

"Ah, yes, Rockbridge Alum Springs, the king among mineral waters."

"They give an analysis of their water and a list of diseases it cures, but there's no scientific connection between the two. I'd like to know how much those physicians were paid to endorse the water. Did the Medical Association of Virginia get to stay at the resort for free?"

Wade shrugged. "And I want to know how they're staying open since their spur line shut down."

The road paralleled a lively stream southward. A sign directed them up a hill to a mountain cove containing two large hotels and a score of cottages. A scattering of guests enjoyed the beautiful day. Wade secured the horse in a shady spot beside the creek. They followed the footpath past a barroom, a store with a post office, the gents' bowling alley, and a billiard room - all empty.

The creases between Wade's eyebrows deepened. "So they're not staying in business."

"Business? Life is not aimless business." A young man jumped off the porch of a brick cottage. He was clean-shaven, and his blazer, shirt, and slacks were neatly pressed. He waved a pencil like a sword. Beneath his perfectly curved brows, his intent gaze focused on Mabel. "You embody all that I ever conceived of beauty, fearlessness, and strange purity."

If she was fearless, Mabel gave all credit to the man beside her who rested his hand on his pistol.

"Could you direct us to the spring?" Mabel asked.

"For the water here is not like the water of other fountains." He stretched out his arms.

"I'm a chemist from the National Conservation Commission, sent by President Roosevelt to test the springs."

He shuddered like a dog shaking off after a swim. "No one speaks the truth here and we're all perfectly happy."

"I'm always truthful," she assured him.

"Veracity is an unpardonable sin against humanity."

"No, the sin is lying about the healing properties of water."

"We're not getting anywhere," Wade said in an undertone. "Let's follow the creek."

"I see with a clarity denied other men." The young fellow bowed low, hands splayed over his heart. "For I am a writer. James Branch Cabell, at your service."

Wade tucked Mabel's arm in his and steered her away. "We'll let you get back to your writing."

"Don't mind if I do." The young man leaped over the porch rail, then waved toward the woods. "Yonder erupts the fount."

A wildflower strewn path beside the lively creek brought them to a large gazebo set into the cliff. Its pillared roof supporting a statue of Hygieia. The spring emerged beneath it.

"Let me guess," Wade muttered, "this water doesn't cure nervous conditions."

Mabel set her equipment on the counter. "I wondered if the Rockbridge Alum Springs had been converted to a sanitarium."

"All the Cabells I know are quite accomplished - governor, professor, physician." He glanced over his shoulder. "None as... unconventional as that one."

"Every family has a black sheep." Mabel glanced over her shoulder to be sure the writer hadn't followed them. "I hope he doesn't put me into his story."

"What better heroine than Miss Maybelle, champion of water

purity?"

"Hush. Don't give him any ideas."

Wade focused his binoculars on the statue. "You're a modern day Hygieia, goddess of health. She looks just like you - holding a pitcher, studious expression on her face, enough muscles to bowl a perfect game."

"Perhaps that writer will put *you* into his story." He could make fun of her all day long, Mabel wouldn't stop working.

They followed the circular drive around a spacious lawn with a band stand, painted light blue with red trim. Two children rode in a pony-cart while their parents played croquet.

Wade peeked inside one of the brick cottages. "Hey, I like this. One chimney serves four corner fireplaces. Cuts down on maintenance."

He couldn't resist taking a look at the main hotel either. "There's no one here."

A kerchiefed woman popped up from behind the front desk. "Well, thank you very much, but God don't consider me no one."

"Pardon me, ma'am." Wade introduced the two of them.

"Well, I'm Camilla and this here hotel building is closed." A hand as dark and strong as mahogany slapped the counter. "Been closed five years now."

"Thanks to the railroad?"

"You got that right." She gave a grim nod. "Cottages for rent, if you want."

"Actually I was hoping we could look around."

"Not much to see no more." Dark eyes assessed them. "How 'bout I give you the grand tour, since this is the Grand Hotel?" She led them down the hall.

"How long have you worked here?"

"All my life." She pointed out the window to a low building with board and batten siding. "Born in the quarters."

148

"Slave quarters?" Mabel asked, doing some calculations in her head. The war ended forty-four years ago and this woman appeared to be in her sixties.

"Yes'm. Freedom come, but no free train tickets. So I stay. Keep the place running."

"You've seen a lot of changes," Wade said.

"Yessir. Heydays of eight hundred guests, sad times of hospital for soldiers, foolish men fist-fighting over two hotels atop one mountain, fancy new gaslights and telegraph. And now shutting down. Who'd a thought?" Camilla took them through the dining hall, parlor, ballroom, and theater. The finest wallpapers and furnishings decorated each room.

"Miss Camilla, right pretty place you've got here. But if you ever decide to move on, Fauquier White Sulphur Springs would be glad to have you."

Mabel began to see how Wade came to his collection of elderly workers.

"Thank you, sir, but I expect I'll stay." She glanced out the window. "Expect you should, too, at least for tonight. You don't want to cross paths with the painter after dark."

"You have a painter?" Mabel asked. "We already met the writer."

"Painter's another name for panther or cougar," Wade explained.

"How much for two cottage rooms?" Mabel asked quickly.

Morning brought scenery so beautiful Mabel forgot to breathe as they descended through Goshen Pass. A boulder-filled river rushed through narrow forested cliffs, attracting a score of fishermen.

"Hear that, Miss Maybelle?" Wade's light touch on her earlobe gave her a shiver. "It's the music of water. Every resort sings it in a slightly different tune."

"Any more poetry from you, Mr. Alexander, and I'll take you back to Rockbridge Alum and that writer."

Wade's satisfied grin increased the restlessness within her.

They turned off the road to a small two-story hotel and a few cottages. Several families camped out of farm wagons. A trio of girls in calico played croquet on the lawn while a fiddler and a banjo player traded songs under a tree.

Wade consulted the map. "Wilson Springs. Captain Drake spent the war here."

"Your guard? The deaf one? He spent the war on vacation, then."

"He defended Goshen Pass."

Wilson's Springs seemed too tranquil to have ever been touched by war. "Was there a battle?"

He shook his head. "Captain Drake did his job."

Union forces probably couldn't find this place. She would have had difficulty doing so had it not been for Wade's skill with a compass and the map. Not that she'd admit it to him.

A sulphur spring issued from an island. They left Traveller beside the river and crossed the log bridge.

Wade sprawled on the grass and reached for yet another way to distract her. "Hear that?"

"Hear what?"

"The birds are talking about you."

They'd been surrounded by birds all morning. "Of course."

He pointed up in the trees. "That little blue fellow is an indigo bunting. One look at you and he started singing sweet-sweet-sweet."

"Really." Mabel recorded her results.

"And I hear a vireo, but he's harder to see. He's singing sweeter-sweeter-sweeter."

"Is that what the University of Virginia teaches in ornithology?" She repacked. "Because I rather suspect the birds are addressing their own species."

They returned to the north bank, past the bowling alley, dance pavilion, and a sparse number of guests, and found the sulphur spring near the hotel.

"I didn't study birds in college," Wade said, leaving open the question of what exactly he *had* studied. "But I've learned a lot from guests who are devotees of Audubon."

"And as their host, you find it important to *appear* interested when they expound on their obsession." He *appeared* interested in her, but was he really?

"It doesn't take much to get me interested in something new. Guess you'd say I'm a bit of a dabbler."

Who dabbled with women, no doubt. Another reason to keep her distance.

Two miles down the road, Rockbridge Baths abutted the road, which hardly seemed conducive to relaxation, but, as Wade said, "was right handy for testing."

Mabel confirmed the springs did indeed contain magnesia. She finished and looked up in time to see him exit the post office. Had he sent another letter back to his staff? He worried more than he let on.

Don't stare. Do not stare.

But she couldn't look away. The sun gilded his hair and the air around him glowed. Wade nodded and waved at the people rocking on the porch. He saluted a boy who'd executed a difficult croquet shot and tossed a ball for a droopy-diapered toddler. Then, this paragon of a Virginia gentleman headed straight for plain Mabel Easterly.

Enjoy it while it lasts.

He caught her watching and bestowed one of his perfect smiles on her. Sharing the local lore, he took her satchel and held out his arm. Mabel was perfectly capable of standing unaided, yet her hand slipped into his and she let him assist her to her feet.

Enjoy that *while it lasts, too.*

CHAPTER SIXTEEN

"Are we lost?" The terrain and Mabel's map didn't match. Had Wade gotten off track?

"Let's ask." Wade stopped the buggy close to a split-rail fence and hopped down. "Good afternoon, sir. Is this the road to Augusta Springs?"

The gaunt man looked up from his hoeing, but his back stayed bent. He tipped his straw hat, hitched up his overalls, then began a lengthy monologue. Mabel made out, "way over yonder cross the crick," and "up along Arminta's place," and "purt near where Reuben shot that Yankee." The waving of his arms and flapping of his beard indicated they should alternate left and right turns, or that the road twisted. Wade's skill as an interpreter and guide proved essential.

"Thank you very kindly, sir." Wade hopped back into the buggy and giddy-upped to the horse. "So now you know, Miss Maybelle."

An equally thin woman tended a caldron suspended over a fire, then called to the man. The man stepped over his fence and they headed inside their small log cabin.

"Why doesn't he build a gate?"

"Mountain folks are independent, relying on only themselves and what they can make, not wanting to spend their limited cash on store-bought goods like latches and hinges." Wade nodded at the cabin. "See how their porch is set up for work -

spinning wheel, butter churn, washtub, chair ready for caning, herbs hanging to dry."

"Not a rocking chair in sight." Mabel pointed to an outbuilding set into the hill. "I recognize outhouses and spring houses, but what's that?"

"Vegetable dugout. Mountain refrigerator to keep cool all the food they put up for the winter."

"They must need money occasionally, say for kerosene for their lanterns. Moonshine?"

"You ask good questions, Miss Maybelle. First off, around here kerosene's known as coal oil. Yes, extra corn might be made into whiskey. Extra apples become brandy. Don't see any young 'uns about, so I suspect their sons have hired on with the railroad or a mining company, and might send their folks some pay. But the big money-maker is right there." He motioned toward the mountain.

What could he mean? All she saw were the spreading giants of Longfellow's blacksmith poem. "Chestnut trees?"

He nodded. "Mountain people sell the nuts. If their pigs eat them first, well, they'll eat the pig. Tanneries buy the bark for curing leather. And they sell the logs for telephone poles and railroad ties."

"Very efficient." Mabel picked up the map. "So did you understand that man's directions?"

"Sure enough, Miss Maybelle." Wade's mouth curved. "Don't you worry none. We'll be there right soon. There's the sign." He turned off at the resort and parked by the spring.

At the Homestead, he encouraged her to finish her research. Yet at Augusta Springs he seemed intent on distracting her into watching ducklings. Down the road at Variety Springs, he tried to talk her into climbing Mt. Elliott. And at Stribling Springs, which he called the grand old lady of the resort circuit, he regaled her with a story about Stonewall Jackson's visit.

Could he be diverting himself, trying to keep his worries about Fauquier at bay? Or was he back to his old tricks, trying to stop her project?

Seawright Magnesian Lithia Springs had a large bottling plant and a new hotel. Mabel finished her tests as the supper bell rang.

Wade loped around a stack of lumber. "Bottled water's paying for the hotel. A mile from the train station, ten miles from Staunton. If they get the place finished, they might make it."

"They claim their water tones the broken system and cures poison oak."

"Worthy goals."

"But not possible given its composition. My favorite line in the advertisement is 'Seawright speaks for itself.'"

Wade nodded at the round pool. "I don't know about speaking, but it sure is enthusiastic about flowing. Wish Fauquier had that much water."

The Tudor-style hotel was so new it smelled of paint and linseed oil. The rest of the guests, a large family from Baltimore, sat at a table stretching the length of the room.

As they paused for the waitress to seat them, one of the children pointed at Mabel. Her face heated and she braced for the boy's words. "Are you the giant from 'Jack in the Beanstalk?'" he asked.

An older child swatted him. "Silly. The giant was a man."

"But she's taller than Papa."

The older one squinted at Mabel. "Papa could beat you up."

The adults, instead of stopping the children's rude behavior, looked on as if Mabel was a side-show act for their entertainment.

Wade took a big step toward the boys, hands raised in claws. "Fum-fo-fi-fe. I smell the blood of a naughty monkey."

The boys whipped back to their food, posture ramrod

straight.

Wade escorted Mabel across the room to a spot for two by the window. Dinner with a handsome and chivalrous gentleman. Mabel would enjoy it while it lasted.

Fortunately he took the reins of conversation. "We always talk about my alma mater. Let's talk about yours, Miss Maybelle. Where did you go to college?"

She aligned her napkin with the seams of her skirt. The situation chafed like a ill-fitting shoe. "Penn."

He blinked. "The University of Pennsylvania? But they don't give degrees to women."

"I have a certificate of completion. And it wasn't a gift. I earned it." Oops, her thin-skin was showing.

"I'm sure you did. Why Penn and not, say Bryn Mawr or Mount Holyoke?"

Mabel squirmed. In Penn's chemistry department, with the ratio of men to women in her favor, she'd hoped to find someone who would overlook her body in appreciation of her mind. Unfortunately scientists were as shallow as the rest of the male population. "They're conducting interesting research in hygiene, sanitation, and bacteriology. And Father taught there."

"Ah, your troublesome father. Always firing housekeepers so you'll have to look after him."

"No, he's not—" But the truth of his statement ricocheted through her brain. Is that why Father kept her close? Then why hadn't he taken her on his Hudson Bay expedition?

"Will the lack of a degree make it difficult to find a job?" Wade asked as if he really cared about her so-called career.

"Father will strong-arm the Lab into taking me back." The Geophysical Laboratory's scientists had shown no interest in her, either. Mabel shook her head. She didn't want to think about her miserable job.

"Are you hoping to follow in your father's footsteps or is

someone else an inspiration?"

No one had asked that question before. "Mary Engle Pennington has an interesting career. She earned a doctorate in chemistry from Penn. Her research on sanitation and food safety has saved untold lives. She's working in the Department of Agriculture's Food Research Lab now."

"Penn awards doctorates to women, but not bachelor degrees? And you think U.Va. is crazy." He shook his head. "So why didn't you keep going with your education?"

How flattering that he thought she should. "Father moved to Washington."

Wade frowned. "Not your biggest booster."

"My only booster. Remember, many fathers allow their daughters only an eighth grade education."

The waiter arrived with their fried chicken dinners.

Wade took a bite. "Not bad. Not as delicious as Fauquier's of course."

"Of course." She smiled back.

He studied his plate. "Since you've been so forthcoming about your education…"

"Your university has an honor code."

"Yes, about my university." He poked a green bean, then looked up without moving his head. "I don't have a degree either. Barely survived a semester."

"I understand it's competitive."

He shrugged. "I missed Fauquier something awful. So much work to be done in the off-season and conjugating Greek verbs wasn't getting it done." He watched the sunset out the window. "Suppose that makes me a pantywaist."

"Not at all. The value of a classical education has come into question in modern times. A business school, like Penn's Wharton, might have been a better match for your interests." What a delightful addition he would have made to their campus.

"I mail-ordered an accounting textbook and figured it out. Wasn't hard."

"You taught yourself accounting? That's impressive."

"Would be if Fauquier wasn't hanging on by a thread."

"With all the broken threads we've seen on this trip, hanging on is an accomplishment." If only his hotel hadn't burned down. Mabel scanned the ceiling, then said, just to please him, "I'm surprised they didn't install a sprinkler system. Their spring certainly has adequate capacity."

Wade's warm hand squeezed hers. "Why Miss Maybelle, you're thinking like a hotel manager!"

"Church?" Wade asked Sunday morning as they rode the B&O up the Shenandoah Valley.

"I wasn't able to find a service that worked into the itinerary. Maybe we'll pass one along the way."

"Selina says God provides good surprises."

Mabel thought God had provided a tantalizing surprise in Wade this summer. "Maybe we'll find another in need of a preacher. Do you have a second sermon?"

He nodded. "Came up with an innkeeper lesson one year when we were snowed in at Christmas."

"There was an innkeeper in the Good Samaritan story, too. Your profession goes back to Bible days."

"So does yours."

"There's a chemist in the Bible?"

"I was thinking more of teachers. But yes, don't you think God had to be a chemist, the way He set up this world?"

"Who else would make water from two gases?" Then Mabel did something she rarely did in Washington - she grinned.

In Harrisonburg, they rented a buggy and a brown horse.

"This here's Big Sorrel, a direct descendant of the Little Sorrel that Stonewall Jackson rode during the war." Wade handed her up.

Mabel narrowed her gaze. "Do you believe that?"

He grinned. "No, but it makes a good story. And what's the harm?"

"The harm is when prevarication is valued more than veracity." Mabel covered her mouth. "Oh, dear, I sound like one of those fuddy-duddies I work with."

Wade pointed the horse south. "When you're dealing with science and measuring what's in the water, best stick with the facts. But for the rest of life, tell a good story."

"But then how can anyone discern if you're being honest or not?" How would she know if Wade really liked her or if he pretended because he enjoyed flirting?

"I'm honest when it counts."

"When does it count?"

He pondered that for a while. "It counts when it affects Fauquier White Sulphur Springs and anyone connected with it."

Well that certainly left her out. "Shouldn't Christians be honest and truthful all the time?"

"You think I'm dishonest? A liar?" He shook his head and gave a low whistle. "Any time Selina caught me in a lie, she took a belt to me. A lie don't care who tells it, but she did." He shot her a worried glance. "What did I say that you count as untrue?"

"Well…" She looked for an example that didn't include herself. "Those two elderly women at your resort…"

"You're talking about a good half of my guests."

"Bridge players. Wide hats."

"Could you narrow it down a bit? Oh, the Dandridge cousins. I lied to the Dandridge cousins? Lord, have mercy." His eyes widened.

"You told them they looked lovely." One reminded her of a small dog with bulging eyes, deeply wrinkled jowls, and nervous gestures. The other had thick glasses, thin hair, and a perpetually damp chin.

"Ah, but they are lovely... inside. When Miss Lucinda's husband started using her as a punching bag, Miss Edmonia took her in. And when Miss Edmonia had an attack of apoplexy, Miss Lucinda got her back on her feet. Both fit as fiddles now. They're the powerhouse of their church - meals and prayers for the sick, sewing clothes for orphans, giving jobs to the poor - and mostly likely a good bit more that didn't make it to my ears."

Mabel fidgeted. Her opinion had been formed by the cousins' looks, just as strangers came to conclusions about her based on her height. "Don't judge on outward appearance. That's kind... and biblical." So what did Wade mean when he flattered her?

"Whoa, Big Sorrel." Wade turned the horse off the road and parked under an oak tree.

Osceola Springs consisted of a bottling plant and a picnic grounds. The water tested calcic and magnesic bicarbonated alkaline.

As she finished the tests, a line of buggies arrived. The men and boys wore white shirts, dark slacks held up by suspenders, and straw hats. The girls and women wore simple cotton dresses in pastels, their hair in braids or in coils covered with white caps, depending on their age.

"Good morning," said a man with a German accent. "We are called Mennonites. Our church in town was too hot, so we came here to worship. Would you like to join us?"

"We'd be delighted." Wade and Mabel exchanged grins. *God provides another good surprise.*

The women pulled Mabel to sit with them. The height of those in front nearly matched hers, making them the tallest women she'd ever met. She couldn't see Wade, but when they sang hymns *a capella* in four parts, her ear tuned to his voice.

One minister spoke for a few minutes in German. They prayed silently accompanied by bird song and the ripple of the waters. A deacon read the second chapter of Ephesians. Another minister spoke on verse ten of that chapter, "We are his workmanship, created in Christ Jesus unto good works, which God hath ordained." A third man prayed in English.

Dear God, what good works do you have for me? Surely You haven't ordained for me to wash chemists' glassware the rest of my life. And if I am your workmanship, why didn't you make me normal sized?

They sang another hymn, received the benediction, and invited Wade and Mabel to stay for lunch. Each family brought out a large basket woven of white oak strips. The picnic featured fried chicken, bread, potato salad, and half-moon pies - which Wade declared the best since he'd left home. So much for her idea to join the Mennonites - Mabel didn't know how to cook.

As they left, Wade called goodbye to each family.

"You memorized all their names?"

He gave her a sidelong grin. "As if you teachers don't have a lot of people to remember."

"It takes weeks." Wait, he'd called her a teacher and she hadn't disagreed with him. Did she still think of herself as a teacher?

"The sermon went with what we talked about earlier," Wade negotiated a turn in the road. "The Dandridge cousins are busy doing the good works God prepared for them."

"So, God's workmanship has to do with what's inside a person, not the exterior? I wish this world, including me, wasn't so obsessed with appearance."

"Are you thinking about how the Mennonites' choice to dress differently draws attention to their group? Or how the Bible says we're supposed to consider lilies and not worry about clothing?"

"Easy for a man to say."

"Miss Maybelle, I'm amazed at how well you manage to

161

clothe yourself out of one little suitcase. You are a wonder."

"Your suitcase is the same size."

"Like you said, it's easier for a man." Wade halted the horse at the sign for Massanetta Springs. "Their hotel looks more like a farmhouse."

"Now who's judging on appearances," Mabel teased.

He grinned. "Unfortunately, hotel guests expect a nice-looking building, flowers along the drive, and a fancy carpet in the lobby. I look for one that's fireproof, has indoor plumbing and electricity, and doesn't require excessive maintenance. And this fails on every count."

The spring had been incorporated into a bottling plant building, so Mabel got right to work as Wade wandered off.

"Haven't made any improvements since Presidents Monroe and Madison stopped by," he told her on returning from his rounds. "They figured out one way to reach full capacity - build only eight rooms. What did you find out about the water?"

She accepted his help into the buggy. "The carbonation is added later."

He joined her on the seat. "That's a problem?"

"They shouldn't advertise it as natural."

A shake of the reins headed them back toward the depot. "Does it harm anyone?"

"No, but... if they're dishonest about carbonation, then how can I trust anything else they say?"

"Are you saying people should stick to the truth all the time? Wouldn't it make for a boring world?"

Mabel thought about the times Wade had complimented her. She enjoyed his words, but she knew better than to believe them. "A safer world."

"We're galloping right into philosophical territory," he said with a crook of his mouth, "where I'll have to admit, being the honest guy that I am, that I paid not a lick of attention to my professor. This is too heavy a topic for such a beautiful day."

Father's expedition team reveled in scientific dialogue, each trying to trip up the other with obscure facts. Conversing with Wade was a relief.

A few train changes brought them to tiny Harriston. Wade emerged from the livery with a black horse and buggy. "Traveler, may I introduce Mabel Easterly, known as Miss Maybelle to those of us lacking the honesty bone."

She rather liked the way he called her Miss Maybelle. "I know who I am, so you may call me by whatever name you prefer."

"You know who you are. Another philosophical discussion." Wade steered the horse out of town and up the ridge. "What about the times you're not honest?"

"How so?" She squeezed into the furthest corner of the seat.

"Like bowling. Trying to pretend you don't play well."

"But men don't like-"

Wade pointed his thumb at himself. "This man thinks you're mighty fine. Emphasis on the mighty." He squeezed her upper arm. "God's great workmanship, right here."

"But I can play well because I'm tall and strong. Isn't that taking unfair advantage of the competition?"

"Nope. It's using the gifts God has given you."

"Only men are allowed to do so." Mabel tamped down her anger, since only men were allowed to express that emotion. "You can't imagine what it's like to be the size of a big, bad giant in a fairy tale."

"Can't I? We're about the same height. Although I outweigh you by a good bit."

"You're a man. You're allowed to be big. You're *supposed* to be big." Her nails dug into her palms. "No one asks if you escaped from a freak show."

He had the grace to wince. "Miss Maybelle. I'm sorrier than I can say. No-'count bullies and ornery drunks will find something mean to say, no matter what size you are."

"Not only the scoundrels." When they thought she couldn't hear, the church ladies had whispered, "It's too bad Mabel is so *big*. No man will take her off her father's hands."

"Who else? Clothing manufacturers? Of course they'll aim their goods at average."

"I'm the only woman this size. I can't buy clothes from the Sears or Montgomery Wards catalogs, or from most stores." Who wouldn't be humiliated after shopping for clothes? A exasperated sigh escaped her. "Professor Dudley Sargent of Harvard and the Boston School of Gymnastics set the ideal measurements for women and none of mine matched."

"First of all, Dr. Sargent was trying to set standard measurements to encourage physical fitness and keep our species from deteriorating into lumps of lard."

"You're familiar with Dr. Sargent's work?"

"I looked into adding a gymnasium at Fauquier." Wade nodded. "And second, the school of gymnastics measured *their* students, not everybody else. While I'd like to say Fauquier's is the standard by which all other water should be measured, it wouldn't be scientific to do so." He tipped his head toward her with a teasing smile. "Seeing as how this is the twentieth century and we're all about being scientific."

"Yes, but…"

"You spent all summer proving advertisements about water were bunk, yet you believe what someone in Boston says about you, someone who's never met you?" He shook his head. "Sorry to disappoint them, but they're wrong."

Speaking of taking advantage, she might not have another opportunity to interview a man on this topic. "But being muscular and strong isn't feminine."

"You're female, so that means you're feminine."

"No, feminine is delicate, girlish, graceful—"

"You screamed when you saw a snake. That should count." His mouth quirked with a silly grin, ending her hope of a serious discussion. "Speaking of which, the kid working the livery says the main activity at Black Rock Springs is shooting rattlesnakes."

She shuddered. "I'll stay in the buggy and you can sample the water."

Wade glanced over his shoulder at the sun. "Afraid we're stuck here tonight, even if it's wood frame."

Which of course it was. The path led up a narrow ravine. A string of summer cottages stair-stepped up the mountain. Young guests gathered on the lawn around the bandstand and stretched out in hammocks strung on the trees.

"Their ad says it's 'good for what ails you,' including rheumatism, gout, and baldness."

"None of their guests are old enough to be bald." Wade parked the buggy at the first spring where they were met by a big yellow dog. Was there some canine telegraph that alerted members of the species when Wade would be in their neighborhood?

Accompanied by the retriever, Wade swished through the underbrush, then raised his arms and bowed. "Free of snakes. Call me St. Patrick of the Shenandoah. But don't call me late for supper."

No saint ever looked so mischevious. Mabel laughed and reached for his hand to climb down. He grabbed her waist and swung her over the grass and onto the flagstones. Was this what feminine felt like? How addictive.

Wade arranged for their rooms while Mabel analyzed the water.

"They have a three-lane bowling alley!" He raced back from the hotel and grabbed her hand. "Hurry, my secret weapon, we've got two other couples to beat before supper!"

Other couples? Was he seeing them as a couple now? Mabel mentally deflated that bubble. Wade hadn't considered the words he used - he merely enjoyed winning.

CHAPTER SEVENTEEN

Wade climbed the boulders at Black Rock Springs to watch the sunrise. Light outlined mountains in all directions and showed the boulders to be more grey than black. If the resort's guests weren't sleeping off their hangovers, he'd expound on Virginia's beauty. By himself, though, he faced an uncomfortable thought: in Miss Maybelle's eyes, he was a liar.

Now, most of the time, Wade didn't worry over people's notion of him. It wasn't that he didn't care for their good opinion - he did - but that he knew how to turn a guest's negative opinion around in no time.

Running a resort was all about making a happy experience. When shoveled out compliments, his guests' days shone brighter and they were more likely to return the next season. No harm in that, was there? It was like the Bible said, think about things that are lovely and worthy of praise… or however that went.

Lord, am I justifying fibbing? Have I gone beyond fibs into falsehoods and outright lies? Just a little sugar—

Instead of God's voice, Selina's words came to mind, "Child, as much sugar you dump, can't see the tea no more."

Well, today he wasn't running a resort. Today he would be as honest as possible. *Gonna need your help, Lord.*

A wiry boy hauled two buckets up the east side of the mountain. He set down his load, shook out his arms, then wiped his face on his shirt sleeve. If anyone needed a whopper of a compliment or tall tale, it was this kid. But Wade had promised God to stick to the truth.

"Help you carry that?" Wade reached for the pail.

"Ain't sharing my pay with you," he muttered, out of breath.

"Agreed." Wade took one bucket, finding it full of butter. "Nice morning for a walk."

"For you maybe." The boy pushed his jaw forward and blew, ruffling the hair over his sweaty forehead. "You ain't gotta do your chores and your brother's, on account of him coming down with the catarrh."

"Catarrh in the summer? What good is that? Can't stay home from school."

The boy gave him a narrow-eyed glance. "Ain't no school hereabouts."

"You learn at home, then?"

"Plowin', weedin', milkin', muckin'."

Grim life high in the Shenandoah mountains. Wade shifted the bucket to his other hand. "Your cows make some heavy butter. How far have you come?"

"'Spect it's about five mile. All uphill. Can't dawdle neither, as they need it for breakfast." He nodded at the dining hall.

"Maybe you can go fishing this afternoon."

"Maybe hogs grow wings and fly." The boy glared.

"Hope not. It's bad enough having bird droppings fall out of the sky, but hogs? Yuck."

Finally got a half smile out of the kid as they entered the kitchen.

Cooks and waitresses rushed about, frying bacon, cutting up peaches, rolling dough, filling coffee pots. A woman with a grey braid handed the boy an egg biscuit and a nickel, and he scampered off. She waved a spatula at Wade. "Breakfast ready soon, sir. Go on around."

Wade took a breath, ready to fling a few compliments about

the kitchen's efficiency and cleanliness, which would be followed by praise for the cook's pink cheeks. All true, pretty much, somewhat. At other resorts, his spiel earned him a chance to eat before everyone else, or at least got him coffee and toast on the porch. His stomach voted for a repeat performance, but his soul said, "Thank you, ma'am." He backed out, taking care to shut the screen door quietly.

Wade sauntered to the dining hall entrance and spotted Miss Maybelle crossing the lawn. She carried herself like a queen, her back straight as if she wore a crown instead of an old straw boater. As feminine as any woman God ever made. No one'd be picking on Maybelle, calling her freak or giraffe or any other nasty names, while he was around. Her eyebrows came together a fraction of an inch as she scanned the gathering guests. He waved and her face relaxed into a smile as pretty as the Shenandoahs. A smile that warmed him more than the sunrise.

The bell rang.

Breakfast with Miss Maybelle. Wade grinned. Might could be an advantage in sticking to the truth.

The train took them to Elkton at the south end of the Massanutten range. Wade pointed out the red brick house Stonewall Jackson had used as a headquarters.

Maybelle pulled an advertisement from her file. "Rockingham's brochure lists medical conditions and matches them to the most beneficial spring."

"Handy." Wade leaned over her shoulder. Anything for heartache? "How many springs do they have?"

"Twelve." She read, "'Allows the pulse to assume its natural condition.' Can you imagine a more ridiculous endorsement?"

"My pulse gallops along whenever you're nearby, Miss Maybelle," he said, being as honest as possible.

"Also ridiculous." Her smooth cheeks turned that delightful

shade of pink. "Gulp down a gallon of number four and you'll survive."

Wade parked the buggy in front of the hotel, checked for snakes and poison ivy, then chewed the fat with an elderly groundskeeper. He popped a cluster of pink flowers from the bunch growing vigorously beside the road. Would they grow at his resort? Would the resort still be his when Robert E finished with it? "Any idea what these are called?" he asked Maybelle.

"I am not a botanist."

"You're not a botanist, but you are a pretty lady." He tucked the flowers in her hat band, then enjoyed the view as her face turned as pink as the blooms. "We should stay here."

Warm molasses eyes gave the wood frame hotel a pointed look - he'd taught her well - then perfectly arched eyebrows raised. "Let me guess - a *four* lane bowling alley?"

"Nope. They're having a piano sing!"

"You are welcome to sing in the buggy." She put her satchel away and he handed her up.

"Hey, this place was good enough for Sidney Lanier."

"The only poet to mention chemists."

"Oh, yes, in that poem about the marsh, 'thou chemist of storms'. He agrees that God is a chemist." Wade shook the reins, then glanced over at Miss Maybelle. Was she impressed that he knew a poem?

"You and your philosophical questions. Yes, of course God is a chemist. And a physicist, biologist, geologist, artist…"

On the way to the next springs, Wade told the story of Governor Alexander Spotswood and the Knights of the Golden Horseshoe who explored this area in 1716.

"So is that why resorts held jousting competitions?"

"Hold. We're still at it. Virginians are awfully fond of Sir Walter Scott's novels." Wade turned at the collection of a dozen cottages forming Bloomer Springs. "Not a bloomer in sight."

"You were hoping for a clothesline of knickers? Sorry to disappoint you."

"No girls riding bicycles or playing basketball either. No, I've been disappointed since the hotel clerk told me 'bloomer' refers to something from the iron works."

A level farm road beside the Shenandoah River brought them to Bear Lithia Springs. A circular stone wall enclosed the spring and a bottling operation was in full swing.

"Not a bear in sight," Maybelle observed as he handed her down.

"Sorry to disappoint *you*, city girl. Rockingham's groundskeeper said it was named after a man named Bear who used to own it."

"You get more information out of the shortest conversations."

"And you get more information out of a splash of water." That compliment seemed to please her - she ran her tests with a smile.

Summer's humidity laid its hand on the day. Mosquitos and flies gave them plenty of reason to hurry back into the buggy. Maybelle loosened another button of her shirtwaist, giving him an enticing view of the delicate notch at the base of her neck.

By the time they reached Elkton, the smudge-darkened western sky had grown into a full-fledged line of thunderstorms, with anvils, lightning, and downpours.

Maybelle cleared her throat. "I'd hate to deprive the Rockingham Hotel piano sing of your fine voice."

Wade turned toward the resort and gave the reins a shake. The horse broke into a trot. "Don't have to ask me or Dixie twice."

Wade helped Mabel into the rig. "Yellow Massanutten scores for best abandoned bowling alley, Sparkling Springs takes the cake for their blueberry pie, and Union Springs gets a loose tooth for worst maintained road. What's next?"

She consulted her map. "Rawley Springs. The first cabin was built by a man who brought his mother here and she recovered from an incurable disease."

"Should bring my mother."

"How long has she been ill?" Mabel asked.

"Been puny as long as I remember, a martyr to migraines." He spoke with a matter-of-fact tone, then clamped his jaw.

"That must have made for a difficult childhood."

One broad shoulder raised an inch. "We were raised by Selina. Remember her?"

"She's a strong woman."

"She said the same about you."

She winced, recalling Selina's words about her hips.

"And your mama?" Wade asked.

Mabel swallowed and studied her clenched hands. She hadn't spoken of this in years, not to anyone. "You're going to think I'm out for revenge."

"Whoa." Wade stopped the horse. He slid forward in the seat and leaned toward her until she had no choice but to look at him. "Your mother died at a mineral spring resort? Here in Virginia?"

"No, Russia." The tall grass growing beside the road faded to the cold white tile of the bathing room where she last saw her mother. Agony rushed through her, spearing her heart and threatening to choke her.

A warm hand closed over hers. "What happened?"

Mabel forced a breath over the heavy lump in her chest. "We were accompanying Father on his research when her pain began. The doctor decided she had female troubles, since she had only one child, and sent her to a sanatorium in the Caucasus mountains. Unfortunately mineral water can't cure appendicitis."

Wade's thumb stroked deep into her palm. "I'm sorrier than I can say. You go ahead and cry, if you need to."

You're too big to cry, everyone had told Mabel, so she hadn't. She straightened and put on her brave smile. "No need."

"That's why I keep Doc Daly around, to make sure I'm not missing anything serious." Wade shook the reins and the horse trotted off. "What was she like, your mama?"

"Beautiful - graceful and dainty."

"You favor her."

Mabel would enjoy his flattery even if she didn't believe it. "At nine years old, my feet were already bigger than hers."

Wade stopped the horse again. He stared at the distant ridge for a long moment, then blinked and faced her. "Are you telling me, your papa expected you to wear your mama's shoes?"

No one else on the expedition thought anything of it. Mabel shrugged. "He was already behind schedule from Mother's illness. He couldn't stop just because I needed—" And she couldn't stop her tears.

"Aw, Maybelle." He took her hat off and pulled to his wide shoulder. His heart beat a steady, soothing rhythm. "Poor little girl. Broken heart and pinched feet. When did he finally realize you needed new shoes? When you started limping?"

"He didn't." Her words caught on a sob. "One of the attendants… At the spa… noticed the blood." Every step squished until her sock couldn't absorb any more and she left a trail on the tile floor.

"Your shoes were so tight your blisters wore through. Lord have mercy."

"Fortunately their waters do help wounds." Mabel sniffed. "The attendant took my shoes and mother's, and brought back thick wool socks and a pair of boots, men's black boots."

"Too ugly for a pretty little girl to wear."

"I've never been little." God loved her. Her father, the famous explorer, loved her... whenever he remembered she wasn't an expedition member. Was it wrong to want someone to love her, someone to take her side and be her champion? To hold her when life dealt her a blow? He wouldn't have to be as handsome and funny as Wade. She dried her eyes. "What choice did I have? I was so afraid Father would leave me in that place with food I didn't recognize and people I couldn't talk to." And here she was again, falling apart on her own expedition. Mabel straightened, immediately missing Wade's welcoming arms. "Embarrassing to have such big feet."

"Not a thing to embarrassed about, Miss Maybelle. God made you just right, feet and all." A hay wagon rumbled down the hill. Wade took up the reins to steer around it, then focused those blue eyes on her again. "Do you have a Selina in your life?"

"We've had housekeepers."

Wade read between her lines. "Hard to keep good employees in the city."

"Father's rather difficult to look after. His research drifts about the house and often appears, to the uneducated eye, to be flotsam and jetsam. The least disturbance in his universe convinces him all is lost." Mabel tried to make light of it, but his tantrums echoed in her memory.

"Ah, I knew he blamed you when plans went awry."

Mabel squirmed. She'd been on the receiving end of Father's ire often enough. "And your father?"

"Train accident." He looked up at the sky. "Twenty years ago this month."

"Oh, dear. Am I keeping you from a commemoration with your family?"

His hands tightened on the traces for a moment. The horse responded with a shake of his head and Wade loosened his grasp. "Mother wallows in mourning every day, more than enough for the rest of us."

"Twenty years ago… Who ran the resort?"

"I did." His chin tipped up, not in an arrogant way, but as if he too tried to hold in tears. "Day after the funeral, Mother handed me the keys to Fauquier. That morning, I made the kitchen circuit, rang the bell, then took Father's place at the entrance of the dining hall." He posed, shoulders back, chest out. "'Welcome to Fauquier White Sulphur Springs, Miss Maybelle. You are a sight for sore eyes. So glad you could join us this week.'"

"You were how old?"

"Thirteen."

"No wonder you're an expert at flattery. You've had twenty years' practice."

He blinked and drew back. "Flattery is false, but I truly mean every word I say. How can I convince you?"

"Scientists need proof."

"You come up with a test and I'll take it."

Mabel might have believed him if he hadn't unleashed one of his distinctive grins.

They crossed a lively river into Rawley Springs as the sun sank below the ridge. Gaslights hanging from the trees illuminated a three story hotel set into the mountain. Ragtime music echoed from the bandstand. A lively crowd descended long staircases to the dining hall. They rounded a cottage and came face-to-face with flames.

"Fire!" Wade slapped the reins into her hands, jumped off the buggy, and raced toward the inferno. "Fire! Fire!"

Mabel pulled the horse to the roadside, set the brake, and ran after him. The blaze grew, reaching as high as the dining hall. Wade yelled for water and a bucket brigade. He found a full pail and swung it toward the flames as a man in a white apron stepped in his way.

"Hey!" yelled the chef as the water hit him. Droplets splashed on the grill beyond, sizzling and smoking. "Fool! Whatcha doing?"

Wade froze, eyes wide. After a long moment, his shoulders drooped. He shuddered as he lowered the bucket. His mouth dropped open and for once he couldn't speak.

The hotel manager took in the situation at a glance. "Sir? You must have thought we had a building burning down. It's a cook fire. No harm done. We can still make our meat. And Manny dries off quickly."

Wade apologized to both men, ran his palms over his face, then trudged back to the buggy. "Now *that's* embarrassing."

"Running toward a fire isn't embarrassing." Mabel slipped her hand around his cool, damp arm. "It's heroic."

CHAPTER EIGHTEEN

After visiting enough resorts to make Wade's head spin, finally one morning Miss Maybelle handed him her poke just like a proper Virginia woman. As they took their seats on the train, a teasing sparkle gleamed in her eyes. "So what would you Virginians talk about if not for General Lee?"

"As Confederate General Jubal Early said, 'We may not have victory, but we do have our honor, our memories, and Robert E. Lee.'" Wade held his hand over his heart, its thumpety-thump due to the prescence of the marvelous Miss Maybelle more than to thoughts of the departed general. "I'd be remiss if I didn't tell of Fauquier County's favorite son."

"And all this time I thought *you* were Fauquier's favorite son." Her lips quirked with a hint of a smile.

"Afraid I don't even make the top ten." He grinned, happy to be spending the day with his favorite scientist. "Turner Ashby came from a long line of military men. His grandfather served under Washington in the Revolutionary War and his father fought in the War of 1812. When The War started, Turner Ashby dedicated his horsemanship to the cavalry under Stonewall Jackson. He became known as the Knight of the Valley or the Black Knight of the Confederacy. He died on a battlefield near Harrisonburg, shot while yelling 'Charge!'"

"Essential last words for any hero. Who else is in the top ten?"

"Number one is Fauquier White Sulphur Springs's guest and

177

chief justice of the United States, John Marshall. His grandson, Colonel James Marshall, lost his life at Gettysburg and his great-nephew was an aide-de-camp to General Lee."

"Lee." She faked a sigh. "Again."

"Another famous cavalryman, John Singleton Mosby, the Gray Ghost, lived in Warrenton."

"He's working in Washington these days."

"Say hello from me," Wade said, although it pained him to think of Miss Maybelle returning to the city. "And then there's Major General and Governor 'Extra Billy' Smith."

"'Extra Billy?' Such nicknames you Virginians invent."

"He earned it during the Jackson administration when he tacked extra fees onto the mail run."

Maybelle shook her head. "How do you keep it all straight?"

"History is in the blood of every Virginian." And he'd never enjoyed sharing stories of the old days as much as he had on this trip. "We have plenty of presidents to brag about. Did you know John Tyler fathered more children than any other president? Virginia also gave birth to Taylor, Harrison, Monroe, Madison, Jefferson, and Washington."

"Gave birth?" Maybelle treated him to a wry smile. "Their mothers might dispute that point."

"I do so enjoy a woman with a sense of humor." Wade congratulated himself for bringing out her fun side. "And you, Miss Maybelle, have a dilly of a funny bone."

"Hardly." She pressed her lips together, but a smile escaped anyway. "Didn't Washington live in Alexandria?"

"He surveyed nearabout the whole state and built forts out here to protect settlers from the French and Indians."

"I don't think of Indian battles in Virginia."

Wade pointed out a stone farmhouse off to the west. "Many a house was built over a spring and had rifle slots in the walls, so it could serve as a fort."

"It must have been a frightening time. Let's hope your state will have peace in this century."

"Amen to that." And maybe the Commonwealth of Virginia, his beloved home, would become hers someday.

They departed the train at Mt. Jackson and rented a buggy and a chestnut mare named Skylark, after Jeb Stuart's horse. They followed a loop of the Shenandoah for a bit, then took off west along a crick. The views showed distant ridges. After an hour or so they left orchards and cattle farms behind and wound high into the mountains. Wade would rate the road as passable, but those that intersected it looked fit for neither man nor mule.

Shenandoah Alum consisted of two old hotels and five cabins on the east side of the road, situated to take advantage of mountain breezes. Wade made sure no varmints would bother his sweet scientist, then crossed the road to check out a stone structure and a tenpin alley. He circled back to Miss Maybelle with a daisy for her hatband.

"A University of Virginia professor analyzed these springs in 1878." She recorded her results. "Look how red these rocks are. I didn't have to wait for the test results to know this is a chalybeate spring."

"Not to mention the iron furnace across the road." The stone tower rose two-stories high from the underbrush, a monument to a departed industry.

Maybelle stared and blinked. Sometimes she focused on work so much, she needed a reminder to look around. "Oh, yes. Of course. All right, on to the next."

A well-maintained road wound through a tiny village, where rag-clothed children hid behind log cabins.

Halfway up the ridge sat Orkney Springs. White clapboard cottages and hotels glowed against the green backdrop of North Mountain. Shade trees sheltered the buildings from the sun. A pedestrian bridge connected the two-story Maryland House with the main hotel, the majestic four-story Virginia House.

"I like this," Wade said as he parked the buggy.

"Even though it's wood frame?" Maybelle asked as he swung her to the ground.

"In spite of it being a fire hazard."

Its lobby nearly matched the Homestead's for size, but instead of pretentious, it felt welcoming. Upholstered chairs and walnut desks offered plenty of places to read and write. Behind the registration desk stood a large safe surrounded by over two hundred mail slots. How close was Orkney Springs to full capacity? And how did the manager keep track of all these guests?

After they registered, the clerk handed Maybelle an envelope from The Homestead.

"We were the least troublesome guests they've had all season," Wade guessed. "They want us back."

Maybelle frowned at letter and shook her head. "The boss wants me back. In the Lab. By Monday. Perhaps I should leave now."

"How'd he know where you were going?"

"Educated guess."

Wade nodded. With so few resorts still in business, wouldn't take more'n a half-dozen letters to find his dishwasher. "Let's see, today's Wednesday. You have time to finish your tests." No doubt her tyrant of a boss would still be golfing in the mountains while poor Miss Maybelle sweltered in the city. "Besides, I'd like to check out this place."

The main spring was called Bear Wallow, a name which didn't seem all that appealing, but who was he to argue with success? He added a spray of wild violets to the daisy in Maybelle's hat band.

While she tested the other springs, Wade surveyed the grounds. Orkney was a good two hour buggy ride from the railroad, yet they seemed to have a reasonable amount of business.

People went to the Homestead to be seen, to move and shake with other movers and shakers, while Orkney's guests met and mingled for fun. The Homestead catered to those who couldn't sit still, but Orkney served those who wanted to relax. Guests knitted and gossiped in rocking chairs, read and napped in hammocks under the trees, and strolled about enjoying the scenery. In the tenpin alley, children made up their own games with the wooden balls and pins.

The perfect place for a vacation. *Dear Lord, wouldn't it be great to stay another day?* Wade paused. What difference would a day make? Maybelle would finish her research and run back to Washington. Not likely a few more hours would help Wade figure out how to keep her in Fauquier. But still... *Dear Lord, if you could work it out...*

As Maybelle tested, Wade studied the Virginia House. The porch railings looked too low to safely contain anyone. He wandered inside and followed a curving stairway up. The railings turned out to be perfectly adequate - the wide space between floors and tall windows created the illusion the rails were unsafe.

From this height, an artist worked to capture the beauty of the forested mountains. In the largest ballroom Wade had ever seen, young girls played duets on a violin and cello. Across the hall in an elegantly-furnished parlor, a quartet of ladies enjoyed a game of pinochle. The back stairs led down to the kitchen where the hotel manager wrenched away on a leaky pipe. Wade introduced himself and they chatted until the cook noticed and shooed him out.

He crossed the road to Maryland House and found his room. It had windows facing both the porch and a courtyard, providing good ventilation. The mattress was woven wire spring.

The pillows were feather. And the woodpecker in the walnut tree assured they wouldn't miss breakfast.

Miss Maybelle finished her calculations on the porch, happier than a starving man at a pie-eating contest. Her neck bent, revealing a spine both delicate and strong, an excellent place for an entire series of kisses. Wade gave himself a shake and took the seat across from her.

"Robert E. Lee slept here and the state revised its constitution here," he reported. "They have the largest swimming pool in the South and the largest wood building in Virginia. We missed the clay pigeon shoot yesterday, but today there's a greased pole race."

"And, most interesting of all, one of the springs is lost." She pointed to a muddy spot in the lawn.

"I've lost dogs, hats, and my common sense. But never a spring."

"You once had common sense?" She flashed a smile.

"If only it came back as easily as your good humor." He wrapped an arm around her shoulders and squeezed - for a second only, as he did have a lick of sense left. "So how did Orkney lose a spring?"

"I can't be certain, but—"

"You have a hypothesis."

"And you know a scientific word." Miss Maybelle raised her eyebrows, as if he actually might have impressed her. "I suspect the water wore through the underlying rock, probably limestone, and made a different path for itself."

Across the lawn in the gazebo, a trumpet player struck up Sousa's "King Cotton" march. Guests filed into the Virginia House.

"So a whole mess of bloodhounds wouldn't be able to find it. Well this bloodhound's nose tells him supper is ready." Wade held out his arm and Maybelle took it. They strolled across the pedestrian bridge to the Virginia House.

The enormous dining room had been decorated in blue and white. In the middle stood a gold statue of a boy, holding a boot which dripped water. Wade surveyed the guests with his hotel manager's eye. No members of royalty or industry bigwigs. The long tables looked to be filled with families and church groups. Wade sent up a prayer that they wouldn't be seated with newlyweds again. He could pretend interest in wedding stories - plenty of guests thought their room and board paid for his undivided attention - but poor Miss Maybelle wilted with every recitation.

"Mabel? Mabel Easterly is that you?" A young woman with a wide smile squealed and hugged Miss Maybelle, then held out a hand to Wade. "Could this handsome man be your husband?" she asked. "I'm Ruth, by the way."

"Unfortunately Miss Maybelle is too smart to have me." Wade shook her hand. Introductions were made.

"Mabel tutored me through Algebra and I helped her diagram sentences. Then we taught together in Washington for a year." Ruth pulled them toward a table full of adults. "We have room for you. These are the teachers I worked with in Mt. Jackson until I married Fred, one of the managers here."

Between bites of chicken and noodles, Wade watched Maybelle talk shop with the other teachers. When the topic was students, she leaned on the table, spoke with enthusiasm, and smiled a lot. When the teachers asked about her job, she slumped, shrugged, and frowned. Didn't she realize she'd be happier teaching? Maybe she did. Maybe her father had pushed her into the laboratory job.

About the time the waiters brought around white cake with a sprinkle of coconut, the hotel manager rang a bell. "Ladies and gentlemen, I regret to inform you the bridge over Stony Creek was hit by a downed tree and damaged. We're working hard to repair it in the next couple days. Unfortunately the band for tonight's dance is on the wrong side of the bridge. So instead, as a special treat, we'll hike up the hill to watch the sunset."

A few male guests pestered the manager, fussing about getting back to the city, back to work. Must be Yankees.

Maybelle leaned close and murmured in his ear, "So to keep the guests from checking out, blow up the bridge? Is this a hotel manager trick?"

Wade leaned even closer and grinned. "It's an answer to prayer."

Father would have read the manager the riot act, demanded immediate repair of the bridge, and scorched bystanders with his volcanic temper. Professor Easterly claimed to like adventure, but he did not like surprises.

Wade, on the other hand, greeted every change in plans with the excitement on the order of a birthday party. "Last one to the top gets dunked in Bear Wallow!" Wade called out, then turned to the manager. "What time do we leave, Fred?"

"Meet out front in ten minutes! Wear sturdy shoes!"

While others questioned his sanity - How would they get down from the mountain at night? - Wade led the stampede.

"You do realize the resort is in a basin," Mabel reminded him as they met seven minutes later. "It's all uphill from here."

"That's why it's important to get the guests all excited."

A rotund man rocking on the porch pronounced, "Only a crescent moon tonight. We won't see y'all again until breakfast."

"Plenty of starlight!" Wade spotted the manager carrying a box. "And Fred's bringing flashlights."

Wade greeted the other hikers, memorized their names, and taught them a hiking song. "Sing loudly enough so the bears hear us coming!"

"Bears?" The mothers pulled their children close.

"Bears have rarely been seen in this county since The War." Fred handed the woman a flashlight. "Black bears are afraid of people."

The mothers did not seem impressed.

Wade held up an adolescent boy's arm and sniffed. "Bears smell you coming and they'll run away."

"Hey, you saying I stink?" The kid pulled back.

His friends giggled and slapped him on the back.

"No," Wade said, "I'm saying all y'all stink. When's the last time you men took a bath?"

"Hey, we went swimming," they argued. "Spent about all day in the pool."

Wade had shifted the mothers' worry to their progeny's hygiene habits. He never stopped thinking like a hotel manager.

Fred studied Wade as if debating whether to hug or strangle him. Finally the man pushed up his glasses, shrugged, and handed out the flashlights. The children grabbed the metal cylinders and flicked the lamps on and off.

"Save it for walk back," Fred cautioned. He turned to Wade. "Could you bring up the rear, make sure we don't lose anyone?"

"Don't mind if I do," Wade said as if delighted with the privilege.

A drummer joined the trumpet player to serenade the hikers with Sousa's "El Capitan" march.

They passed cottages and old cabins from the time before the resort was built. A large grey dog watched the group pass, then leaped off the porch and joined the pack when she spotted Wade.

The road narrowed to a trail bordered with rocks. The forest smelled damp with leaf mold. Other guests spotted robins, crows, and an indigo bunting coming in to roost. Fred identified four different oaks, three types of pines, plus maple, hickory, chestnut, and birch trees.

Mabel stopped. Was that lump across the trail a snake? No, it didn't move therefore it was a tree root.

One of the younger boys sidled up to her and eyed her head to toe. "Are you... Well, I've never seen..."

"Yes, I'm a woman." A woman who hoped Wade didn't hear this conversation.

"How tall are you?"

"Can you keep a secret? The number of days in a year, minus the ninth prime number, divided by two, plus the square root of sixty-four is my height in centimeters."

"I love math puzzles." The boy scrunched his face and talked himself through the problem with a little help for the centimeters.

"Well done," Mabel whispered when he reached the correct answer. "Remember, it's a secret."

The boy zipped his lips closed and raced ahead to join the pack.

"You can take a teacher on vacation, but she won't stop educating," Wade said behind her. "Well done, Miss Maybelle."

She held an overhead branch out of his way. "Enroll the boy in the University of Virginia."

"He's ready," Wade agreed.

The trail rose steeply. Ruth's teacher-friends huffed, puffed, and threatened to return to the resort.

"Stop and catch your breath, ladies," Wade told them. "We still have an hour before sunset."

The oldest one plopped down on a boulder. "I'm not fond—" She gulped air. "Of being dumped—" Another breath. "In the springs."

Wade shook his head. "Everyone in your honorable profession is excused from such nonsense."

"In that case, we'll carry on." Ruth turned to Mabel and whispered, "So why haven't you married him? He's Prince

Charming."

As if it was her choice. As if *she* could ask *him*. As if he might say yes. Mabel muttered, "My foot is too large for a glass slipper."

Ruth softened her teacher's glare with a hint of a smile. "Fraidy cat."

They reached the summit as the sun slipped behind Great North Mountain, the border with West Virginia. The ridge turned from emerald to cobalt and the birds quieted. Behind them to the east, a few lights sparkled from the resort. The valley filled with mist. Before them radiant streaks of sunlight rippled upwards. The cirrus clouds turned from hazy white to bronze, then brightened to gold as the sun lit them from beneath. The sky deepened to blue-grey and the sun was gone.

Mabel turned to watch Wade in the last of the light, expecting him to say the sunset at Fauquier was better. The grey dog leaned against his knee as he scratched behind her ears.

Instead of his usual silly grin, he met her gaze with a serious look, as if studying her. "God sure made a beautiful world."

"Thank you for helping me see it."

"Oh, Miss Maybelle." He tipped his head, then lifted his face to the sky and sang, "For the Beauty of the Earth." The rest of the group joined in. By the time they finished - no one remembered more than the first two verses - the stars had come out. An owl hooted and night's insects added their chorus.

"Can we use our flashlights *now*?" asked one of the children.

The adults laughed. Fred led the way down the path.

Wade held out his elbow. The temperature dropped and Mabel moved close to share his heat.

"Aren't you going to turn on your flashlight?" she asked.

"Let's try it without. I don't want to make it too easy for the bears to find us."

The dog investigated a rustling in the underbrush. "What

time do snakes go to sleep?"

Wade squeezed her hand. "Their mamas sung their lullabies right after supper. Don't you worry."

What could be more romantic than a starlit night in the mountains? Could she try for a kiss now? No, not with the bridge down. If it didn't go well - and with her lack of experience, it wouldn't - she'd have difficulty avoiding him at Orkney and for the rest of the trip.

Wade sauntered along, keeping her from stumbling over the rocks or slipping on the leaves. "Miss Maybelle—"

A loud growling roar erupted overhead. Mabel jumped backwards and braced for Wade to shoot. But instead, he flicked on his flashlight and caught a half-dozen youths standing on a boulder with arms raised and mouths open. Even the grey dog seemed to grin.

"Hey, we can't see with your light in our eyes!" they yelled. "You scairt? We scairt you!"

Wade shook his head. "That distinctive odor of ripe boy gave you away."

"Hey, our mamas making us take baths tonight on account of you."

"You'd better get, then." He motioned the boys to move ahead on the trail.

"But you said last one to the top gets dunked." The smallest one pointed. "And that means you!"

How would the noble and honorable Virginia gentleman wriggle out of that promise?

"You're right." Wade grinned. "Tell you what, let me escort Miss Maybelle safely to her hotel, then I'll meet you at Bear Wallow."

"The water is only 59.7 degrees," Mabel cautioned.

"Four point seven degrees warmer than Fauquier." Starlight lit his grin. "And I'm bringing soap."

GILDING THE WATERS

* * *

Magnificent Maybelle played tennis even better than Wade had expected. She had the strength to slam the ball over the net. Her scientific mind studied the court, the wind, and his weak backhand to keep him running. And her stamina wore him down until he plopped flat on his back.

"Wade, are you injured?" She raced around the net and fell to her knees beside him. Her face had pinked up so pretty and she smelled like warm peach pie.

He wanted to pop up and plant a kiss on those dewy lips. But instead he shook her hand. "You win."

She rocked back on her heels. "You said not to hold back."

"I meant it." He rolled upright. "And I enjoyed every point you took. Thank you."

She stood. "Perhaps we should have played doubles."

"Then I wouldn't have been able to watch you. What a backhand. How do you do that?" She hesitated and he teased, "Or maybe you'd rather not share your secrets."

"No, it's not that. Most men don't appreciate advice from a woman."

"Most men don't realize how thorough your analysis is. I'll take all the help you're willing to give."

"All right. Try adjusting your grip palm down a little." She demonstrated on her racket. "It will give you more power. As the ball comes toward you, shift your weight to your back foot. Bring the racket up from below the ball to give it the lift necessary to clear the net."

"There's a cure for my net balls?" He scooped upwards, following her demonstration.

"Then follow through, weight on your front foot—"

The Sousa-fixated trumpet player tooted out "The Liberty Bell" march, signaling the approach of the next meal.

"How about another lesson this evening?" he asked.

189

"Certainly." No reclining on a fainting couch for this majestic woman.

They stowed the equipment and washed up with the basin and towels the resort set out. Then they strolled across the lawn toward the Virginia House. Finally Miss Maybelle had slowed her Yankee pace.

Wade's toe caught in a tree root. He pitched forward, catching himself on his palms. He'd already lost in tennis. Did he have to look completely clumsy? Or was that what he deserved for not paying attention to the path and focusing on Miss Maybelle?

She frowned. "Are you kidding around again or injured?"

"Not bad enough to miss supper." He stood and tried to take a step. "Ouch. Believe I'll need a raincheck for my tennis lesson."

"Put your weight on me." She wrapped his arm over her shoulders and held onto his belt, which took his mind off the pain. Miss Maybelle was strong enough to lean on - one of the many things he liked about her. "Twisted ankles plague our expedition."

"Better than plagues twisting our expedition." Between the rail and Maybelle's support, Wade hobbled up the steps into the dining room.

The waiter took one look at Wade, directed him to the closest seat, and brought an extra chair to prop his foot. Wade was delighted to discover they'd been seated with the resort manager, his wife, and their two children.

"You get a chance to eat?" Wade asked Fred.

"For the moment." He nodded to a fellow near the kitchen door. "Charley's on duty tonight."

"How's the bridge repair coming?" Wade hadn't dared ask God for another day - Maybelle needed to get back to Washington.

"Fixed."

"So tell me about managing Orkney Springs. What's your biggest challenge?"

"Our biggest challenge is ironically the reason for our existence: the water. Seven springs gushing away - all that water has to go somewhere."

His wife kicked him under the table when he started talking sewage, so they discussed staffing, fire-proofing, and the endless quest to fill the resort's rooms.

At the end of the meal, the waiter provided a wheelchair.

"Thank you, my good man," Wade said. "But believe I'll manage without."

"Stay off it, and it will heal faster." Ruth's teacher voice had Wade in the wheelchair in two shakes. She pulled the footrest up. "You must keep it elevated until the swelling subsides."

"I've heard that," Maybelle said with a teasing smile.

"You can take the pedestrian bridge back to your rooms." Fred did indeed keep track of his guests.

Maybelle pushed him back to their hotel.

"You've been working so hard, Miss Maybelle," Wade said. "Time you set a spell."

Since sitting was the only activity he could participate in, she kindly agreed. She positioned him facing the sunset and sat in a nearby rocking chair. A mist rose from the valley as the stars came out. A bit of romantic nonsense came to mind, but he kept it in, out of respect for Miss Maybelle.

Cool air spilled down the mountain, easing the day's warmth. The clapboard buildings glowed in the evening sun.

"Dear Lord, spare them from fire." Wait. He hadn't meant to say that aloud.

Maybelle leaned toward him. "What happened to your hotel?"

"It's not a happy story."

She tilted her head. "Wade," she said with a soft voice. "I'm not one of your guests."

"But you could be. Any time." The last rays of light showed the strong lines of her face. Her gaze held his. No, Maybelle wasn't one of his guests. Guests might ask when the hotel would be rebuilt, but none asked about the fire. Even if they had, he couldn't speak of it with them. With Maybelle, he didn't have to wear his happy mask. He could be honest. He *had* to be honest. He glanced at her from the corner of his eye. Yes, she was still there, watching him, waiting for him to drum up his courage. He sucked in a breath. "What do you want to know?"

"Were you there?"

He shook his head. "I was in Warrenton, loading up a new piano at the depot. When the alarm came in, I thought they were kidding. Our hotel was fireproof. I unhitched Captain and raced home bareback." The horse lathered, pushed nigh to exhaustion, as he'd run him full out into the smoke.

"Was anyone hurt?"

"No one, thank the Lord." His off-season staff and friends from nearby farms had started a bucket brigade, but the fire burned out of control. Sheets of flames had swallowed the building. "We lost the entire hotel, our tenpin alley, and some storehouses. Selina saved a card table."

"What's your theory?"

He shifted, pushing on the arms of the wheelchair, setting off a spasm in his ankle. "Your boots aren't tall enough to wallow in our mess."

"You're not involving me. You're testing your hypothesis."

He glanced around. No one was close enough to overhear, but he lowered his voice anyway. "The last person in the hotel was Robert E. He was tinkering with the gas lights."

"Your brother. Oh, no. An accident, then?"

"Robert E always hated the resort. He hides from the guests, complains about them invading his woods and disrupting his routine."

"What did he say?"

"Of course he denied it. Spouted some nonsense about one of the Bethel students leaving a magnifying glass in the tower."

"It's possible-"

"If he saw a magnifying glass up there and didn't bring it down, it's still his fault." Wade rubbed his head. Shouting matches echoed in his ears, even after all these years. "He left, moved to Norfolk. When he visited in the summer of '03, one of our cottages burned to the ground. The guests escaped in time."

"He's a firebug, an arsonist? Yet you've seem quite calm on our trip."

"My staff's keeping watch."

"Those elderly soldiers? Aren't they blind?"

"Only Colonel Vance. The other two see well enough to bag a 'possum with a pistol." Wade flexed his foot. Would he be able to walk in the morning? "Then there's Selina. The way she swings a cast iron frypan, Ty Cobb could take lessons. 'Sides, I told him, if'n anything else burns, I'll send the law after him."

"Were you insured?"

"Yes. For less than half the cost to build it in 1878." Wade rubbed the spot between his eyebrows. "Not enough, needless to say, to rebuild."

"It must have been difficult to leave."

"You know what the Bible says about worry - it can't add an hour to our lives. And I sure wouldn't want to fret away my time with the world's prettiest water analyst."

"Wade." She used her teacher voice, quiet with a warning hint of disappointment.

"Yes'm. Leaving Fauquier pained worse than a toothache."

An owl hooted from the highest porch of the Virginia House.

Wade straightened and scanned the darkness. "Ssh. Moonshiners," he breathed.

A gangly boy towed a heavily-laden mule out of the forest and across the road to the side door of the Virginia House. A fellow in dark clothes met him and carried the load into the hotel. No one lit a lamp.

Wade checked his pistol, glad he and Maybelle were hidden in the porch shadow.

The owl hooted again. The man disappeared into the building. The boy hopped on the mule and raced into the trees. A moment later, three men on horseback galloped up. White shirts made them visible for miles. They peered between the buildings, then, empty-handed, trotted down the mountain.

"Revenuers," Wade murmured.

"Who knew life in the mountains could be full of such drama?"

"Us hillbillies might could stir up a passel of trouble just for fun." Wade pivoted the wheelchair, heading inside. "Thank you for not chasing down the moonshiner, offering to test his water."

She held open the door. "Not without my side-kick. How's your ankle?"

"I'll be fit tomorrow." He echoed her words and she smiled in recognition.

"So how did you know a moonshiner was coming?" Miss Maybelle had to have her facts.

"Firstly, this here's an ideal location, close to the state line, a fair number of customers right handy. Second, tonight's punch had a mountain-made kick of apple brandy." He turned to watch her expression. "But most of all, owls aren't fluent in Morse code."

The rare and musical sound of Miss Maybelle giggling blessed him right down to his sore ankle.

CHAPTER NINETEEN

Mabel woke to the disappointing realization she had been cuddling her pillow and not Wade. As if she could mistake a bag of feathers for his narrow waist and the shift of muscles beneath his shirt. After playing tennis in the hot sun, she'd expected to be repulsed by his body odor. Instead his salty masculine scent intrigued.

And not just his scent. Everything about him intrigued her. He reminded her of those unknowns chemistry instructors were fond of giving to students. Mabel could analyze Wade for the rest of her life, under every condition, and still make surprising discoveries. Unfortunately she didn't have the rest of her life - she only had tomorrow before she had to return to Washington. Might this be her last opportunity for... a kiss? Could his proficiency at flirting correlate with skill at kissing? He had to be better than her organic chemistry lab partner with his fish lips. Instead of that debacle of a kiss, Mabel could have a happy memory of kissing an expert like Wade.

After she finished her research.

Mabel asked God to help her stay focused instead of longing for what would never be... a relationship with Wade. Might he need her again this morning? She hurried to dress and rushed out, ready to slip her arm around him and feel the warmth of his body next to hers. *Dear Lord, please forgive me - I'm thinking of Wade again.*

Wade stood beside the bridge to the Virginia House, chatting with two other men, his weight on both feet. Mabel blew a mental raspberry at her foolish heart, pasted a smile on her face, and greeted them.

Sousa's "Washington Post March" had the guests processing into the Virginia House for breakfast.

"How is your ankle this morning?" she asked as they crossed the bridge.

"Fit as a fiddle." Wade took her hand and tucked it into his elbow. "Don't want to misplace you in this crowd. Fred has us sitting with some folks you might find interesting."

Their breakfast companions turned out to be ceramic artists from a workshop in Strasburg. They showed a surprising interest in and knowledge of chemistry. Their questions had Mabel reaching for a pencil and paper to work out formulas and calculations. So by the time she and Wade left Orkney Springs, Mabel was talked out and content to watch the hawks spiral over the mountains.

Wade, of course, was never talked out. "Miss Maybelle, reckon you're good at puzzles."

"I do enjoy them."

"But you're too modest to admit you're good at them." He glanced at her with a warm smile. "I'll tell you the pieces I've figured out, see if you can put together the rest. First, you enjoyed your time with your teacher friends. Ever think about going back to the classroom?"

Nearly every day, but she wouldn't admit it. "The Geophysical Laboratory conducts important research on the earth's structure."

"And that's the second piece. I'm more'n a little worried about these scientists you work with, if'n they'll ever let you join in."

"Well, I am the newest staff member." Although she couldn't imagine them hiring a male scientist and relegating him to dishwashing duties. "If President Roosevelt includes my research in the National Conservation Commission report, perhaps they'll gain a better understanding of my abilities."

"Hope so. Do any teaching there?"

"Not with the staff being so much more experienced than I." And not to mention male.

"If you could get one of them to take you on as an apprentice…"

"A mentor? Yes, I've broached the subject with several, but they're rather…"

"Jealous? Stuffy? Boneheaded?"

"Concerned that I might slow their research."

"Hah. Obviously they haven't seen you in action."

Mabel smiled back at him. No one encouraged her like Wade. He steered the horse across the newly repaired bridge. "And the third piece is your papa."

She shifted, turning away from Wade. "He's a distinguished scientist, highly respected in his field."

"Is this his first trip without you?"

Mabel checked her watch, but of course she'd wound it already. "I suppose it is."

"Seems odd he'd get you a job without a summer vacation, a job where you'd have to stay behind."

"Well…" She'd thought so too. She'd expected Father to ask the Lab to let her go for the summer. When he didn't, she'd reviewed their last expedition, trying to see if she'd made some mistake justifying her exclusion. Perhaps this expedition's sponsorship by the Smithsonian, instead of by a university, precluded her involvement. "I helped with the planning."

Wade stayed silent for a long moment.

Mabel crossed her arms, holding back a ridiculous impulse to cry. "It's quite an honor to be the first woman hired by the Lab. There are so few opportunities for female scientists. If I quit, they'll say women are not suited for research and never hire another. I must make the best of it."

Wade frowned at the horse's back side. "I know how to make the best of Fauquier's lack of a hotel. I give more personal service. I remember who prefers tea to coffee, who wants which newspaper, and so on. And we focus on activities for small groups like tennis and bridge, instead of jousting and balls." He turned to her, his mobile mouth held in a straight line. "I don't see how you can make the best of your job."

"Well, at first I tried to guess what chemical would clean each piece of glassware. But it seems sulphuric acid dissolves most anything."

"Sulphuric acid? Isn't that dangerous?"

"Certainly." How kind of him to be concerned. Father wasn't. "I wear a rubber apron, gauntlets, and a face mask."

"Unbearable on a humid day." He leaned forward, so she had to meet his gaze. "Put the puzzle pieces together and reckon you're stuck in a job you hate."

"Of course a Virginian would be the expert on Lost Causes," she said, referring to the Southern veneration of the Confederacy. She caught his wince. "I'm sorry. That was uncalled for."

"No, I'm sorry. Smart as you are, you'd have found a way out if there was one." He settled back on his side of the seat. "Best stop fretting and fussing, and enjoy the beautiful day God's given us."

He whistled as they rode to Mt. Jackson, took the B&O to Woodstock, and followed a twisty road through the bends of the Shenandoah River and over Massanutten Mountain into Fort Valley. Mabel could think of a better use for his lips.

Wait— what was she thinking? Scientists did not think about kissing. The scientists at the Geophysical Institute talked about their research - what fieldwork might be planned, which equipment should be purchased, whether the results proved their hypotheses. They never spoke of love or wives or children. If she hadn't met their families at the Institute's opening ceremony, Mabel would have guessed they were a flock of desiccated bachelors. So what sort of scientist was she, obsessing about kissing Wade?

Then Wade stopped whistling and studied the meadows. "Ought to be right about here… somewhere."

They bent their heads over the map - a good time for a kiss if Mabel had been willing to settle for a cheek. But no, nothing less than lips would do. "Should be around this curve."

A few lonely farms dotted the shallow dale, but no signs for Burner's White Sulphur Springs or Seven Fountains.

"There's a springhouse." Wade turned the horse off the road.

Mabel made the rounds of the seven springs - three sulphur, plus chalybeate, magnesium, lithia, and limestone.

Wade returned before she finished. "This is the closest resort to Fauquier and they never recovered from the War. All that's left are a few summer homes. Guess I should be thankful for the years we had."

Mabel couldn't see anything that resembled a resort. "What was here?"

"Hotel buildings for six hundred guests. Stagecoaches met three different trains. Then during the War, Sheridan came through and burned it all down."

"How did he find it?"

A flicker of a smile crossed the lips Mabel planned to kiss. "Got me."

Mabel wished she had.

On the train north to Winchester, Wade asked, "So have you reached any conclusions from your research?"

"Yes. Resorts owners, for the most part, accurately reported analyses of their waters."

"That's bad for you, isn't it? Uncovering scandalously false results would make better press and prove you right."

"Research isn't about right and wrong. It's about uncovering the truth."

Wade gave a satisfied grin. "Fauquier's water was never in doubt."

"What is in doubt are the health claims."

He motioned for her bag. "Do you have my most recent advertisement? If not, I'll tell you what it says, since I wrote it." Wade took a deep breath and recited, "'Only 56 miles from Washington, D.C. The popular Fauquier White Sulphur Springs near Warrenton, Va. Now open for the season. The finest Summer Hotel in the South. Surrounded by 550 acres of beautiful Groves, Shady Walks, and Drives. Famous Hot and Cold Sulphur Water Baths! Fine Orchestra for the Entire Season!' And the rest tells which train to take."

"No health claims." Mabel found his advertisement. "You stuck to the truth."

"I tried. You're right, science has ended the era of water cures. I don't know what we'll do to survive, but claiming mineral water cures everything isn't the answer."

Mabel studied the drawing in his ad. "Your hotel had an unusual design."

"Scottish baronial."

"Sir Walter Scott again. Did you have jousting tournaments?" Her goopy brain imagined Wade in tights. "Did you wear a costume?"

"No suit of armor, but I did wear a tunic with an embroidered Scottish lion over my riding clothes."

"Is it dangerous, stabbing each other with lances and such?"

"Couldn't have guests injuring each other. No, civilized jousting consists of trying to snag a ring on a pole while galloping across the field. We awarded prizes - everything from a

Fauquier White Sulphur Springs umbrella to a gold watch. Afterwards we'd have a coronation ball." He sent her one of those glances that made her insides dance. "I would have crowned you my Queen of the Summer."

Only the summer? Mabel wanted to be queen of his whole life, in every season. Who was she kidding? Those awards always went to the pretty girls, the accomplished flirts who studied courtship instead of chemistry.

Mabel struggled to keep her mind on her work as they hurried from Rock Enon to their last stop, Jordan White Sulphur Springs. Afternoon sun brought out the copper in Wade's brown hair and added a green tint to his blue eyes. His lips rested, ready to curve into a smile at any moment. Were they ready for a kiss?

By this point in previous expeditions, Mabel had tired of the other members and hoped to never see them again. Wade evoked the opposite response - she liked him more every day and desperately didn't want to let him go.

"What?" He wiped his bandanna across his chin. "I have something on my face?"

"I'm sorry. I didn't mean to stare. It's—" She couldn't admit to dreaming about a kiss. "I was thinking about microscopes. A poor lens distorts light so the image is blurred - spherical aberation. But a properly ground lens magnifies the object accurately."

"So…" He blinked and tipped his head to the side. "I'm under your microscope?"

"Expeditions grind the lens of life into focus. You're a lot harder working and a lot smarter than I first thought."

"Thanks, but…" He pondered her words a moment, then leaned forward, elbows on his knees, a pair of creases between his eyebrows. "What about honest?"

What about honest? Could she trust him? "Yes, you're more

truthful than I expected."

The conductor called out their stop.

He slid his hands around hers. "And you, Miss Maybelle, are the finest woman ever. God's best workmanship. Don't sell yourself short." Wade released her hands with a gentle grin, then stood to gather their suitcases. "And that's what I learned on this expedition."

Mabel's heart pounded like an automobile engine, generating a ridiculous amount of heat. Perhaps Wade wouldn't object to being kissed?

Sunrise and bird song took away Jordan White Sulphur Springs's sinister air. Mabel shouldered her satchel and followed the path to the springs.

Working out a plan had given her a restless night. Wade wasn't a chemical that would fit in a formula. He was an unknown that made predicting results impossible. All she could do was watch for an opportunity.

"Morning, Miss Maybelle." Wade leaned against one of the pillars of the black gazebo, more handsome than any man had a right to be. "The springs are ghost-free, snake-free, and ready to be tested."

"Thank you kindly," she said, her approximation of a Virginia accent earning a smile from him.

As she analyzed, he broke off a pine tree branch that scraped the gazebo's roof, then brushed its floor clean, working as if he ran the place.

"You're ready to return to your duties at Fauquier?" she asked.

Instead of the enthusiastic "yes," she expected, Wade stared at the mountains. "Of course I miss Fauquier. But... it's been..."

Mabel paused in writing up her results. She'd never seen him at a loss for words. "Your work is quite stressful."

"It's a heap of fuss, keeping all my guests happy, all my staff working and all those old buildings from falling down." He turned to her with a gentle smile. "I'm finding it's a good bit easier taking care of one pretty chemist."

He thought she was pretty? Was this her opportunity? Alone at the final spring had a certain romantic allure. And her research was complete, which merited a celebration. She stood, took a deep breath, and tried to figure out the sequence. Should she ask for a kiss? Or wrap her arms around him, bring her face close, and see what happened?

The hotel proprietor rang the bell. Wade turned toward the dining room. Perhaps over breakfast? But no, they were seated with the only other guests.

After introductions, the tool salesman, his hair slicked tight to his scalp, asked Wade, "So, you find something wrong with the water, then sell them a device to fix it?"

"To purify it?" The encyclopedia salesman's stiff collar poked him in the chin.

"Miss Easterly is in charge." Wade motioned toward her. "I'm merely her guard."

"No 'mere' about it. You've provided essential logistical support," Mabel told Wade, then explained to the others, "This was a research expedition for the president's National Conservation Commission."

The salesmen stopped chewing and stared.

Wade put down his fork. "Was? Are we done?" His stare pierced. "What about Paradise Springs in Clifton and Berry Hill Dyspepsia Water? Didn't we miss some down south, in Mecklenburg County?"

"I tested Chase City, Buffalo Lithia, and Cluster Springs prior to your joining the expedition. And Clifton and Berry Hill earlier on the day we met." She dared a glance at Wade. "Truly,

I cannot impose on you any further." One more day with him and she'd lose all control.

The tool salesman recovered from his surprise first. "So where to next? Moving on to another state?"

"West Virginia?" Wade's straight eyebrows rose an inch. Didn't he want to go home?

"The survey of Virginia springs is conclusive. All that remains is to write up the results." Mabel fiddled with her toast, unable to contemplate fieldwork without Wade. "Although we've noted in our travels that mines fill watercourses with sludge."

"Mess with their water, mine owners like to shoot you," the tool salesman observed.

Wade propped his fist on his hip, showing his holster. "Might."

"They won't suspect a female," said the book seller.

What would they think she was doing with the water? Making tea?

"Ohio River reeks," the tool dealer said. "Don't need no test to tell it's gone bad."

"Pointless," the encyclopedia man said. "How would you clean it up?"

"Roosevelt could do it," the other salesman rapped his knuckles on the table. "Remember the coal miners' strike? Square deal for every man."

Mabel checked her watch. "Pardon me, gentlemen. We have trains to catch."

Their last moment alone, on the way to the depot, Mabel took a deep breath to launch into her prepared speech.

Wade seized the initiative. "You know, Miss Maybelle, I've been praying God would keep Fauquier White Sulphur Springs going."

He wanted to talk about God *now*? So much for her planned kiss. "I'll pray for you, too."

He stared off in the distance, as if his heart had already returned home. "Look how many other resorts have already closed: Augusta Springs, Yellow Massanutten, Mountain Top, Basic City, Brunswick Inn. Fauquier's still in business. God has answered my prayer." Blue eyes turned her way for a too-short moment. "You suggested I do some research and now I have plenty of ideas for a new hotel."

"But what if you don't find investors? What if the answer really is no?"

He shook his head. "Fauquier's my life."

"Wade." Mabel put her hand on his arm. "Any other business would be glad to have someone with your range of skills."

"That's kind of you to say, but I hope I never have to find out." He gathered the reins, guiding the horse through the mix of automobiles and delivery wagons to Winchester's depot.

Wade returned from the livery and Mabel handed him his ticket. "Your train is leaving."

"My train?" He grabbed his suitcase. "No, I'm escorting you to Washington."

"That's hardly necessary. The B&O is perfectly safe. No snakes." She managed a smile in spite of the lump in her throat. Taking his dependable arm for the last time, she steered him toward the Richmond and Danville line. "I've kept you away from your resort too long."

The conductor called, "All aboard for Strasburg, Edinburg, New Market, and points south."

"But TR-"

She gauged the distance across the platform to the passenger car, estimated their pace, and slowed her steps. Timing was essential. "I'll send you a copy of my report."

"Well, of course, I want to read it, but—"

"Let me know how you get on with Robert E. I hope your mother feels better. Give Raleigh a scratch behind the ears from me." Mabel choked up.

"But—" Wade stepped into the passenger car.

Now here was the part she was unsure of about. Her blood bubbled as if filled with dry ice. "I want to thank you for everything you've done, Wade. You've made this trip... a pleasure."

The engine hissed. Hurry.

Wade set his suitcase on the top step and faced her. "Miss Maybelle..."

The whistle blew. Hurry, hurry.

Now!

At long last she found a use for her height. She took hold of his collar and slid her other hand around his nape. Curls brushed the back of her hand. She raised up on tiptoes. He didn't resist. Her mouth reached for his, twelve inches away, then six inches, three inches, until his face blurred. Her eyes drifted closed. Air skimmed her lips as his breath hitched. Their lips touched. His were dry and warm. For a fraction of a second, he didn't react. Then he adjusted for perfect fit.

Detonation! Like a million potassium nitrate explosions in every cell of her body!

The earth moved. No, the *train* moved, wrenching Wade away from her. His mouth dropped open. He blinked three times, then his eyes opened wide. He swayed in the doorway and for a moment she was afraid he'd tumble out. "Miss Maybelle!"

The train rounded the curve and he was gone.

Mabel closed her eyes again and ran her tongue over her lips, committing every element to memory. He tasted salty with a hint of his morning coffee and Septol toothpaste. Contact had initiated an exothermic reaction, releasing significant amounts of heat in her body. His lips had pressed gently, tentatively, then with more authority, perhaps desire. Yes, her reminiscence would note he'd been attracted to her.

GILDING THE WATERS

The B&O conductor called the train to Harper's Ferry, connecting to Washington. Mabel turned, picked up her suitcase, and walked off into the colorless future of life without Wade.

CHAPTER TWENTY

Wow!

"Sir?" said a voice somewhere behind Wade.

Miss Maybelle kissed him!

"You need to take your seat."

One lollapalooza of a kiss!

"Mister? I'm fixin' to close the door."

She'd set his heart aquiver. He couldn't leave her now!

Strong hands grabbed Wade by the scruff of his neck, or perhaps his collar, and hauled him into the passenger car.

"Now, mister, don't you be a-thinking of jumping from my car. You get hurt and I lose my job. Neither of us be a-wanting that." The conductor pushed him into a seat and leaned over him. "If you don't mind my asking, what's a matter with you? Coming off a bash? Sick in your head?"

Wade pressed his palm to his chest, where his heart thumped, "May-belle, May-belle, May-belle." He was in love. No, that wasn't new. He'd been in love since the moment he saw her bending over his spring, but now, *now!*, he thought, it seemed, Miss Maybelle might love him back. "She kissed me."

"Whupped by a woman. I should of known. Now you just sit there and think about how you're going to pay for a wedding, and setting up house, and the babies coming along. Have I reined in your wild horses?"

"Yessir." This was more exciting than a fully booked hotel,

more exciting than winning at jousting or steeplechase or even bowling.

Wait a minute. Did the conductor say something about a wedding? His Maybelle wouldn't carry-on like those brides at the resorts, would she? Well, Wade had helped with his share of weddings at Fauquier. Let's see, they'd have it as soon as her father got back from the Arctic Circle.

Her father. Now there's one wild horse Wade couldn't rein in. He would have to talk to Miss Maybelle's father. Professor Easterly would give his permission, wouldn't he? Wade got along well with all sorts of folks, old men especially. Professor Easterly wouldn't take a dislike to him, would he? Surely not. Course not. He'd won over the daughter, he could win over the father.

So when would his expedition return? September, October? The weather would still be nice, the trees colorful, and the summer guests gone. They could have their wedding outside, by the spring where they first met. Miss Maybelle could wear that blue dress she'd worn at The Homestead. He'd wear his suit. They could invite that nice couple from Orkney Springs, Fred and Ruth. Selina would give him a haircut, with plenty of unsolicited advice. Advice a-plenty would be coming from the colonel, the major, and the captain.

And Mother.

Oh, no. Wade was fixin' to marry a Yankee. Lord have mercy.

"Strasburg," the conductor called. He hefted Wade off the seat, out of the car, and pushed him toward the waiting C&O train. "You're Rusty's problem now."

Wait, should he go back, try to catch up with Maybelle? No, her train left minutes after his. She was on her way to Washington. And besides, he had a wedding to plan. He got on the eastbound to Manassas.

What else was involved with planning a wedding? Music - friends in Warrenton played for other occasions at Fauquier.

Minister - his would be happy to do the honors. Flowers - the roadsides were filled with yellow ones at the height of fall. Food - Mrs. Fitzhugh could cook up Virginia ham, corn on the cob, Chesapeake bay oysters. The apples would be in, so they'd have cider. But most of all, in honor of his Miss Maybelle, they'd have peach pie.

If Mother didn't whup him into next week for marrying a Yankee.

Then after the wedding... *after the wedding...*

"Calverton," the conductor hollered.

Usually Wade knew someone on the spur line, but today he was relieved not to recognize a soul. He had a dilemma to think on. Miss Maybelle was used to working a fancy job at the Geophysical Laboratory, rubbing elbows with the live-wires of the nation's capital, traveling the world to research all sorts of fancy chemicals. What would she do in Fauquier County? On one side, the train passed shacks with a dozen chickens, a vegetable patch, and a woman hanging laundry while a naked baby clung to her skirts. On the other were white fenced farms whose owners could talk Thoroughbreds and little else. Best he could hope, they wouldn't mind having their water tested.

The train pulled into the Warrenton station. Wade grabbed his suitcase and shuffled off to face Mother. And see what Robert E had done to his resort. And figure out how soon he could go get Miss Maybelle.

A hand from a nearby farm was waiting for a delivery. Wade helped him load his shipment and hitched a ride with him.

"So, Finn, what's new?" Even as slow as life moved in the country, something might have changed in the past sixteen days.

The man answered with a language that might have been Irish or Gaelic, but certainly wasn't anything Wade recognized.

"Expect you're right," Wade said and they rode the rest of the way in silence. The corn reached for the sky, about ready for harvest. Occasional leaves of gold mixed in with the green. The halfway point of summer had passed.

Fauquier White Sulphur Springs looked the same from the road. Golfers whacked at their little white balls. Still no hotel, but all of the cottages stood as he'd left them. Wade thanked Finn, grabbed his suitcase, and jumped down. The day had turned hot and the elms provided a welcome shade.

He opened the door of Warrenton House and stepped inside. Empty. Where was Clayton? Usually Major Holston sat in for the desk clerk if'n he had to be away. "Hello?"

Stowing his suitcase behind the desk, Wade went out the back door.

His hound emerged from beneath the porch with an enthusiastic woof.

"Raleigh! Hey, old boy." The dog welcomed Wade home with a thrashing tail and slobbering tongue. "Someone's glad to see me. Now where's the rest of our crew?"

"Gone." Robert E leaned on the porch rail of the Fairfax cottage like he owned the place.

"Afternoon, Robert E." With no more answers forthcoming, Wade went up the chain of command. "Mother around?"

"Yep." He turned and went inside.

Good to see you, too, brother. Moving faster than was wise in the heat, Wade hurried into the Fairfax.

Mama reclined on a chaise, looking especially fragile after Miss Maybelle's vigor. "Wade Hampton." She opened her arms and Wade hugged and kissed her, getting a nose-full of rose-scented powder.

"How are things around here?" Wade perched on a stool.

"While you've been gallivanting around, I've been working," Robert E said from the staircase behind him.

"That so?" Wade asked his mother.

"Robert E took a business class in Norfolk."

"Since when does one class trump two decades of experience?"

"I made some changes," Robert E said. "To help Fauquier's finances."

Wade braced. He wasn't going to like this. "Our finances have been sketchy for years, and they'll stay that way until we can get another hotel built."

"Anyone who wasn't pulling his weight is gone."

"Who?" Wade's gut clenched. "Colonel Vance, Major Holston, Captain Drake?"

"The Confederate Soldiers' Home in Richmond," Robert E said with what passed for a smile on his mealy face.

"But they liked working here. And guests liked them." Could Wade bring them back? "They'll die of boredom and the heat in the city."

His mother's cool hand patted his. "They were old men, too old for the work you asked of them."

"All I asked was that they keep an eye on things." Wade pressed his fingers into his forehead. He hadn't had a chance to say goodbye. "All they expected in return was a warm place to sleep and three meals a day."

"No more meals."

Wade jumped to his feet. "What are you saying?"

Robert E leaned on the newel post, his arms crossed. "Kitchen wasn't making any money, so it's closed."

"Kitchens make food, not money." Arms waving, Wade stomped over to his brother. "So what are guests supposed to eat? What about the staff? I promised those girls work all summer."

"The cottages have kitchens. Golfers can make themselves a picnic lunch."

"Picnic lunches?" Wade's hands fisted. "This is the finest resort in the South." It had been, before the hotel burned down.

"Our guests expect to be served a proper dinner, in a dining room. Not sandwiches. Not cooking for themselves." Robert E *knew* that, the swine. "Who else? Mrs. Fitzhugh?"

"Quit."

Who'd blame her? Wade paced the floor. "Selina?"

This time his mother answered. "Went to live with her granddaughter. With the size of that brood, she'll be a help."

With that many children, Selina would work herself into the grave. "Doc Daly?"

"Confederate Home needed a physician."

"Clayton?"

"Golf course." Robert E pointed up the hill. "No need for a desk clerk. Don't rent rooms no more."

Wade shoved his fist at his brother's face. "I've only been away sixteen days, just a little over two weeks, and you manage to undo all my years of hard work, break all my promises, and drag the family honor into the mud. I ought to whup you back to Norfolk."

"Wade—" His mother's tone warned him off.

"You were losing money every summer." Robert E's eyes narrowed. "Face facts, the resort is gone."

"Couldn't burn it down, so you chopped it to pieces." Wade swung at him, but tears blurred his aim.

Mother crossed the floor in record time and stood between them. "I'll not have my sons fighting."

Robert E backed up against the wall. "I helped build that hotel. It was our legacy. I swear to you, on Father's grave, I did not burn down the hotel or the Marshall cottage."

A memory flashed through Wade's mind, of Robert E toting buckets of nails up the stairs. His brother had poured his energy into the construction, working hard enough to grow from a scrawny kid into a muscular man.

"Robert E, go on upstairs, so I can talk to your brother."

Mother's voice held a note of steel Wade hadn't heard since she caught him in a lie about kissing the Bradley's curly-haired daughter.

Robert E stomped hard enough to break the treads.

Mother waited until the door slammed overhead. "The morning of the fire, Robert E didn't go near the hotel at all. He wasn't even here. Truth is, after you left for town I had another episode of neurasthenia. This was afore Doc Daly came to work for us. I sent your brother to Jeffersonton to fetch Selina's mama."

"Miss Lulie?" Wade remembered a hundred year old bundle of wrinkles and rags who smelled of sage. "But she was a midwife."

"She knew a lot of herbal remedies and she was close enough to come directly." Mother had kept to her room for weeks afterwards. Wade had blamed the fire.

"I'm sorry I was too busy to tend you."

"You were a young 'un doing a man's work."

Wade pressed a knuckle to his forehead. His thoughts spun like gnats on a still summer day. "Yes, I remember Miss Lulie bandaging up more'n a few blisters and burns. I figured she came when she saw the smoke, like all our other neighbors."

Mother shook her head. "We'll never know why it burned, but I know Robert E had nothing to do with it. You owe your brother an apology."

So Robert E hadn't caused the problem in 1901, but he sure stirred up trouble today. "Mother, please, can't you see? We've got to have guests. No investor will build another hotel here if the place is abandoned. We'll end up like Seven Springs or Montgomery, a wet hole in the ground." He shuddered.

She rubbed his hands. "Wade Hampton, tell me, how many mineral springs resorts did you and Miss Maybelle visit these past two weeks?"

"A little over forty."

"And how many are successful?"

Wade shut his eyes. Wind slapped an unlatched door at Healing Springs. Footsteps echoed in Rockbridge Alum's elegant halls. Brunswick Inn's fancy new building had turned into a boarding house.

"Wade Hampton." Mother had a good grip for someone who'd been poorly for so long.

"The Homestead..." He gulped. "And maybe Orkney."

She wiped a tear from his cheek. "You've done your best. It's time for you to hang up your keys. Father wouldn't have wanted you fussing and fretting your life away."

Fussing and fretting? Hadn't he just told Miss Maybelle to stop fussing and fretting?

"Come sit a spell and tell me about your travels."

"Mother." He couldn't, wouldn't put up with this. There had to be another way. "I need air." He stumbled out the door, Raleigh at his heels. "Good thing you don't eat much," he said to the dog, "less'n they farm you out somewhere." Or worse.

Wade hiked up the hill, feeling like he'd been sucked through a knot hole. This should be their busiest season, but instead all the cottages were empty, abandoned. He couldn't bring Miss Maybelle here. Not like this.

How soon before Robert E convinced Mama that Wade wasn't pulling his weight, wasn't bringing in enough money to count for his room and board?

Wade entered the stable where they kept the golf equipment and found Clayton squinting at the gears of the lawn mower. "Hey."

"Oh, Wade. I'm sorrier than I can say." The older man rested a hand on his shoulder. "I tried to talk him out of it. I told him your father'd never approve."

"Probably flipping over in his grave."

Clayton shook his head. "Robert E got everybody so riled, they all up and left, guests and workers. I don't know how much longer I can hold on."

"Could you—" He'd never thought it would come to this. The hound leaned against his leg and Wade scratched behind his long ears. "Would you mind Raleigh for me?"

"Be glad to." The man wiped his grass-stained hands on his britches, then scratched the dog behind the ears. "Where you off to?"

"I'm thinking…" Wade shook his head. He looked around at the rolling hills he'd called home his whole life. "It's time to call on some of our guests… the ones who are lawyers… If'n I can find them."

The town of Harper's Ferry had been built on the cliffs above the confluence of the Potomac and the Shenandoah rivers. Most buildings were stone, yet the depot was wood. It's a wonder it hadn't burned down already. Mabel shook her head. Wade again. She'd never been so concerned with fire safety.

Mabel gathered her bags and crossed the platform. She was perfectly capable of carrying her own load. She had every other trip. But Wade's help, being pampered as if she was delicate, certainly had been lovely.

She boarded the B&O to Washington, slumped onto a seat, and barricaded herself with her satchel. Etiquette dictated she seek a female passenger to sit with, but Mabel didn't feel up to conversing. And she certainly didn't want some overfamiliar man to sit beside her and attempt a dialogue. Wade had shielded her from that sort of nonsense.

Stop thinking about him.

The train pulled out, crossed the river, and passed through a tunnel, not as long as Rockfish Gap where Wade—

Mabel gave herself a shake: focus on research. How should

she word her report and recommendations for the president? Would he agree to a mobile water testing laboratory? She opened her lab notebook and started a list on the back page.

She'd need a large wagon, like a tinker's or an ambulance. Inside would be a lab table with compartments to secure the equipment against jostling. Father's lab on the Nile had microscopes, an autoclave, and an incubator, plus all the usual flasks, porcelain dishes, retorts, crucibles, and fermentation tubes. A Marsh apparatus would be handy for determining precise arsenic levels, but would it travel well?

Had MIT scientist Ellen Richards used a mobile laboratory in her research? Mabel made a note to write to her.

Farm roads were beset with potholes, deep ruts, and washouts, so she'd need a sturdy wagon with heavy springs. All that weight would require a team of horses. She could focus on water analysis if she had a driver to manage the team. Wade had been perfect for the job, but he was on his way back to his resort and she *must* stop thinking about him.

"Look, there's the Washington Monument!" The boy across the aisle pointed out the window. "Is that the Capitol?"

Mabel peered through the haze and identified the clock tower of the post office, the smokestack of the Potomac Electric Power Company, and several churches. The air thickened with humidity and the reek of sewage and trash.

Washington and the Geophysical Laboratory were still here. Mabel gave herself a mental kick. Had she actually wished the city and her employer had disappeared? No, but she had wished she was still in Virginia. Wouldn't Wade grin about that?

The train pulled into the recently opened Union Station. Wade would applaud its fireproof construction.

Enough already.

Mabel hefted her bags, and trudged through the arched corridors into the steamy afternoon. The salted nut vendor had deserted his post and the newspaper vendor had fallen asleep in his. During the summer, few stayed in the city, fewer visited, and nobody offered to carry her luggage.

Before she could stop herself, she wished for Wade again.

A cable car trundled her across the city and up Connecticut Avenue to the row house she and Father shared.

Mabel set her luggage inside the front door and plopped her hat atop the mail on the hall rack. She had sent a telegram alerting the housekeeper- what was this one's name? -to her imminent arrival. A sluggish breeze pushed half-heartedly against the curtains. The refrigerator had been filled with fruit, eggs, and a bowl of her favorite chicken salad. Mabel ran her palms along the edge of the ice block, then patted her face.

The ceiling lowered and the walls closed in. Mabel went out the back door, plopped onto the small bench beneath the oak, and unbuttoned her collar and cuffs. Smoke from a cooking fire tainted the air. On the other side of the tall fence, a man and woman argued in a language Mabel didn't recognize. High in the leaves of the tree, a cardinal called what-cheer, what-cheer.

No cheer at all.

Her hypothesis had been that one grand and glorious kiss from an expert would hold her for the rest of her days. She'd kissed Wade to stop thinking about kissing him. She had hoped that the allure would be reduced by removing the mystery, so that she could focus on unraveling the mysteries of the earth.

When nosy friends spoke of prospects, she could respond with an enigmatic smile. "There goes Mabel Easterly," the neighbors would say as she passed on her way to the Institute. "She had a romance one summer."

Mabel leaned back, her heart as heavy as a bowling ball. No, she would *not* think about Wade bowling.

Further research would not be necessary or even possible. Her hypothesis was totally bunk.

CHAPTER TWENTY-ONE

"Get off." The hay wagon lurched onto a lane and its driver kicked Wade's foot. "This is as far as you go."

Wade didn't blame the fellow for being irritable. He'd dozed off or been too down in the dumps to make conversation - either way, not good company. He surveyed the countryside from the wagon's seat. "This isn't Warrenton."

"Ain't running no cab business." The farmhand shot a wad of tobacco south. "Warrenton's twelve miles." Another spit north. "The Plains is that away 'bout a mile." A third spit west. "Marshall's four miles."

"What's east?" Besides the wind, which would make for an entertaining spit.

"Dunno. Never been that way."

Wade thanked him, grabbed his suitcase, and climbed down. The farmhand giddy-upped before he had both feet on the ground and about ran him over. Since it was getting on to late evening, Wade headed north.

A few short hours ago, Wade had ridden by on the train, thinking he still had a resort to run, still had a home for Miss Maybelle. Now he plodded across these same tracks, out of a resort, out of a job, out of money. Wade trudged by a couple churches, a post office, a doctor's and dentist's, a dry goods store, a wheelwright's and a blacksmith's - all closed for the night. In spite of the village's sleepiness, several large structures were under construction on the west side.

Near as he could recollect, and confirmed by the age of most buildings, The Plains hadn't suffered any battles during The War, although troops had marched past. Nor could he recall anyone he knew in the area, so, force of habit, he wandered over to the Southern depot. A familiar figure sat in the shade wearing a new set of store-bought clothes, including shoes. "Mr. Absalom, how are you doing this fine evening?"

"Mr. Wade, back from your wanderings." Arthritic knuckles knocked on the bench beside him. "Set a spell?"

"Don't mind if I do." He should find supper and a bed for the night, but he could spare a moment for an old friend. "You left Calverton? Better trains here?"

Absalom's clouded eyes turned skyward. "My son got a job at a fancy horse farm here."

"Congratulations to John Henry." Wade patted the man's shoulder. Yes, he was eating better. "Those horses sing Yankee Doodle when they drop their dung?"

"Indeed they do." The elderly man wheezed when he laughed. "So tell me, what you gonna do now the resort's closed?"

"Word gets around quick." Wade leaned his aching head against the stuccoed wall. "Might could stay here, keep you company."

"Best you go to the Chinn Hotel, ask for a room in the back, and say your prayers." The elderly man grabbed his walking stick and pushed upright with a groan. "Then talk to the money man about business."

"Say my prayers? You been talking to Selina?" Wade guided him to the steps. "Wait— Money man? Where?"

Absalom paused and whispered. "Mr. Edward Harriman's newest thoroughbred arrives here in the morning."

"The wizard of the railroads?" Wade's heart jumped. Could

this be the opportunity he'd been looking for? "The guy who runs the Union Pacific, Southern Pacific, Illinois Central, and who knows what else?"

"Wells Fargo and a steamship company." Absalom reached for the railing and made his way down to the dusty street. "But he's real fond of horses."

"Mr. Absalom, you have friends in high places."

"Mr. Wade, it's your Friend in the highest place you need listen to." Stick tapping the street, he headed home.

After an expedition, Mabel usually celebrated waking in her own bed. But not this time. Her sojourn in the mountains had made her less tolerant of summer. The city had become an incubator, growing rank odors and buzzing flies. The sounds of traffic, automobile and horse-drawn, echoed from the street.

Sunday she dressed in her lightest clothes and attended church with the few hardy souls who hadn't escaped the city. The junior minister gave the sermon and suffered considerably in comparison with Wade. Mabel prayed for Wade, asking God to help him find the investor he needed, and asking Him to replace her wanton thoughts with pure ones.

At home, Mabel peeled off her damp clothes and found a prickly rash around her middle. She took another cold bath - in this instance, Wade was right about the healing power of water. Since no one would visit in this heat, she dressed in only a sleeveless vest, knee-length drawers, and the kimono she'd brought back from their trip to Japan. She sorted her laundry, then organized the pile of mail. The only envelope addressed to her came from a corset shop. "Are you too stout?" asked the enclosed advertisement. "The Sahlin form reducer will do for you what an abdominal corset cannot. The lower or reducing part is fitted with twelve separate adjustments which can be tightened or loosened to fit every figure."

Mabel crumpled the ad. No amount of steel boning could reduce her form in any way that counted. She was oversized all over. She'd been too big from birth, damaging her mother so she couldn't have more children.

And yet, instead of scorning her, Mother had loved her. She had been her champion. Mabel remembered playing outside their house in Boston. She had tripped, tearing her stocking and knee open on a cobblestone. Her wailing had drawn every woman on the block. You're too big to cry, they said. Why aren't you in school? Hush, now, you're frightening the younger children. Big girls must set an example. Mother informed them Mabel was only four, then, in spite of predictions of breaking her back, Mother had carried her home.

Was Mabel too big to cry now? With no one here to scold her, she let a tear slip.

When third grade found her half-a-head taller than everyone in her class, Mabel had stopped eating. Mother had taken her to a doctor who tried to sell her a body brace so she'd develop "properly." Father had put the kibosh on that, calling it a medieval torture device. He put a plate of roast and potatoes in front of her and told her to eat. Abraham Lincoln had been tall and so was he and it hadn't harmed them. Of course not - they were men.

Mother had sewn clothes for her with extra length in the hems and sleeves. Then she was gone, leaving Mabel to fight her own battles. Mabel away wiped another tear. To fight with Father for money for clothing, to fight with dressmakers for less style and more function, to fight with bullies who called her giraffe and worse. No one had stood up for her… until Wade.

Could he… Was it possible Wade loved her? Mabel shook her head. Foolish notion. His role as a hotel manager and Virginia gentleman required him to treat everyone with kindness and respect. When he did marry, he'd choose someone pretty, not an aberration.

If only Mabel had been normal, maybe she and Wade could have had a future. She would have married him, escaped her boring job, and… and what? What would she do in the rolling hills west of Warrenton? Besides kiss Wade. No, she had to stop thinking about *The Kiss*. It only made her feel warmer.

Mabel went upstairs to lower the shades on the west windows. The thermometer in the hall registered 98 Fahrenheit.

But that night, it wasn't the heat nor the noise, keeping her awake. It was memories of Wade.

Wade hurried up to The Plains depot, dodging puddles and horse apples. Wouldn't do to meet Mr. Railroad all spattered with muck. "Good morning, Mr. Absalom. Any sign of Mr. Harriman?"

"Not yet, sir." The man patted the bench beside him. "How did your prayers go last night?"

"Very well." Too excited to sit, Wade dropped his suitcase beside the bench and handed the elder a package. "For old time's sake."

"Thank you kindly." The elderly man broke off a bit of the biscuit, ham, and fried egg sandwich. "You were telling me about your prayers."

"Oh, yes. Mrs. Davis runs a nice little hotel." Wade paced the platform, footsteps loud in the Sunday morning quiet. "Appreciate the recommendation to ask for a room in the back. The builder must have expected passengers to walk right off the train and into his lobby, close as he put the hotel to the tracks. 'Course, back before The War, trains didn't run at night."

Absalom shook his grey head. "Mr. Wade…"

"Our days of glory are coming back, Mr. Absalom. I picked up some great ideas in my travels - heated spout baths, baseball, sunset walks, fireproofing. Once Mr. Harriman's on board, I'll head back to Fauquier, give Robert E the boot." Then he'd head to Washington and save Miss Maybelle from the city. She would help him lead the revival of Fauquier White Sulphur Springs, greeting the guests, sitting with him at the head table, helping continue the family line. Wade danced a jig, his shoes echoing on the platform.

"Mr. Wa-a-ade…"

A gleaming-new black coach pulled by four perfectly matched Cleveland bays rounded the corner. "Is that him?" Wade asked before he remembered Absalom was blind. "Has to be. Only Yankees can afford a fancy rig like that."

"I'm praying, even if you're not."

"I thanked God that I packed a Fauquier brochure." Wade pulled out the green-covered booklet, bound and stitched, printed in a fancy font with an engraving of the resort before the fire. Wade smoothed his hair, straightened his clothes, and met the coach.

An elaborate silver "H" had been monogrammed on either side of the windows. The footman jumped off the back and opened the door. A spectacled man with thick grey hair and mustache swung down. His straight posture showed off an English style riding jacket in dark green, buff breeches, and boots that had never stepped in manure.

"Mr. Harriman?" Wade introduced himself.

The railroad baron allowed his hand to be shaken, but kept his gaze on the tracks.

Wade held out the brochure and launched into his presentation.

Mr. Harriman raised his arm, palm out. "We already have the land we need."

Wade's heart dropped. "Fauquier has many advantages—"

"Which I'm well aware of, since I looked at all available property in the area. Beautiful land, but lacking proximity to the railroad."

"You could put in a spur line, like the Homestead."

"Here I don't have to. I'm sorry, Mr. Alexander." At the sound of a train whistle, the man strode away. "Now if you'll excuse me, I have a new horse to meet."

Wade slumped onto the bench beside Absalom and watched as a lively mare pranced off the freight car. Her shining chestnut coat reminded him of Miss Maybelle's hair, which rolled him even further into the dumps. The train, the horse, and the coach left, taking with them Wade's last hope.

"I didn't get to tell him about race course beside the river."

"You didn't get to praying either." Absalom stood, ran his hands down his fine-looking suit, then shuffled across the platform. "I'm gone to church. You close your eyes, listen real hard until God speak to you."

What else could he do? Wind fluttered the stack of newspapers Absalom had been sitting on. Wade folded them into his suitcase so they wouldn't blow away. He leaned forward, his head in his hands, eyes closed. Church bells rang and he remembered worshipping with Miss Maybelle. Clip-clops on the pavement of Main Street reminded Wade of introducing Miss Maybelle to all the livery horses and the stories behind their names. Bird song brought to mind Miss Maybelle laughing at the bird watchers.

"I'm sorry, Lord, but my mind's hopping around like a foxhound puppy." For once, Wade ran out of words. "I don't know what to ask for."

"Hey, mister, need a ride?" A barefoot kid perched on a farm wagon pulled by an ox team.

"Sure." Wade climbed up beside him. The load of grain smelled like barley. "Where are we going?"

"Chapman's Mill."

"Answered prayer. That's where I need to go."

A skeptical squint wrinkled the boy's freckles. "God's answering prayers, even though you skipped church this morning?"

"I'm in for a talking-to far better than any sermon." Wade grinned. "Guess you know all about the history made right here in August of 1862?"

Five miles of split-rail-fenced meadows rolled by as Wade entertained the young farmer with the story of the Battle of Thoroughfare Gap. A lively stream named Broad Run roared through the cleft between Mother Leather Coat Mountain and Pond Mountain, then spilled eighty feet over a mill wheel. Gears thumped inside the five-story stone building and the miller's hammer ping-pinged as he dressed the grindstone.

Wade said goodbye to his young friend, then followed a path up the hill to a slave cabin. The chickens noticed him first and commenced cackling. Shining dark eyes peeked through chinks in the cabin's door. Someone giggled and another voice said, "Hush, now."

"Hello!" He propped his suitcase atop the rain barrel to keep the hens from nesting on it. "I'm here to visit Miss Selina."

The woman in question hurried from behind the house and enveloped him in a fierce hug. "Oh, Wade. Thought I'd never see you again."

"Miss Selina." He hugged back, wanting to put his head on her sturdy shoulder and have a good cry. "How y'all doing?"

She patted his cheek. Her hand smelled of red Piedmont clay. "Garden's never looked better. Come, see." She towed him around back. Neat rows of tomatoes, beans, and cucumbers crossed the hillside. A yoke of water buckets sat between the pumpkin and squash vines.

Seeing as how the strange white man didn't hurt their granny, the grandchildren emerged from their hiding places. Wade lost count at eight. "These babies all belong to your daughter?"

"They're all my grandchildren. Five from my daughter, six from my son." Selina relieved a young girl of a chubby baby. "Naomi, Mr. Wade be walking a long ways. We got something cold to drink?"

With a "Yes'm" the girl scampered off. Selina led him under a brush arbor and set the baby on the pallet in the corner. She lowered herself onto a wobbly stool and motioned for Wade to take the stump.

The baby stared at Wade, probably the first time he'd seen a white fellow. Baby rolled toward the edge and Wade scooped him up. "Miss Selina, they make you sleep out here?"

"It's to my liking. I'll move inside for the winter."

Wade eyeballed the cabin. Fifteen feet square, he guessed. A row of end logs midway up showed it had a loft. How many people fit in there? At the resort, Selina had her own room with a bed, nightstand, chamber pot, and curtains. "Oh, Miss Selina."

Naomi returned with a dripping jug and two glass jars. She filled the jars with iced tea, then with a delicate motion worthy of a Homestead waitress, topped each with a mint leaf. "Here you go."

"Thank you kindly." His parched throat welcomed the cool liquid.

"Expect you been by the resort." Selina raised an eyebrow as she sipped.

He set his jar on the crate, but kept hold of the baby as he paced. "I'll make the rounds of the lawyers and judges in Warrenton. Surely there's something we can do to get your job back. I'll go to Richmond if I must. Well, I have to on account of our soldiers. Do you think the kitchen staff would come back, once I give Robert E his walking papers?"

Selina raised her eyebrows and shook her head. "I don't know about no papers, but you sure enough doing the walking."

"Trying to get this here baby calmed down." The baby stared, a crease between his brows, lips tucked in, but didn't make a peep. Wade ignored Selina's tell-me-another eye roll. "This is no kind of life for you squeezed in that cabin, treated like a—" He stopped himself himself before he said "slave."

"Wade." Her voice held a note of warning.

"Can you imagine Colonel Vance, Major Holston, and Captain Drake at that soldier's home? They'll be lost, not knowing what to do with themselves. All the stink and disease of the city. It'll kill them."

Selina grabbed his wrist and forced him to sit. "Oh, child."

"I can't believe, after everything—"

She pulled scissors from her workbasket and commenced cutting his hair. "You looked at those account books six ways to Sunday. Tried purt near everything. And lost money faster than you could burn it."

Mention of money had the baby giving him a fierce frown.

"The Homestead's still packing them in."

Selina's strong fingers grabbed his chin and forced him to meet her gaze. "I'm on your side. Always. But you're frittering away your life—"

"Frittering? I work my fingers to the bone every day to bring back the finest summer hotel in the South. Then Robert E throws it all away in two short weeks." He slapped his knee, which roused the baby to do the same.

"You pouring out your life on your daddy's dream, doing what your daddy wanted, instead of asking your Heavenly Father what He wants for you."

She was talking about Miss Maybelle, not him. "It's my dream, too."

"You ever prayed for God to show you His will? Or you just pray to keep that resort open?" She waved her scissors in his face, then resumed clipping. "Don't lie to me while I've got your hair in my hands."

"Yes'm." He swallowed and watched the children. They were supposed to be checking the tomatoes for worms, but, realizing their granny was otherwise occupied, they pelted each other with dirt clods. "But you have family…" And he'd lost even that.

Selina stowed her scissors, then called the children. They formed a solemn circle around him. One of the little boys closed his eyes, pressed his hands together, and in one breath said, "Bless this food for the nourishment of our bodies in the sweet name of our Lord Jesus Christ we pray."

The other children fought to hold in their giggles.

"Right prayer, wrong time, Isaiah." Selina put one hand on Wade's head and raised the other toward the sky. "Merciful Jesus, comfort this man in his sorrow. Show him your way, guide him along Your path."

Naomi must have heard this prayer a time or two, as she added, "Keep his feet on the righteous road, Precious Savior, away from the temptations of this world, such as liquor, gambling, loose—"

Selina stopped the sin recitation with a firm "whisht."

One of the boys added, "And no more burning money, Lord."

Burning money? Shock rippled around the circle, followed by whispered questions. Selina wrapped up the prayer with an "Amen," and the children scattered to their play.

She blew on the back of his neck. "It's a right fur piece to town. You know trouble rain on our heads, if'n you caught here."

Not to mention, they had no place to put him. Wade drained his tea and stood.

"How's that nice woman you traveled with?"

The thought of Miss Maybelle had him wanting to cry again. "What do I have to offer her?"

"Yourself." She patted him on the cheek firmly enough to say she'd like to slap some sense into him. "Yourself. With fresh-cut hair."

"Thank you." Wade gave Selina another hug and thanked the children for keeping him in their prayers. He retrieved his suitcase from an irritable rooster, then strolled down hill to the railroad platform. The wooden bench made for hard sitting. How did Absalom manage and him with so little meat on his bones? The newspapers. Wade pulled them from his suitcase. Instead of old editions, he found the latest issues of the Fauquier *Democrat*, Washington *Evening Star*, Washington *Post*, and Richmond *Times-Dispatch*.

The first Wanted ad in the first paper caught his eye. He leaned back and blew out a deep breath. Well, then. This morning's rustle of the wind through the newspapers must have been the still small voice of God.

CHAPTER TWENTY-TWO

Mabel tossed off her covers and scratched her latest mosquito bite. What was Wade doing today? No doubt he'd returned to the innumerable duties of a hotelier, too busy to think of her. She turned off the alarm clock. Plenty of time to write her thank you note.

After breakfast, which made her think of Wade saying, "Not bad, but not as good as Fauquier's," Mabel sat down in Father's office with a sheet of stationery. *Dear sir.* Oh for heaven's sake. She'd traveled with the man for two weeks. She knew his name. Mabel drew a line through the first two words. This would be her rough draft. *Dear Mr. Alexander.* Still too formal. *Dear Wade.*

Dear, dear Wade, How I miss you! Scratch that, even though it was true. What must she say? *Thank you for traveling with me. Sorry about The Kiss.* Mabel tossed the pen down, leaving a blot of ink the shape of a retort.

Wait, Mother's etiquette book had sample letters. Mabel hunted through his bookshelves until she remembered Father had stashed it in the kitchen with the cookbooks he never read. She located the book and flipped through the pages. Letter of introduction, breaking an engagement by letter, love letter - Oh, how she wished! - and, thank you letters. Thank you to the hostess for a weekend at her estate, thank you to the hostess of a luncheon, thank you to the hostess of a dinner party. Mabel blotted the perspiration from her forehead and turned the page.

231

Letter of apology. Close enough. She could reword it to fit the situation. *I do deeply apologize for my seeming rudeness in kissing you.* No, that drew more attention to her action and might be interpreted as criticm of his ability - and he was nothing less than perfect. How about, *Every moment of our journey was a perfect delight - especially the last. Thank you so much for the pleasure you gave me.* Whoa, entirely too forward and easily misconstrued.

Letters of friendship. Yes, she counted Wade as a friend. Correspondents were advised to avoid excessive formality or too great familiarity. "Write cheerfully, considerately, honestly." Dare she risk sharing her honest feelings? No, not with Virginia just across the river. She'd have to sail for the East Indies if she ever confessed her infatuation.

The hall clock chimed the hour. She'd have to finish the letter at work. Using the Geophysical Laboratory's stationery would give her letter a professional tone.

"Get your fresh blackberries, raspberries, blueberries!" called the fruit vendor from the street. Would he be selling any of those pippin apples Wade recommmended?

As she locked the front door, one of the neighbors played "Ye Banks and Braes of Bonnie Doon" on the piano. Mabel's head echoed with Wade's baritone.

She shouldn't have kissed him. No, she was glad she did. Wade would hold a place in her memories for the rest of her life. For this summer, Wade had been the cake and The Kiss was the frosting.

Last night's thunderstorm brought a few degrees of relief and a few more puddles for breeding mosquitos. Like the rest of the city, Upton Road was under construction. Mabel nodded to the men shoveling gravel, and picked her way around wheelbarrows and piles of dirt. She slogged up the hill, scraped mud off her shoes, and entered the Geophysical Laboratory.

The building had been in use for only a year, but in spite of its highly touted forced circulation of air, it had already developed a distinctive odor. The heavy smell of paper, the vinegary acids, and the taint of overly heated metal compounded into the smell of serious research.

The other highly touted feature - thermal insulation - had turned the building into a giant autoclave. Mabel held her breath, listening. No one else had come to work today and she suspected no one would. She hurried up the stairs, opening windows, lowering shades, and turning on fans.

On the top floor, Mabel peered south. Humidity and smoke limited the line of sight to nearby houses and trees. Neither the Washington Monument nor the post office building pierced the haze. She hoped Wade and his guests were enjoying cool mountain breezes.

The janitor's closet was empty - not even Mr. Brown would work on a day like this. Mabel donned her protective clothing, estimating the heavy rubber increased perspiration two hundred percent. She made her rounds of the sinks, finding a Nessler tube here, an Erlenmeyer flask there. When she first started this job, she'd tried to identify the chemical residues and reason out which agent would dissolve it. Since then she'd fallen into a rut of using sulfuric acid and potassium bichromate, with an occasional resort to alkaline permanganate, or an oxalic and sulfuric acid mixture, rinse and dry. The routine left far too much time for her thoughts to wander to Wade. Who was he flirting with this morning? Who would kiss him next?

Enough! Mabel fanned herself with a copy of the director's research on high temperature measurements in *Annalen der Physik*. She must finish her letter to Wade and put this experience behind her, then start her report for the National Conservation Commission.

Mabel sat at the secretary's desk. A set of reference works stood between geode bookends - a dictionary, *Palmer's Guide for the Amanuensis*, and, yes, *The Twentieth Century Guide to Business Letters*. Her arrangement with Wade had been business, not social - she should find something here that would apply. But no.

Dear Wade. What exactly did she want to thank him for? For saving her from copperheads and moonshiners, for dancing and bowling, but most of all for believing she could complete her research, for seeing her as a scientist... and as a woman. No, not those last four words - they'd remind him of The Kiss.

What was that smell? Was something burning or had spending time with Wade heightened her worry about fire? No, she definitely smelled smoke.

Mabel followed her nose to the basement. She found a scientist puffing away on his pipe as he sat cross-legged on the concrete floor. He stared up at a chalkboard covered with his atrocious scrawl.

"Dr. Stephens?"

He blinked. "Ah... Miss Marble."

No sense correcting him. He never would learn her name. She motioned toward the half-filled sink. "Shall I clean?"

"If you must." He rummaged around in his beard, as if searching for something. He spoke with the rate of speech used to address the simple-minded. "I suppose you're wondering why I'm working here instead of the U.S. Geological Survey lab. It's cooler."

Actually Mabel wondered why he smoked in the laboratory when he knew the vapor would damage delicate instruments, including this lab's collimating compass, gas thermometer furnace, and expansion coefficients apparatus. She scrubbed seven Gooch crucibles, thirteen petri dishes, and several plates covered with food residue. For a moment, she contemplated smashing the dishware on the man's head.

The chicken-scratches on the chalkboard caught her eye. What a mess. Before she could consider if she was making the best or worst of this dull job, she picked up the chalk. "Dr. Stephens, four plus five is…" she said in her best teacher voice.

He didn't respond. She strode to the chalkboard, corrected a four to a nine - what handwriting! - and moved a decimal point one place to the right. She reworked the final calculation in her head, drew a line through his answer, and wrote the correct result in large clear print. As she strolled out of the room, she heard the distinct thump-clatter of a French briar pipe hitting the wall.

Not what you'd call an auspicious beginning, Wade thought as he rode into Washington sitting on a mailbag surrounded by milk cans. But riding with the freight fit his budget. He climbed off at the gleaming new station, shaved in the restroom, woke up the newspaper vendor to get directions, then stepped out into the city.

Whoa, steam bath. The sun rose over his shoulder, raising a layer of haze from last night's showers. Humidity mixed with smoke from thousands of chimneys to form a lid of noxious fumes over the city. This was misery and Fauquier White Sulphur Springs was… no more. Wade sighed. Uh-oh. Need to breathe in. He inhaled a garbage dump's worth of foul odors and a mosquito or two. He switched to shallow breaths through his mouth. No wonder everyone leaves for the summer.

Well, not everyone had left. Pigeons perched on statues and thronged the sidewalks. Flies swarmed and buzzed. He saw a few people, too. Working folks, those who couldn't afford to leave and didn't have a place to go. None of Wade's guests would be around. None except Miss Maybelle and he couldn't face her as a penniless bum.

His eyes adjusted to the soupy light and he realized the new train station had been built far from the city's center. Someone should put a hotel here, someone with money, which left him out. Wade started to sigh again, then caught himself. Pant like a dog. No. Thinking about dogs would remind him of Raleigh and make him homesick. Fauquier White Sulphur Springs had been the only thought in his head for his entire life. Now he had to think about getting a job.

Lord, how'm I gonna manage? I always worked at Fauquier, working with people who knew my family, doing the job my father taught me. I don't know this city or these people or what work awaits me.

Every moment the temperature climbed a degree, so Wade hefted his suitcase and headed west. The city didn't have mountains to provide direction, so he navigated by the Capitol and the Washington Monument. After a block, he removed his jacket. The street cleaner dragging a shovel along the gutter didn't give him a second look.

Rows of wood frame firetraps gave way to blocks of four-story brownstones. Fancy limestone buildings flying the flag must be government offices. A few blocks south stood the red brick castle of the Smithsonian.

A US Mail wagon stood in the middle of the intersection. A streetcar stopped beside it. The mailman swapped bags from the car for ones from his wagon as the passengers watched, then the two parted without a word.

A white-coated proprietor stepped out of the Peoples Drug Store on the corner. Wade expected him to wash the windows or sweep the sidewalk, but instead he lit up a cigarette. Wade wished him a good morning and got a grunt in response.

A gent on a bicycle passed and also ignored Wade's greeting. The air must be too thick for talking.

At the Sanitary Grocery Company, a boy set a bin of peaches in his window, bringing Miss Maybelle to mind. She'd be back to work this morning. How soon could he see her again? He wanted another kiss. Then his stomach reminded him he'd missed breakfast. Best wait. Wouldn't do to ask for work with sticky hands.

He turned toward the clock tower of the post office. Across the street shone a limestone building fancy enough for Paris, the Raleigh Hotel.

Aw, Raleigh. Wade's hunger pangs changed to heart pain. He mopped his face with his handkerchief, put his jacket back on, and crossed the street. Clayton would take good care of the old hound.

The main entrance was locked, seeing as how the hotel was closed for the summer. Wade circled around to an alley and found a basement screen door. Someone had oiled it recently, which seemed a poor security measure. Wade slipped inside and set his suitcase down. The hallway was empty, if you didn't count the dead crickets, but in the first room on the left, a man drowsed behind a Burroughs adding machine, slowly fanning himself with a ledger.

"Mr. Leerlauf?"

The ledger hit the desk with a thump. The man scrambled to find his spectacles in the mess of papers and ashtrays. "Yes. How may I help you?"

Wade introduced himself. "I'm here about the advertisement."

The hotelier flinched. "Which one?"

"All of them. I'm experienced with painting, plastering, wallpapering, and fitting keys."

Eyeglasses located, the manager gave Wade a thorough inspection. "You'll have to excuse me, I meet so many people in my line of work. You look familiar. Have we met?"

Wade grinned. "Yes sir. You were a year ahead of me at U.Va."

Since college, the man's middle had thickened and his hair thinned. He returned Wade's smile, and offered him a seat and a bottle of Coca-Cola from his ice chest. "Fauquier White

237

Sulphur Springs, right? It's been rough going for those old resorts lately. Not that it's easy here."

Wade took a long swallow of the cold liquid. "I'm used to hard work."

"I'm sure you are. But a building this size requires a crew and therein lies the problem."

Therein? Oh, yes, Leerlauf had studied the law. Wade tried to hide a belch behind his fist. "The problem?"

"No one wants to work. Laziest bunch of bums you ever want to see. Destructive, deceiving, devious. If you don't monitor them every moment, they'll sit around doing nothing all day."

Wade would have pointed out Leerlauf had been busily engaged in doing nothing minutes ago, but he needed the job. He settled for a sympathetic "Sorry to hear that."

"No doubt you have higher class workers in the country." The manager led him down the hall. "The last supervisor quit after three days. Only a month to go before we reopen. I don't know how we'll do it with this bunch of good-for-nothings." He flung open the door.

The dim light from a vent window showed a fellow dark and large enough to blend in with the furnaces and boilers. He hid something behind his back and met their gaze.

Leerlauf glared. "Where's the rest of the rabble?"

The man crossed his enormous arms and spoke slowly. "Don't got no idea."

Red-faced, the manager turned to Wade. "See what I must contend with? Of course he knows where the others are, he merely refuses to say."

"I'm not lying." The worker's chin raised. "I don't know where they are now. They left since you got no work for them."

"I have a whole hotel full of work for the willing. This is Mr. Alexander. See you treat him right." The manager handed Wade a key. "Have to keep supplies and tools locked up around these thieves. Take a look and tell me what you think." The manager's footsteps echoed as he returned to his office.

Wade stepped into the boiler room and held out his hand. "Pleased to meet you."

The man's eyes widened a fraction of an inch, then narrowed. His arm extended slowly to give a firm handshake with a full set of calluses.

Wade said, "I'm sorry. I didn't catch your name."

"Hoban."

"Is that your first or last name?"

"First name Jim."

"Any relation to James Hoban, the guy who designed the White House?"

His slow blink asked if Wade had lost his mind. "Do I looks like him?"

"Since he's dead and you're not, I'd say not especially." Wade stepped into the hall. "How long have you been working here?"

"A while."

"Longer than me at any rate. All right, give me the grand tour, show me what needs doing."

Jim pushed to his feet. An *Evening Star* slid to the floor behind him. So, the man could read, a rare and welcome skill.

"Anything in the news?" Wade asked.

"No."

"Too hot, I suppose."

Jim took him up the service stairs, making the rounds of each floor. Fluted columns, inlaid tile floors, and mural-painted walls made for an elegant lobby, even with the furniture piled in the middle and the rugs rolled up. The hotel had been added onto several times, resulting in a variety of rooms and a variety of problems. Each flight up lessened the stench from the street, but increased the heat. Sunlight poured through the windows, turning the building into an oven.

"Mercy. I can see why no one wants this job." Wade wiped his forehead. "Where are the curtains?"

"Laundry."

"In this weather, the only thing more miserable than painting would be stirring heavy curtains over a hot fire. My sympathies to whoever ended up with that job."

Jim made a sound in the back of his throat and Wade turned to him. "You know the laundress?"

"My wife."

That's why he'd stayed. If Leerlauf fired him, likely he'd send the curtains elsewhere and the whole family would go hungry. "Very clever, Mr. Hoban. Now I see why you stuck around. Go home and you'd be roped into washing."

The man's mouth twitched as if he considered smiling, but thought the better of it.

"Could we hang sheets or something to keep the sun out?"

Jim reached into the top of the window frame and lowered a shade.

"Much better. We may live after all." Wade pulled down the rest. "Painting, scraping wallpaper, plaster, keys. What do you like best, Jim?"

"This and that."

How many bad bosses had this man endured? Wade nodded. "Yep, I like variety, too. So long as it doesn't involve overflowing toilets."

He thought he heard the man snort.

The hallway corner by the elevator shone white with globs of plaster. "Who did this?"

"The boss who quit."

"My minister says we're not supposed to speak ill of the departed, but this is the most miserable excuse for a patch job I've ever seen."

"Hmm."

Wade's fingers bumped over trowel marks. "I'd rather add a bit of extra water to the plaster, do neat work, and not have such a mess to clean up."

"You done this before?"

"Yes." Wade mopped his face again. He needed to bring his bandannas to work. "Never in summer though."

The top floor had a second kitchen. Shelves held enough tableware for every person in the city plus the full array of serving dishes. Each piece was decorated with the letter R and tobacco leaves, for Sir Walter Raleigh himself. Wade turned over a delicate plate and found the insignia of Haviland. He whistled. No doubt these custom dishes cost a lot more than than the run-of-the-mill ware sold in the Sears catalog. "Wonder how much they charge to eat here."

"Dunno." Jim opened the door to a banquet hall as opulent as The Homestead, with a vaulted ceiling and a balcony for an orchestra. Large windows would overlook the city if the air ever cleared.

Wade circled the room, checking the walls and woodwork. "Could do with a touch up. Do we have paint?"

"Yeah."

"This place is too fancy for plain old green and white. What is it, pine needle and snow? Grass and cream?"

Jim's mouth quirked. One of these days he'd laugh. "Myrtle and ivory."

"Thanks. Hate to get canned for picking the wrong color."

They trudged back to the relative cool of the basement. The padlocked room was well-stocked. Tools were organized by task.

"I'll change into my work clothes. Let's save the painting for tomorrow morning—" A noon whistle blew somewhere and Wade's stomach echoed its complaint. "First, let's eat."

"I waits for you here." Jim said, reminding Wade he wasn't allowed in restaurants.

"Where do you take your meals?"

Jim pointed to a rag-covered metal bucket on the cement floor of the boiler room. A squad of flies flew circles over it.

"How very kind of you to share your dinner with the mice, Mr. Hoban."

He smothered his laugh with a cough.

Wade rapped his knuckles on the office doorframe.

The manager looked up from his invoices and motioned for Wade to take a seat. "Will we be ready to reopen on time?"

Wade sank into the chair. "It's possible. Right off the top of my head, I can think of three things to make it more likely."

The manager scowled and Wade remembered he wasn't in charge here. "And that would be?"

"Start at sunrise and stop when it's too hot."

"Sunrise? Good luck getting those boys to show that early. They stay up all hours drinking." He pulled a ring of keys from his desk. "You'll need these since I don't arrive until nine."

"Get fans to help the air circulate."

"Electricity's off."

"Sears catalog has a battery-operated model."

"I'll look into it." Leerlauf scribbled a note to himself. "And third?"

"Provide lunch."

His mouth twitched. "They bring their own."

"Which sits on the floor all day, getting warm. I'm surprised you haven't had trouble with rodents."

Leerlauf shuddered. "I don't know, Wade."

"Nothing fancy. Sandwich, apple, cold tea. Or you could get another icebox." Either one would cost less than one of those place settings in the banquet room. Wade leaned forward. "Working in this heat is asking a lot. We need their cooperation."

The manager glanced at his adding machine, then nodded.

He quoted an acceptable rate of pay and recommended a boarding house nearby. "Wade, if you can pull this off, I'll see you have a job when we reopen."

"You've got yourself a deal."

At the nearby store, Wade bought sandwiches, peaches, and Cokes for himself and Jim. They spent a couple hours patching, scraping and sanding, then finished the day fitting keys. From his skill and knowledge, Jim's "a while" of experience figured to be a good number of years. He worked steadily, but the job was bigger than the two of them could manage.

As they stowed their tools, Jim cleared his throat. "My granny worked for James Hoban."

Likely his granny had been enslaved to Hoban. "You're a credit to his name."

Jim nodded, gathered his pail, and left for home without making any promises about the rest of the crew. Wade splashed his face with water, grabbed his suitcase, and headed up the street to the boarding house.

He needed a dunking in a crick, a breath of cool mountain air, and a decent night's sleep. But most of all he needed Miss Maybelle.

CHAPTER TWENTY-THREE

It wasn't proper for Wade to call on Miss Maybelle, not with her living alone. Best he could do was meet her at the Geophysical Laboratory and walk her home. He'd studied the map and figured he could hike up 14th Street and cross over through Rock Creek Park, but the guys at the boarding house thought he'd make better time taking a streetcar up Connecticut Avenue. Now all he had needed was to finish work early enough to give himself a good scrubbing and change clothes.

Jim held up another sheet of wallpaper, heavy with paste. "Best stop thinking about your girl, Mr. Wade. Boss man coming."

When it came to the hotel manager, Jim Hoban had more than a lick of sense - he had a sixth sense. Wade grabbed the tape measure and tried to look busy.

Leerlauf emerged from the stairwell, out of breath even though he'd only climbed two flights. "Another convention."

Wade glanced at his crew, a half-dozen men from age fifteen to fifty, all kin one way or another. They were smart enough not to react to anything the hotel manager said. And tired enough they'd all been looking forward to an early night. Wade groaned on their behalf. "First the Republicans, then the Democrats. Now who?"

"The Interstate Association of Live Stock Sanitary Boards," Leerlauf read from a slip of paper. "They're meeting about tuberculosis. Tonight. I know you're all tired. So I asked the waiters to come in early. Arrange the tables and chairs, and they'll do the rest." The stairwell door slammed as the manager hurried back to the less humid basement.

"Go on down to the dining room, get set up," Jim told two who'd been working on locks and still had clean hands. "Now don't you worry, Mr. Wade. Your girl still be pretty tomorrow."

"Let me go talk to the boss." Wade took a rag to his hands.

"Don't get yourself fired now," Jim said.

"I'll do my best." Wade trooped downstairs and found Leerlauf at his desk. "Boss," he said to remind himself of who's in charge, "all these conventions sure get in the way of finishing the hotel."

"Have a seat." Leerlauf popped the cap off a Coca-Cola and handed it to him. "I know it's an interruption, but conventions are confined to the first floor, out of the way of the rest of the work, and they bring in revenue."

"But it's off-season." Wade cooled his hands on the bottle, then ran them across his neck. "At least for another week."

The man handed over his ledger.

Wade opened it to the most recent entry. "Is this the real one or the one you show investors?"

The hotelier's jaw nearabout fell onto his desk.

With remarks like that, no wonder Maybelle thought Wade fell short in the honesty department. "Just kidding. Your mama taught you better."

"Uh, well, yes." Leerlauf's exhale ended with a chuckle. "The owner has high standards. He expects income every quarter."

"Income every quarter? Is he off his rocker? You'd have to have a full house every night in September to pay for July and August." Between gulps of the cold drink, Wade paged back through the months and years. The numbers looked good, better than good, with a steady stream of income outpacing expenses. If Fauquier had shown this much profit, it would still be open.

"It's how he keeps the Raleigh in business. How'd you manage with your resort's long off-season?"

"We did all right in the 1880s." But never as good as the Raleigh Hotel did in its worst month. "Bethel Military Academy took over the hotel starting in 1895, until it burned down."

"You haven't had a profit since 1901? It's a wonder the owner didn't shut you down years ago. How did you pay your staff, keep up with maintenance?"

Wade raised a shoulder, sending a shooting pain down his back. "Sold off an acre here and there." Not to mention the pocket watch his father gave him for his eighteenth birthday and his favorite horse. "Labor costs are lower out in the country." Good portion of his employees, like the old soldiers, were desperate enough to work for room and board.

"My guess is you nearly died trying." Leerlauf squinted at him. "When's the last time you paid yourself?"

Wade squirmed. "Been a while." Thirteen years, to be exact. He stood and set the empty bottle in the divided box beside the door. "Thanks for the Coke."

"Thanks for staying on the job."

Wade made it down the hall and into the stairwell before he choked up. The door shut behind him. He collapsed on the bottom step and tried to keep his head from falling off.

And here he'd thought Maybelle was the foolish one, toiling away on a project doomed to the ash heap, all to earn the respect of a bunch of bonehead scientists.

For two weeks.

While Wade had poured his entire life into Fauquier. Sweating on leaky roofs and in clogged ditches. Pinching pennies so tight his Scottish ancestors would shake their thrifty heads. Making nice to nit-picking guests, especially the well-heeled. And every season he'd lost more money.

For thirteen years.

Maybelle thought he had an honesty problem and she was right. But his biggest lie was the one he'd told himself, that Fauquier White Sulphur Springs was a going concern. He'd worked so hard for so long, he hadn't recognized it had become hopeless. But Robert E had.

Lord, I don't know how or when, but I need to forgive my brother. And apologize.

For now he had to check on his crew, make sure the meeting room was ready. Wade wiped his face on his sleeve and hauled his weary carcass up the steps. A glance at the meeting room showed all was in order.

The lobby door opened to a familiar pair. Selina would say this was God telling him to "hop to it and no dilly-dallying." Maybelle would tell him to be honest. He crossed the carpeted floor. "Mother? Robert E?"

"Wade Hampton." Mother spun around like a dancer. Her face lit up. "How's my boy?"

"In need of a bath." He kissed her cheek.

"And a decent meal." She grabbed his chin, her grip nearly as firm as Selina's. Looking at her now, no one would think she'd ever had a ill day in her life. "Do they ever feed you?" she asked.

"Too hot to eat." Wade spotted his brother lingering in the shadows and extended his hand for a shake. "Robert E. We have a lot of catching up to do. What brings you to Washington?"

"To see you, of course." Mother wore all new clothes from her hat down to her shoes. "What a lovely hotel, Wade. Quite impressive."

Robert E was decked out in a new suit. Where did the money come from? "Our local veterinarian is speaking at a meeting here, so we rode up with him. Thought to visit you, see what our capital city is all about, and pay a call on Colonel Mosby."

A waiter ushered them into a private dining room set up with iced tea.

"I hope we're not interrupting." Mother poured.

"Work'll wait. You both look wonderful." Better than he did in his workman's clothes. "How've you been?"

"Fit as a fiddle." She put a slice of lemon in his brother's glass. "Robert E and I moved into Warrenton. We have rooms at Mrs. Norden's."

"Glad to hear it." Mrs. Norden's boarding house was brick.

"Robert E is working for Mr. Jennings, collecting rent, making repairs." Mother dosed his tea with a good bit of sugar, just the way he liked it. "I've been teaching piano and attending women's Bible study."

"All those things you never had time to do before."

Mother stopped fussing with the sugar bowl and met his gaze. "We both feel... free of the burden of the resort. And you? How're you doing, Wade Hampton?"

"Lower than a cottonmouth in bottom land." Wade sent up a prayer, grasped his mother's hand, and nodded to Robert E. "Please forgive me, both of you, for all my fighting words when I was home last. And for running out without even a goodbye. I was so caught up in saving the resort, I couldn't see the truth in front of my face."

"You did your best," Mother said.

"The resort business has changed," his brother added without his usual gloat.

Wade nodded. "The truth finally drilled into my hard head. Between taking a gander at the account books here and touring other resorts with Miss Maybelle—"

"Oh, before I forget." Mother opened her new purse and pulled out an envelope. "You have a letter from Miss Maybelle. Doesn't she know you're here?"

Wade tucked it into his pocket to savor later. "I've had no time to call on her. This place needed a heap of work. Got one more floor to go."

"Then we'd best let you get on with it." Mother stood. "We're staying at the Ebbitt."

And then Robert E extended the olive branch. "I hope you'll join us for dinner."

The secretary met Mabel at the front door. "The director is back."

Mabel tightened her grip on her purse, waiting to hear *and you've been fired.*

The older woman pointed upstairs. "You're to report to his office immediately."

Mabel headed for the janitor's closet across from the entrance.

"Miss Easterly, immediately." The woman tapped her foot on the tile floor.

"Thank you." Mabel hung up her hat and purse on her allotted hook. She had been brave enough to kiss Wade Hampton Alexander, why should the director scare her? Mabel grabbed her file folder from the highest shelf, then climbed the steps to the second floor, perspiration breaking out under her corset. Silence wouldn't change her job for the better. She had to speak up. She had to be calm and confident.

Even if her stomach felt like she'd eaten dry ice for breakfast.

You are God's workmanship. Mabel straightened her shoulders and marched down the hall.

The director's tan had darkened to bronze and he looked rested… until Mabel entered his office. "Miss Easterly." His tone conveyed the distaste usually associated with finding a fly in one's soup. "Have a seat."

Mabel perched on the edge of the chair, then realized the sun beaming through the director's window landed right on her face. She squinted and leaned to the side.

Before she could ask how his vacation was, the director said, "You left your position without proper notification."

Her eyes watered, which undoubtedly would be misconstrued as tears and further proof she was unsuitable for research. "Who should I have notified?"

"Did you tell anyone?"

She pushed with her feet, but the chair wouldn't slide on his Aubusson carpet. "Mr. Brown."

"The janitor." His eyes narrowed.

Mabel stood and repositioned the chair with an ungainly thump. "If I'd known where you were," golfing at the Homestead, "I would have asked you."

"Scientists must follow directions and you did not, Miss Easterly. You neglected your duties."

Mabel removed the diagram from her folder and placed it on the stack in front of him. "This graph documents the number of pieces cleaned daily since I started work. As you can see, the amount dropped to near zero in June. July's accumulation barely reached double digits. I cleaned all within an hour of my return. The quantity has only this week returned to normal levels."

The director scowled over the top of his eyeglasses as he pinched the corner of the graph, dragged it across his desk, and dropped it into the wastebasket. "Miss Easterly, are you trying to prove the Geophysical Laboratory has no need of your services?"

"I'm showing you no work was neglected in my absence." Mabel set her report in front of him and hoped he didn't notice her hand shaking. "And this is to show you The Geophysical Laboratory can trust me with greater responsibilities."

"The Geophysical Laboratory did not request this report and has no interest in—" He glanced down. "—*An Analysis of Virginia's Mineral Spring Waters.*"

She should have let Wade shoot him. "The US Geological

Survey—"

"I'm well aware of their research. It was done while I was in their employ." He jabbed her report with his pen, leaving an ink splotch. "And I'm well aware of your credentials and your father's estimate of your skills, however none of our scientists are willing to take you under their wing. Their wives object to a woman in the lab."

Mabel's mouth dropped open. Their wives? Mabel had made a point to meet the scientists' wives at the lab's opening. They had nothing to fear from her and they knew it. And what about those who were single?

Uh-oh.

Another stab of the pen spattered ink on the cuff of his white shirt. Obviously he didn't do his own laundry. "I'd hoped you could assist one of the chemists who's not married. Your legible penmanship would be an asset. However, before I even returned to Washington, Dr. Stephens felt it necessary to wire me about your behavior. A donnybrook, he called it."

Mabel forced her words through clenched teeth. "Apparently he didn't express gratitude for correcting his arithmetic or cleaning his breakfast dishes." One good tattle deserves another. "At least he stopped smoking in the lab."

The director's moustache rippled. "Miss Easterly, your father's esteem in the scientific community does not excuse you from exercising appropriate tact and diplomacy."

"Of course not." Mabel returned his glare, fighting the rising heat of anger. He'd never lecture a male scientist this way. "Perhaps I could use the chemistry lab at the end of the hall? There's only space for one scientist in that room. I could continue the alumina-silica studies."

"Impossible. That lab is reserved for a German chemist."

Who had just been hired, but would never have to clean his own equipment. Mabel ran her thumb over the final item in her folder. Should she? In for a gram, in for a kilo. She set it on top of her report. "Well, then, a mobile water testing laboratory is a good match for my skills and wouldn't inconvenience any other scientists."

The director propped his head on his fingers. "Miss Easterly…"

His telephone rang, saving him from deflating yet another dream. Fighting the anger women weren't allowed to feel and the tears women weren't allowed to shed, Mabel returned to the janitor's closet and her rubber dishwashing gear. The open window breathed in fresh air and the voices of children. Mabel leaned on the frame and watched a trio of students hurry down the hill. Today was the first day of school.

If only she'd been fired…

Wade raced through his work, hurried to clean up, then dashed to Ebbitt House to dine with Mother and Robert E, all the while wondering what Maybelle had written. Her declaration of undying love, A promise of more kisses? A plea for relief of her loneliness? He'd been hankering for her something fierce.

He returned to the boarding house late that evening. Wade sat on the edge of his cot and held his mail. A letter signed by several friends urged him to run for Virginia's House of Delegates. Another from the owner of the Warrenton House asked if he'd be interested in managing the town's best hotel. He set those aside and opened the letter that held his future.

Maybelle wrote with a neat script, without any extra twists or curls. She didn't seal the envelope with wax or douse it with perfume. The postmark said she'd mailed it on her first day back to work. Wade lifted the flap. Only one page. One sheet of stationery embossed with the name of the Geophysical Laboratory. A few brief lines:

Dear Wade,

GILDING THE WATERS

Than you very much for providing guard services for the mineral springs of Virginia fieldwork. Your assistance was greatly appreciated.
I wish you all the best in your future endeavors.
Yours truly,
M. Easterly

What? The letter dropped to the floor. What was she thinking?

The man across the hall thumped up the steps on his wooden leg, dropped into bed, and commenced snoring. The chickens in the backyard settled on their roost. The cook opened the kitchen door and emptied the dish water.

Wade snatched up the letter and read it again. It sounded familiar, like something he'd written. No, like something he'd copied... more than once... from *The Twentieth Century Guide to Business Letters*. Now why would Miss Maybelle Easterly, one of the smartest people to walk the planet, resort to copying a letter from a business book? No mention of her job - must be the Geophysical Institute continued to be miserable. Not a word about her report for the National Conservation Commission - guess that didn't earn her any respect. And, worst of all, no mention of the kiss that made angels weep and church bells ring. Had she given up - given up on her work and given up on him?

Maybelle had asked for his honesty. It was time to ask for hers.

CHAPTER TWENTY-FOUR

September brought cooler weather and cold shoulders from the scientists as they returned from fieldwork. Mabel had more glassware to clean, but not enough work to keep her from worrying about the president's reaction to her report. Would she ever hear back from the National Conservation Commission? Or had they tossed her research in the nearest wastebasket?

She didn't have enough work to keep from worrying about what Father would say. His most recent note, sent from Hudson's Bay in early July, reported he'd won a debate about continental drift with a Canadian geologist, which Mabel thought was rather discourteous to his host.

And she definitely didn't have enough work to keep from thinking about Wade. She missed his watchfulness. Someone her size didn't need a protector, but Wade's vigilance made her feel treasured. She longed for his warm hands helping her in and out of buggies and passenger cars. She missed the way he drew out her name, almost turning it into a song. But most of all she missed their conversations.

Leaving work after another lonely day, Mabel joined a group of students, teachers, and government clerks waiting to cross Connecticut Avenue. The city's population increased every day, yet Mabel had spoken less in the past two months than she had during her two weeks with Wade. The one time she had crossed paths with her housekeeper, the woman had been in such a hurry Mabel felt guilty for speaking to her. Once again, she returned to an empty house.

Mabel pushed the key into the lock and the door swung open. She gasped, breathing in a mix of campfire smoke, moldy canvas, and fish. "Father!"

"In here."

"Woof!" A mass of grey fur bounded from the study, planted large paws on Mabel's shoulders, and engulfed her in a cloud of rancid breath.

"No! Down! Off!" Father grabbed for the beast, ending up with handfuls of hair. The animal raced into the study and emerged dragging a large white object. Father pried apart the massive jaws, then handed her the bone. "Scapula of a juvenile bowhead whale. Sorry, she's just a pup and doesn't recognize commands in English yet. She was a gift from our guide. Her name is Maheegan."

"A wolf?" In the city? What was Father thinking?

"No. Well, not purebred. Mostly sled dog we think." Father tied the dog to the newel post. "Maheegan, sit."

The canine wagged her tail, panted, and stepped in the tin pan from Father's camp kit, spilling water all over the floor. Father pulled a piece of dried meat from his pocket and the pup sat. The dog gobbled her treat, then her mouth pulled back in a grin. She may not recognize English, but she knew food.

"Welcome home, Father." Mabel kissed a spot in front of his ear. Hollows under his cheeks showed he hadn't been eating. According to her nose, he hadn't bathed the entire trip. And in spite of the stinky ointment he still wore, mosquito bites pockmarked his skin. "When did you arrive?"

"Just now." His eyes sparkled - research must have been successful. His beard reached the second button of his vest. Trunks, sample boxes, and equipment, all coated with grey fur, littered the study. A pelt - dark brown edged with buff, possibly a wolverine - draped his chair. The neat stacks of correspondence on his desk had been reduced to rubble. He'd tossed his hat atop the lamp; Mabel removed it so it wouldn't catch fire.

Wade… I'll always remember you.

"How was your summer?" Father returned the whale bone to a box bristling with long pieces of baleen.

"I'll tell you over supper. Shall I run your bath first?"

"Splendid idea. The streets feel like magma."

"This is the coolest it's been since you left."

"And the warmest I've been since May."

Halfway up the stairs, the doorbell rang. Perhaps Father's crew had brought more of his luggage.

The man on the front step wiped his glasses with a handkerchief, then shoved the bridge back onto his nose. A walrus moustache framed an impossibly large set of teeth. He grabbed her hand and pumped it as if she was allowed to vote. "Miss Easterly, delighted, just who I wanted to see."

Mabel blinked at Theodore Roosevelt. Had he come about her report? Was a personal visit a good or bad sign? "Good evening, Mr. President."

"Woof!" Maheegan tapped into her sled dog genes, pulled the newel post from the staircase, and charged the president. The post smashed into the umbrella stand, which fell with a loud clatter, spilling its contents across the tile.

"Oh, no!" Mabel lunged for Maheegan and missed. She stomped on the rope, but it slipped from under her foot. The post hit her ankle, toppling her into the hall rack, knocking off three hats. She lost her balance and landed on the floor.

"A wolf!" Roosevelt boomed. "Where's my gun?"

"Sit!" a familiar voice drawled. A much admired long leg flexed. A highly regarded knee met the dog's chest and stopped her from launching herself at the president. Maheegan plopped into position and looked up with an expression of adoration that undoubtedly mirrored Mabel's.

"Look who I found at the Raleigh Hotel." Roosevelt puffed out his ample chest. "Well done, Lieutenant."

"Miss Maybelle." Wade Hampton Alexander flashed one of his heart-igniting grins.

She had thought she'd never see him again. And now, here he was, elegant in a dark suit, catching her at her ungainly, awkward worst. She straightened her skirt, smearing the black fabric with grey dog hair.

"You all right?" Wade reached down and helped her to her feet. His hands were warm and strong and oh, too wonderful for words. Mabel had to force herself to let go.

She stood and stared, unable to move, unable to speak, unable to breathe. She considered fainting, except swooning remained yet another female skill she hadn't mastered. Instead her body lit like an Edison lamp. Electricity flickered beneath her skin until she was sure she glowed.

Her father's heavy footsteps thumped over the obstacle course of umbrellas. "I thought I heard a familiar voice. Good evening, Mr. President. Please come in."

The men filled the entry. The president was large, her father lanky, and Wade, of course, was perfect. For once, Mabel's size wasn't so unusual.

"The professor has returned." The president pounded Father's back. "How was your expedition? The zoo tells me you brought back a pair of snowshoe hares and a lynx. Bag any polar bears? I'll have to make that trip once I get back from Africa."

Father watched Wade pop the newel post back into place, then focused on staying upright around their boisterous president. "One of my crew shot a splendid *Ursus maritimus*."

"Bring him over once the taxidermy's complete. I'd like to compare him to my grizzly."

"Have you ever seen ice algae? Arctic jellyfish?" Father led the president into the study, leaving her alone with the man she had assaulted with her lips.

A foul odor filled the entry.

"I don't know what the professor has been feeding you," Wade told the dog as he returned the umbrellas to their stand, "but you need to go out."

Yes, quickly before more odiferous events occurred. "I suspect whale blubber is the culprit. The yard is fenced." Mabel led them to the back door and the dog galloped outside.

The closet-sized kitchen brought Mabel in excessively close proximity to the object of her desire. She glanced at Wade's shoes, a polished pair he hadn't worn on their trip. "I should... serve something."

"Miss Maybelle—"

She stuck her head into the icebox, hoping it would cool her face. "So what brings you into the city? Isn't your resort open until December?"

"Robert E shut it down."

She popped up. His face showed lines of fatigue, but not defeat. "Oh, no. I'm so sorry. Did you—?"

Now it was his turn to study his shoes. "Fight? No. Kicked and squirmed a bit though. Finally had to face facts." He met her gaze with an expression of resignation mixed with relief. "It was time."

"But... Fauquier White Sulphur Springs was everything to you. It was your life. Are you all right?"

He pushed the icebox door closed and gave her a sad smile. "Better. Like a thousand acre weight was lifted off my shoulders."

"So what have you been doing? And why are you in the city?"

"Working at the Raleigh Hotel."

"By the post office building? You've been here in Washington since—"

"Since shortly after we parted." Wade took her hands. If she'd known hand-holding was coming up, she'd have used lotion more often. He tipped his head. "I wanted to see you right away, but we had to cram three months of work into three weeks. I wouldn't have gotten tonight off if TR hadn't sprung me."

Take a breath. Oxygen is essential for speech. "But—"

Father called from the study, "Mabel, something cold to drink, please."

Mabel tried to collect the careening electrons of her thoughts as she peered into the icebox again. She had kissed Wade Hampton Alexander. And now he was here, in her kitchen. Would he mention it? Had he forgotten? Would it be awful if he had? Perhaps she should bring it up. But what could she say?

Wade reached over her and grabbed a pitcher. "Lemonade. Perfect."

"Wait. It's the president. I should put that in a different pitcher. Except the cut glass one is in the parlor."

"No need." Wade filled two tumblers, then found a can of salted peanuts on the shelf and emptied it into a berry dish. He reached for the Coca-Cola tray, but Mabel stopped him.

"Let's use this." Let's? As if they were in this together? If wishes were horseless carriages, she'd own a fleet of Buicks. Mabel grabbed a cut glass tray off the top shelf, showering them both with dust. "Oh, dear. Mrs. Hoban is short. She must not have—"

"Mrs. Hoban?" Wade held his hand up midway across his broad chest. "About this tall? Big smile, big eyes, big hair. Three children. I work with her husband. She washed the hotel's curtains."

"You've learned more about the Hobans in two months than I've found out in a year." She wiped off the tray and loaded it.

Wade stood in her way. "Your hat."

259

Mabel gasped. How many ways could she be inept in the feminine arts? She reached for the pin, but couldn't find it in the loops of milliner's mull, ribbon, and rosettes.

"Hold still." Wade slid the pin out, untangling it from her hair. "Not every day you come home from work to the razzmatazz of a returning explorer, a wolf puppy, and a rambunctious president."

And the man she'd kissed. "And you. I've missed you." She managed a smile then picked up the tray.

"I've missed you, too." Wade held the door for her.

Father and the president continued their examination of malodorous bird specimens without acknowledging her. She set the tray on his desk. Outside the kitchen door, she paused, wishing she had a mirror, a hairbrush, and a half hour to primp. Should she run upstairs? No, it wouldn't help. No amount of fussing would change her in any way that counted.

The kitchen door swung open. Wade handed her a glass of lemonade. "How's your job?"

"The same, unfortunately." She sipped, then clamped both hands around it so she wouldn't run the cold glass over her hot face. And so she wouldn't grab Wade for another kiss. "What happened to your staff? And your dog, Raleigh?" She tried to concentrate on his answer, but all she could think about was The Kiss. She caught something about the Soldier's Home, a brick building, and the Virginia House of Delegates. He tilted his head and leaned toward her - did that mean he might entertain the possibility of yet another kiss? No, she couldn't think about that with her father and the president on the other side of the door.

Wade pried the glass from her fingers, set it beside his, then wrapped his hands around hers. "So I guess what I'm trying to say is my prospects are good. But Miss Maybelle, none of it means anything without you."

Her breath caught. He couldn't be talking about— For once his expression was serious.

"Miss Maybelle, you kissed me."

She focused on his dark green silk necktie, since looking at his mouth disrupted her thought processes. "I didn't mean to."

He let go and stepped back. Creases shot up from his eyebrows. "Two months ago you went crusading across the Old Dominion in the name of keeping resort owners honest. What happened to telling the truth?"

Mabel swallowed and fidgeted with the buttons on her cuffs. "Well, yes, I did mean it. I planned it, even, to thank you for your kindness on the trip. I didn't mean to offend you. I hoped you'd forget about it."

"Forget?" His incredulous tone of voice indicated he didn't believe a word she'd said.

"Since you have so much experience win that department." She dared a glance at him. "Mine must be forgettable."

He shook his head and stepped close, forcing her to look him in the eye. "Miss Maybelle, you strike me as a woman who does not dally with another's affections. A woman who would not give a kiss unless it meant something, and, as the one on the receiving end, I believe I'm entitled to know what you meant."

She gulped in a breath. He was right - she owed him honesty. "My hypothesis was one good kiss, from an expert, would satisfy me for the rest of my life."

His mouth crooked up with the onset of a smile. "So I was part of an experiment. And your results?"

She pressed her lips together. Dare she admit how very much she wanted to repeat her experiment? "My theory proved false."

He pretended to be shocked, but his grin burst through. His drawl stretched each word by a syllable or two. "Miss Maybelle, your kiss had me seeing shooting stars and hearing brass bands." His hands slid up her forearms, past her elbows, up to her shoulders, as if he might embrace her. He narrowed the space between them and whispered, "The only thing wrong with that kiss was it ended way too fast. And should have started sooner, much sooner, like the day we met."

She shook her head. "But I didn't trust you when I first met you."

"You do now? You know I'll tell you the truth?" He answered her nod with a warm smile. "Well then, reckon I'd best tell you —"

"Mabel!" Father yelled from the study, making her jump. From the harsh tone of his voice, she guessed the president had told Father about her research. She hurried from the incubator into the autoclave.

"Another rotten interruption." Behind her a low and confident voice said, "We will finish this conversation later."

The men stood in the midst of crates spilling with fossils, specimens floating in jars, and boxes of microscope slides.

The president plopped a hand on Father's shoulder. "You must be so proud of your daughter."

Mabel gulped. "Father returned home moments ago. I haven't had the opportunity to tell him of my work."

The president thumped Father on the back again. "Lewis, your daughter completed a thorough investigation of the mineral springs of Virginia, comparing on-site tests with results from resort owners and the US Geological Survey."

Father scowled. "You left Washington?"

"Briefly." Mabel's face heated.

"If my children would make themselves this useful, I'd be delighted." The president worked her arm like a bicycle pump. "It's a grand investigation, bully research, well done, Miss Easterly."

Mabel heard the letdown coming and braced.

"But it won't be included with the National Conservation

Commission report. The rest of the members opposed its publication due to your lack of credentials."

Wade piped up. "But Miss Easterly's certificate of completion from the University of Pennsylvania is the equivalent of a degree."

Father frowned at Wade. "And you are?'"

"Oh, that's right, you haven't met." Roosevelt threw an arm around Wade's shoulders. "Lewis, this is Lieutenant Wade Hampton Alexander, one of my Rough Riders, who kept your daughter safe on her expedition."

Wade stepped forward, hand extended. "Professor Easterly, welcome back to civilization."

Father returned the handshake with a narrow gaze, clearly putting Wade under his mental microscope.

"Miss Easterly, it's hardly your fault Neanderthals are running our universities." Roosevelt patted her hand.

Father's frown deepened and Mabel wished she'd gotten a bit of food in him before this volcano erupted. "Just a minute now. You're saying Mabel's research was adequate—"

"More than adequate. Distinguished, exceptional, using the latest technology."

"But unacceptable because she's female." Father pulled his beard. "Should have submitted it under my name."

Which would completely negate any benefit to her own career. "You were out of town," Mabel reminded him.

Roosevelt rocked heels to toes. "Now the idea of a mobile laboratory - sanitary survey, microbiology, and chemical analysis on site - has considerable merit. Got to keep an eye on those mining operations, ensure safe water for rural areas, especially farms. The Secretary of Agriculture wants to give it a trial, but he plans to send his own team of scientists. This is the kind of project your Geophysical Lab likes to fund. Have you run it by your director?"

263

Mabel shook her head. "He has yet to forgive me for leaving the city this summer."

Father gave her a fierce glare. "You left without the director's consent?"

Roosevelt's laughter shook the chandelier. "These modern girls. Alice never asks permission either."

Father's glare could melt granite. "What about your research? What project are you assigned to?"

"I'm not. I'm still cleaning."

"What? Those halfwits haven't given you a lab?" Father harrumphed. "You could have accompanied my expedition after all."

"Next time I see Andrew Carnegie…" The president thumped his fist into his palm.

She straightened her back, raised her chin, and tried for a confident tone. "I'd prefer to return to teaching."

Father scratched the mosquito bites on his neck. "You're a good researcher, but you did enjoy teaching. Maybe the Friends School would take you back."

Mabel grimaced. The school had viewed her departure as betrayal. "They seem pleased with my replacement."

Emphatic barking echoed from the backyard. Mabel excused herself to check on the dog and Wade followed. Maheegan jumped on the oak, paws scrambling for a toe-hold on the trunk, trading taunts with a squirrel on a high branch.

"Maheegan!" Mabel called without any result.

Wade whistled, bringing the pup came to his heel. "You are a dog—"

"—And perhaps part wolf—"

"—You are a canine of some sort. You're not supposed to climb trees." With one word, Wade had the dog lying beside the back steps. Then he took Mabel's hand in his and walked her across the yard. "I imagined many different ways to propose to you - at Rock Creek Park, the Washington Monument, the Smithsonian - but never guessed TR would take over the show."

Her whirling thoughts settled on one word. Her feet planted, unable to take another step. "You *proposed* to me?"

"I'm doing my best. If we set a spell, reckon I can get the words out." He motioned toward the bench.

"But you can't marry me." She waved up and down her body. "I'm big and gawky and—"

"Who says?" He picked up an acorn. "If I have a hankering for peaches, a nut just won't do. Packaging. Much as I surely do admire your package," he winked, "it's what's inside that counts."

"But I fell—"

"And I fell at Orkney. We helped each other up and kept going. I'd say we make a good team." He guided her to the bench and they sat. "You, Miss Maybelle, are made in the image of God. I try to avoid arguing with the Almighty as I always lose. You're in fine fettle and that's nothing to sneeze at. You can work and bowl and whop a tennis ball with a powerful backhand. You climb mountains without wheezing, eat a healthy diet without succumbing to dyspepsia. You're always thinking, coming up with ideas and plans and questions. And your spirit's even more beautiful, sharing your knowledge so people can live better."

"Oh, Wade…" Hope ignited an exothermic reaction in her heart. Mabel squeezed his hands. "To be totally honest…"

One side of his mouth crooked. "Appreciate it."

"My experiment didn't work at all as I expected. Kissing you…" Was the best experience of her life. "Kissing you strengthened my memories and made me yearn for you even more, beyond infatuation."

He nodded. "And my feelings for you go far beyond a crush, all the way to love." He knelt in front of her and clasped her hands. "Miss Maybelle, let's spend the rest of our lives together."

She closed the distance. His lips met hers. Her heart expanded like rubidium hitting water, complete with red splashes and purple smoke. This second kiss eclipsed even the first.

"Now where's your wolf? Oh! Bully! Wade's proposing." President Roosevelt burst from the kitchen door and hustled across the yard. "Excellent choice. Delighted. Young people like you keep America great."

The dog jumped up, barked, and raced to tackle the president, but Wade put her back in her place with a word. He stood without letting go of Mabel's hand. She rose on wobbling knees and braced for her father's reaction.

Father propped his hands on his hips and narrowed his eyes at Wade. "So what is it that you do? Are you with the Secret Service?"

Wade faced her father without flinching. "Currently I'm the night manager at the Raleigh Hotel."

The kitchen door opened again. Mrs. Alexander swept out, followed by Robert E. Could this day have any more surprises? Mabel gave the Wade's mother a second glance. She looked much younger and not in the least perturbed by the scientific detritus littering the Easterly house. "Wade has the the opportunity to return to Warrenton to manage a hotel there."

"It's brick," Wade told Mabel, then introduced his family to Father. Maheegan bounced up, bringing her muddy paws within inches of Mrs. Alexander's violet skirt, but a snap of Wade's fingers returned her to sitting.

"The Warren Green, a lovely hotel." Roosevelt patted his substantial midsection. "They set a fine table."

"And he's been asked to run for the Virginia House of Delegates," Robert E said.

The president thumped Wade on the back. "I'll endorse you."

266

"But…" Mabel's thoughts scattered like bowling pins. "You can't run for office in Virginia if you marry a Yankee." She glanced at Wade's mother, expecting horror, shock, or, at the very least, an attack of the vapors.

Mrs. Alexander clapped her gloved hands and gave Mabel a warm smile. "Wade proposed? What delightful news!"

Roosevelt weighed in, as the reigning political expert in the Easterly backyard. "This is a whole new century. The War's been over forty-some years. We're one country again."

"If it comes down to you or wrangling in Richmond, I'd choose you any day, Miss Maybelle." Wade squeezed her hands.

Mrs. Alexander crossed the lawn. "Both the Fauquier Institute and the new Warrenton High School are in desperate need of science teachers."

Robert E followed. "Virginia has plenty of water that needs testing."

"And if you'd rather stay here in Washington, I can make a fine career at the Raleigh Hotel," Wade said. "I'd be happy anywhere, as long as we're together."

The dog barked and raced to the fence. Wade called her to heel again. Two Secret Service agents poked their heads over the pickets, breathing heavily.

"Blast! They found me!" President Roosevelt gave Wade another whack, then hurried to the gate. "Have the wedding at the White House," he demanded. "We have plenty of frou-frou left over from Alice's."

Mabel couldn't imagine anything worse than the pandemonium of Alice Roosevelt's wedding. Yet, how did one turn down the president?

Mrs. Alexander and Robert E accepted the president's offer of a ride to the White House, and the yard quieted.

"Well, this is a surprise." Father pulled a handkerchief from his pocket, frowned at its filthiness, and tossed it, giving

267

Maheegan something to pounce on. He wiped his eyes with his knuckles, then stepped forward. Mabel held her breath. She had considered herself essential to the running of his household and expeditions... until this past spring. He narrowed his eyes at Wade. "Roosevelt endorsed you. But I want to know if you attended college."

"One semester at the University of Virginia."

The scowl deepened and he shocked Mabel by saying, "My daughter is quite intelligent."

"Yes, she is, sir."

Father pulled on his beard. "So, you met on this expedition?"

"Traveling with Miss Easterly gave me the chance to see her perseverance and courage."

"You're forgetting the copperheads," Mabel muttered.

Wade gave her a wink.

"She's logical, precise, and creative. She appreciates nature and beauty. She—"

"I know that. You're the unknown here." Father made an impatient wave of his arm then turned to Mabel. "Expeditions are a crucible for character. What have you learned about this fellow?"

At her glance, Wade broke into the grin that warmed her heart. Mabel said, "He's calm in the face of adversity, gentle with horses, plays the piano and sings, can preach a good sermon with a moment's notice. He's respectful, especially to the elderly and needy. He—" *His kisses cause spontaneous combustion.* No, she couldn't think of that in front of her father. "He's resilient, finding joy in the most difficult days, and... he's honest. The ultimate Virginia gentleman."

"You kept my daughter safe. And fixed the stair rail. Many thanks." Father nodded and turned toward the house, setting off a flurry of tail-wagging and barking. "And got this rambunctious puppy to behave. Let me wash up, then we'll have dinner. I want to know more about my future son-in-law."

"And your daughter's research."

"Absolutely." The door closed behind him.

Wade rested his hands on her waist. "Do you suppose we could sneak in another kiss?"

Mabel put her hands on his shoulders and drew him closer. "Maybe more than one, if we get started right away."

CHAPTER TWENTY-FIVE

"How you doing this fine morning, Miss Maybelle?" Selina carried a tray loaded with coffee, fried ham and eggs, and biscuits into Mabel's room at the Warren Green Hotel. The elderly woman wore a new white apron and kerchief with her dark green housekeeper's dress.

Mabel stopped pacing and rubbed her hands down her dressing gown. "Selina, you're not supposed to be working this morning. Wade said you were a guest."

"Lord knows a certain amount of work keep me out of trouble. Now let me see how this dress of yours came out." She inspected the gown hanging from the wardrobe. The cream satin flowed through her fingers. "Mighty fine, from the stitching to the ironing. Now let's see about you. What are you planning for your hair?"

"I wish I could fix it up like they did at The Homestead, fluffy with twists and rolls and loops." Mabel twirled her hands around her head. "Best do my usual."

"No Homestead maid going to outdo me." Selina grabbed the hairbrush and pointed to the seat in front of the dressing table. "Eat your breakfast and I'll have you all fancied up in no time."

Mabel lost track of the number of hairpins Selina used to pouf and curl. Wade would have to help her find them tonight. *Tonight*— Her blood warmed. *Stop!* She couldn't think about *that* in front of the woman who'd raised Wade.

Selina added a spray of tiny white flowers producing a style that would delight the pickiest Gibson girl. Mabel brushed her teeth, powdered her face, then Selina slid the gown over her.

"Oh, Miss Maybelle, you do this gown proud." Selina made a low hum as she fluffed the embroidered elbow-length sleeves. A "V" of lace ran from each shoulder to the band of satin at her waist. Mabel had been concerned the design would make her look even taller, but, as the dressmaker promised, she looked slender, willowy even.

Selina approached with a damp washcloth. "Child, you got something on your face. Let me get that for you."

A woman in a violet gown glided in.

"Good morning, Mrs. Alexander."

"My word, Miss Maybelle. You are radiant." Wade's mother pressed her hand over her heart, but no one worried about her health these days. Since the engagement had been announced, she'd left her couch to steer Mabel into Warrenton society. She'd hosted teas, addressed invitations, and arranged flowers. And this morning, Mrs. Alexander supervised the dining room decorations. Now she opened a black case and lifted out a gold chain. "George Washington gave a necklace just like this to Martha on their wedding day. This one has been in the Alexander family for a hundred and twenty-three years. The gold was mined right here in Fauquier County. And now it's yours."

"It's beautiful. I'm honored to wear it." Mabel sat so Mrs. Alexander could fasten it around her neck.

A warm cheek pressed hers. "Welcome to the family."

"Thank you." Mabel managed to say without choking on her rose dusting powder.

Selina peeked out the window. "Haven't seen so many people in town since The War."

"I'm sorry." Mabel stood and peeked over her shoulder. "I

wanted a small wedding."

Selina straightened the pleat in the back of Mabel's skirt, then helped her into elbow-length silk gloves. "No chance of that, seeing as how Wade never met a stranger and all your students want to wish you well."

The courthouse bell tolled the hour. Wade's mother paused at the mirror to check her hair. "Time to put your father out of his misery."

"Is he nervous?" Father seemed anxious to get her married off this past month.

Mrs. Alexander headed for the door. "I left him out in the hall with the minister."

Mabel slid her feet into satin slippers. "I hope he's not debating evolution."

The door opened to two beaming gentlemen. The minister escorted Mrs. Alexander downstairs.

Father tucked her hand into his elbow. Since a clipping at his barber's, consuming a healthy diet, and having a new suit made, he'd traded his wild-eyed explorer demeanor for that of a distinguished professor. "You're as beautiful as your mother."

If only she were— No, Wade loved her just the way God made her and that's what counted. "Thank you, Father."

Selina handed her a bouquet of golden mums and purple asters. "You're ready."

"Is Wade?"

Selina grinned. "Oh, child, Jesus has been getting the two of you ready all your lives."

"You ready?" Robert E entered the Warren Green Hotel's office.

Wade waved his tie in surrender. "No. I need you to run outside and find someone who knows how to fasten this nonsense."

His brother took the offending waste of silk and worked it

under his starched collar. "Hold still."

"Don't saw my head off." Silly thing had him all broken out in a sweat. "How'd you learn this?"

Robert E twisted the loop. "Hanging out with sailors in a seaport."

"Did I warn you my bride is a stickler for honesty?"

"Used to attend church with the ship owners." Robert E's mouth quirked. If his brother wanted to strangle him - and he had in the past - this would be his opportunity. "Thought to catch me a captain's daughter."

Wade's mouth dropped open, although he couldn't say which was the bigger surprise - church attendance or looking for a girl. "How'd that work out?"

"Chin up. Turns out captains' daughters are smart enough not to throw in with a lowly ship's carpenter." He turned Wade toward the mirror and stepped back. "There you go."

The tie lay in elegant folds, thanks to his brother. His hair sat flat to his head, thanks to Selina's trim. He wore a morning suit with tails and creased slacks, thanks to Mother's guidance with the tailor. His shoes shone thanks to himself. "Ready to meet the King of England."

"Fortunately neither he nor our president showed up today. Are you ready for the brilliant, but blushing bride?"

"She is awful smart, isn't she?"

"Lord only knows what she sees in you. Best get out there and marry her quick, afore she comes up with a better plan." Robert E pulled the door open then paused. "Papa would be proud of you, Wade."

Wade gave a grim sigh. Much as he loved his new job and the liveliness of the county seat, he still missed Fauquier White Sulphur Springs. "Even though I lost the resort?"

"He'd say, 'only Jesus walks on water.'"

"I thought that was Selina's saying."

"She always added 'and you ain't Him.'"

"You ain't Him, but He is here today." Selina pushed the door open all the way. She pinned a yellow flower to each of their lapels. "You boys looking mighty fine. And your mama is ready to burst her buttons. Come along, now."

In the courtyard, the orchestra tuned up. Wade had told them they couldn't play "Dixie," "Carry Me Back to Old Virginny," or the "Rough Riders' March." They settled on a lively version of the Celtic "Haste to the Wedding." Usually Wade didn't hold with haste for any reason, but in this case, the wedding couldn't be hasty enough. He patted his pocket where he'd tucked the key to their honeymoon cottage. *Get along, now.*

Selina handed them over to the minister on the hotel porch. A clear blue autumn sky shone over the crowd on the lawn. Wade recognized a passel of neighbors, longtime guests of the resort, former employees. Miss Maybelle's students filled the last two rows - they'd fallen in love with their teacher about as fast as he had.

Those standing at the back turned. Over their heads - thank the Lord for his bride's height - he spotted a meringue of chestnut hair topped with a sprinkle of sugar. His stomach growled.

"Did I eat my breakfast?" he whispered to Robert E.

His brother nodded. "And mine."

Professor Easterly turned the corner first. The old explorer had cleaned up nicely. Then Miss Maybelle came into full view. A knockout! Humdinger! No, she seemed too majestic for slang. Wade's bride glowed like the Statue of Liberty. She had taken to small town Virginia life like a peach to a pie crust.

Sunlight caught on the gold chain around her neck. Mother had given her the Washington necklace? He glanced at the first row of guests and Mother gave him a reassuring smile. The Lord was coming up with miracles left and right these days. First

Robert E and he had buried the hatchet. And now Mother accepted a Yankee into the family. *Thank you, Jesus.*

The minister gave a welcoming speech. Maybelle breathed evenly, maybe a little quicker than usual. Was she nervous? She reached toward him. Oops. The minister had told them to join hands. Wade grabbed hold. Beautiful, magnificent, amazing in every way… and his. He really should be paying attention, but oh…

His bride took a deep breath to say her vows, which was ever so distracting. "I, Miss Maybelle Easterly—"

Maybelle? She's calling herself Maybelle? Wade grinned so hard he could barely say his own vows. Fortunately, when it came time for the kiss, their lips worked just fine.

Haste to the wedding indeed!

Acknowledgements

With thanks to editors Jennifer Fisher and Larry Collins, and to my critique group, Nebraska Novelists, especially the sharp-eyed Katherine Barnett.

Author's Note

In the spring of 2014, I took a research trip to the mineral springs of Virginia with my mom, Sara Collins. Her expertise as a Virginia history librarian provided context for the tour, yet it was her personal stories I cherish the most. She'd explored most of the state while lost!

A few months later, Mom made her final journey, to a place even more beautiful than Virginia. Grief hit like a shotgun blast to my heart and I stopped writing. Readers encouraged me to finish this story and share it with you. Many thanks to all who wrote! I treasure your letters more than I can ever say! Keep them coming! http://CatherineRichmond.com

https://www.facebook.com/catherinerichmondfans

And if your mom's on this side of heaven, give her a hug!

Also by Catherine Richmond:

Spring for Susannah   http://amzn.to/1KO1MJz

GILDING THE WATERS

* * *

Through Rushing Water *http://amzn.to/ 1Ws1Ztf*

If you enjoyed *Gilding the Waters*, a review would be so appreciated!

44983214R00158

Made in the USA
Middletown, DE
22 June 2017